WINNING THE WIDOW'S HEART

WINNING THE WIDOW'S HEART

Sherri Shackelford

CHIVERS

British Library Cataloguing in Publication Data available

This Large Print edition published by AudioGO Ltd, Bath, 2013.

Published by arrangement with Harlequin Enterprises II B.V./S. à r.l.

U.K. Hardcover   ISBN   978 1 4713 2576 2
U.K. Softcover   ISBN   978 1 4713 2577 9

Printed and bound in Great Britain by
TJ International Limited

God setteth the solitary in families: he bringeth out those which are bound with chains: but the rebellious dwell in a dry land.

— *Psalms* 68:6

To Mothers:

To Rita Rounds Shackelford,
for the beautiful soul
I never had a chance to meet,
for all the extraordinary books she
never had a chance to write.
Thank you for giving me the most
precious gift of all: my husband, Todd.
Your generous spirit shines
through your children.

To Bonnie Preble, for
always believing in me,
even when I didn't believe in myself.

To the three greatest
characters ever conceived:
Jocelyn, Shawn and Noah

CHAPTER ONE

Outside Cimarron Springs, Kansas, 1870s

A shrill scream from inside the homestead split the frosty air.

Jack Elder flattened his back against the cabin's rough-hewn logs, his Smith & Wesson drawn. Icy fear twisted in his gut. He couldn't think about the woman inside, couldn't let himself imagine what had ripped that tortured sound from her.

Head cocked to one side, he strained to hear voices over the howling wind. How many men were inside? Was Bud Shaw one of them?

Dense clouds draped the afternoon in an unnatural twilight. Fat, heavy snowflakes sheeted from the sky, pillowing in heaps on the frozen ground. Jack nudged the deepening slush with his boot. No footsteps showed in the fresh covering. No animal prints, either.

The glass-paned windows had been covered with oilcloth to keep out the cold air and curious eyes. He cautiously edged toward the rear of the house, his shoulders hunched. A sharp gust of wind sucked the breath from his lungs. He stretched one hand around the corner, relieved to feel the raised surface of a door latch.

Another harsh shout mingled with the raging blizzard. The desperate cry hardened his resolve. He didn't care how many men were inside — he couldn't let that woman suffer any more.

Mustering his fortitude, he whipped around to face the door and kicked. Hard. Wood splintered. A gust of warm air scented with fresh-baked bread knocked back his hat. He lunged inside, his pistol arm leveled. A woman's startled blue eyes met his shocked gaze over the silver barrel of her Colt .45.

Jack froze.

The lady standing before him was young, and nearly as round as she was tall. Her pale hair clung damply to her forehead, and a shapeless gingham dress in drab hues swathed her from head to toe. She kept her body partially obscured behind a tall chair, as if the flimsy wood might somehow repel a lead bullet.

Her hands shaking, the woman wrestled

back the gun's hammer. "Take one more step and I'll blow your head off, mister."

Jack thought he'd planned for everything, but staring down the barrel of a quivering Colt .45 was proving him woefully wrong. An armed woman hadn't been on his list of contingencies.

Carefully pointing his own weapon at the ceiling, he cleared his throat. "I'm a Texas Ranger," he called out loud enough to reach anyone who might be hiding. "You're safe now, miss."

Her face screwed up in pain. She tipped forward, clutching her stomach. Her gun weaved a dangerous path in the air. Fearful of a wild shot, Jack extended his arm toward her.

"Don't touch me!"

He searched her panic-ridden features for any sign of injury. "Where are you hurt?"

"Nowhere." She warned him back with a wave of her gun. "So get out."

His instincts flared. She was obviously in pain, not to mention she'd been screaming loud enough to wake a hibernating grizzly moments before, yet she still refused help. Was she trying to warn him? Had the outlaws set a trap?

Jerking his thumb, he indicated a door on the far side of the room. "Is he in there?" he

11

asked, his voice hushed. "Where's Bud Shaw?"

"No one here by that name," she gasped. "Now get out. I don't want any trouble."

Liquid splashed onto the wood plank flooring at her feet. Her face paled, and her eyes grew as large as twin harvest moons. Frigid air swept through the broken door.

The truth hit Jack like a mule kick. She wasn't plump, she was pregnant. Very pregnant. He hadn't stumbled into Bud's hideout — he'd barged into a peaceful homestead. The lady of the house was understandably spooked, and about to give birth at any moment.

He didn't need a sawbones to tell him the woman's bag of waters had just broken. Jack raised his eyes heavenward and offered up a quick prayer for guidance.

"Lady, you got a heap o' trouble," he said at last, "but I ain't part of it."

She staggered to the left, the weapon still clutched in her hand.

With a quick sidestep, he dodged the business end of the barrel. "Ma'am," he spoke, keeping his voice quiet and soothing, "I'm holstering my weapon."

She aimed her gun dead center at his chest.

Anxiety rose like bile in his throat. Nothing was more unpredictable than a frightened civilian with a firearm. Not to mention she was unsteady on her feet and in obvious pain. The sooner he disarmed her, the better.

His decision made, he crept forward, his arms spread wide to display his empty hands. "Where's your husband? Has he gone to fetch help?"

She glanced away, as if considering her answer.

His stomach clenched. "You're alone here, aren't you?"

Her full, rose-colored lips pursed into a thin line. She shook her head in denial.

Annoyed by her refusal to look him in the eye, Jack grunted. He could guess the meaning of those loaded pauses and hesitant answers.

His sharp gaze surveyed the room once more. An enormous cast-iron stove dominated the space to his right. A single pine table and four crude chairs filled the corner behind the woman, a side cupboard and a pie safe flanked the open kitchen area. No masculine boots rested on the rag rug. No overcoat hung on the sturdy hooks beside the door. Ten years as a Texas Ranger had given him a heap of insight into people.

Everybody lied, just not for the same reasons.

He assumed his most charming smile to put her at ease. "I'm Jack Elder, and I'm not going to hurt you. I've been tracking a gang of bank robbers through Kansas. You haven't been robbing any banks, have you?"

She scowled at his joke, then another pain racked her body. She doubled over, pressing her free hand beneath the shelf of her belly.

Taking advantage of the distraction, Jack caught her around the forearm. Her startled gaze flew to his face. Though her wild, frightened eyes pierced his rigid control, he held firm. Careful to keep his touch gentle, he pried the Colt loose from her trembling fingers, swiftly releasing the hammer with a seasoned flick of his thumb.

She narrowed her eyes. "Are you really a Texas Ranger?"

Jack stepped away, hardening his heart against her suffering. Emotions clouded judgment — and poor judgment got people killed.

After hooking his finger into the gun's trigger guard, he flipped back the collar of his jacket to reveal the silver star he'd carved from a Spanish coin. Uncertainty flitted across her face, followed by reluctant acceptance of the tarnished evidence of his profession.

"Ranger or not," she said. "You have no right to be here."

Habits honed from years on the trail had heightened his senses. The woman had a curious lilt to her voice, the barest hint of an accent in the way she spoke. She wasn't from around these parts, but then again, who was?

He let his coat fall back into place. "Ma'am, you need to lie down. That baby is fixing to come."

"No," she cried, stumbling away. "It's not time. I checked the calendar. It's too soon."

"I don't think your baby is on the same schedule."

"But I can't have the baby now. I'm not ready."

Jack heaved an inward sigh. *Marvelous.* She was delusional and in labor. He definitely hadn't planned for this. She appeared oblivious to the telling mess at her feet, to the growing chill in the cabin, to — well — to everything. As if ignoring the situation might somehow make it all go away — make him go away.

He shifted his weight, considering his options. Best not to push her too hard. Mother Nature would deliver the full realization of her circumstances soon enough.

15

She mumbled something beneath her breath and vigorously shook her head. "No, it's definitely too soon. I have everything planned out for the last week in November."

Another glance at her rounded belly heightened his trepidation. A little nudge in the right direction never hurt. "You look plenty ready to me."

Her expression turned icy. "And what do you mean by that?"

"Well . . ." he stalled. "You're, you . . ."

A flush crept up his neck. While there was no polite way to indicate the most obvious symptom of her condition, she was a little too far along in the birthing process for his peace of mind. Wherever her husband had gone, it didn't appear the man would be returning home anytime soon. Without another person to watch over the woman, Jack's options were limited. Unless he took control of the situation and found a reasonable way to extract himself, they were *both* in a mess of trouble.

"Do elaborate," she demanded. "I'm what?"

Suddenly hot, he slid the top button of his wool coat free. He'd just come from Cimarron Springs, and it was forty-five minutes to town for the doctor. Leaving the woman alone that long was out of the question. Grateful for the breeze from the busted door, Jack released the second button. Surely someone was watching out for the woman? Even in this desolate land a person was never truly alone. She must have friends or family in the area.

A teeth-chattering shiver rattled her body, buckling her defensive posture. She wrapped her arms protectively around her distended stomach. "This is my home, and I want you to leave."

"You and me both."

He'd rather face an angry rattler than a fragile woman any day. But the sight of her pale face tugged at his conscience. Of course he'd do the right thing. He always did the right thing, especially when it came to women and children.

That code of honor had been ingrained in him since his youth. "I can't go until I know you're settled."

Conscious of the dropping temperature and her growing discomfort, he backed his way to the broken door, his attention riveted on the woman. Snow swirled around his ankles, dusting the cabin floor with white flakes.

Her gaze skittered to the gun in his holster. "You're trespassing on my property." She tightened her arms over her rounded belly,

17

highlighting the swell. "Return my gun this instant."

He nudged the sagging door closed with his heel. Wind whistled through the cracked hinges. "I can't do that. You might need my help, and I can't have you shooting me."

He rested her Colt on the sturdy worktable before the stove, then covered the weapon with his hat. "I might be a Texas Ranger, but my family owns a cattle ranch. I haven't delivered any babies, but I've brought a passel of calves into this world, and I've got a fair understanding of the process. Once your bag of waters breaks, there's no going back."

She started, as if noticing the wet floor for the first time. "Oh, my goodness. What a mess. I — I need a cloth."

She waddled to the side cupboard, swinging the door wide to rummage through the shelves.

Jack blew out a hard breath, letting her prattle about her chore. He'd seen that same vacant stare plenty of times before. His first year as a Ranger, he'd come upon a homestead after a Comanche raid. The woman of the house was setting the table for supper, her clothing torn and bloodied, while her husband and three young children lay slaughtered on the dirt-packed floor.

His chest constricted at the memory. He'd never forget the mother's dark footprints circling her dead children's bodies. From that moment on, he'd hardened his feelings to the suffering he witnessed in order to preserve his own sanity.

The pregnant woman faced him, her chin set in a stubborn angle, a square of linen clutched to her chest. "The man you're looking for isn't here, so you can leave now, mister."

"What's your name?" he asked, his tone deliberately brusque. Most decent folks responded honestly to a direct question.

"Elizabeth. E-Elizabeth Cole."

He offered her another friendly grin. His questions had the added benefit of keeping her distracted. "See, that wasn't so hard, Elizabeth." He also found people answered to their own name, even when they ignored everything else. "Where's your husband?"

Her eyes welled with tears. Sniffling, she blinked them away. "He's dead."

Jack bowed his head, shielding himself from the agony in her steady gaze. She definitely wasn't lying now. The way her emotions paraded across her expressive face, she'd make a terrible criminal.

"I'm sorry for your loss," he replied.

She was awfully young to be a widow. Jack

sometimes felt the good Lord had let evil concentrate west of the Mississippi.

He opened and closed his mouth a few times to speak, finally deciding to give her a moment to collect herself before any more questions. Judging from her condition, the man couldn't have been gone for too long. In this harsh land, it was best not to get attached to anything, or anyone.

When she finally glanced up, he asked, "Do you have any family or friends in the area?"

"The McCoys live just over the rise."

Hope sparked in his chest. "Is there a Mrs. McCoy?"

"There's a Mrs. McCoy, a Mr. McCoy —" she ticked off each name with a finger to the opposite hand "— and five little Mc-Coys."

Relief weakened his knees. Delivering babies was best left to women and doctors — and he didn't qualify as either. "Thank heaven for the McCoys."

He'd find a way to contact the family as soon as Elizabeth was settled. With his immediate worry eased, he stepped forward, motioning with one hand. "Let's get you someplace where you can rest, Mrs. Cole."

She eyed him with obvious distrust.

Flummoxed by her stubbornness, Jack

paused. Now what? Give him a raging outlaw or a drunken killer any day. He wasn't equipped for this kind of sensitive situation. Those teary blue eyes were sorely testing his vow to remain detached.

She lurched to one side, clutching the ladder-back chair for support. "Oh, dear," she moaned.

Feeling helpless and out of his element, he cupped her elbow. Her wary gaze swept over his thick wool coat, lingering on his stamped, silver buttons. Her jaw clenched. He had the uneasy sensation she had just sized him up, and found him lacking.

Jolted by her odd reaction, he dropped his hold. "I'm not going to hurt you, Elizabeth."

She pinched shut her eyes against another pain, then fumbled for his hand, threading her fingers through his in a silent plea for comfort. His heart stuttered at the unexpected gesture.

How long since her husband had died? How long had she been pregnant and alone, solely responsible for the grueling work required to run this homestead?

After a long, tense moment, her delicate features relaxed. The grip on his hand loosened.

"That one wasn't so bad," she said, though

her wan smile indicated otherwise.

"Let's get you away from this breeze." He nodded toward the back of the house. "Someone near broke your door in two."

"I hope that same someone repairs the damage before he leaves."

She lowered her head, then yanked her hand free, as if surprised to see their fingers intertwined.

Keeping his gaze averted, he flexed his fist a few times to shake off the lingering warmth of her skin. He didn't want to look at her, didn't want to see the raw edge of fear in her eyes. Didn't she realize he was one of the good guys?

Following the strangely intimate moment, an awkward silence stretched between them. The widow was a curious mix of bold courage and heartbreaking vulnerability. She'd been in labor, isolated and alone, yet she'd met his forceful entrance with rare fortitude. Despite her blustery grit, he sensed her reserve of energy was running lower than a watering hole in July.

She brushed the hair from her forehead with a weary sigh. "Maybe I will have a rest."

"That sounds like the best idea I've heard all day."

She leaned heavily on his arm as he eased her past the cast-iron stove, through the doorway to another room. An enormous four-poster bed dominated the space. A wedding-ring quilt in faded pinks and dull greens covered the mattress. An old porcelain doll with matted chestnut hair rested between two fluffy feather pillows.

Jack scratched his forehead. "That's quite an impressive piece of furniture."

Her cheeks flushed pink. "My husband and I bought the homestead from another family along with the furniture. They made it almost six years before they gave up." Avoiding his curious gaze, Elizabeth shuffled to a sturdy oak dresser. A red kerosene lantern with a floral-etched, fluted cover lit the room. She tugged on the top drawer, sending the flame flickering, then glanced at him askance. "I'm sorry I lied to you earlier. I didn't want you to know I was alone."

"I didn't give you much choice."

She kept her eyes downcast, her discomfort palpable. While he appreciated the awkward impropriety of the situation, his nagging concern for her welfare took precedence over their mutual embarrassment.

They had a more pressing problem to solve. "Is this your first baby?"

She nodded.

"How long have the pains been comin'?"

"About four or five hours."

The knot of anxiety in his chest eased. The birthing processes often took hours, sometimes even days. "If there's one thing I do know, it's that first babies take their good sweet time in coming. I've got three older brothers, and they've blessed me with two nieces and six nephews. Not a one of them took less than twelve hours to be born."

She met his gaze, her pale blue eyes full of hope. "Then you can go to town. Cimarron Springs has a doctor. Two of them."

"Ma'am, there's a snowstorm blowing in. I'll be lucky to make it to the McCoys, let alone town."

Her shoulders slumped and his heart went out to her. Pain and fear had a way of sapping a body's strength.

"This isn't exactly a church social, I know that." He paused, searching for a way to alleviate her fears. "Tell you what. I'll get my horse out of the weather and check on the animals. Won't take me more than a minute. You can change and lay down for a rest. Keep track of the pains, though. They should keep coming closer together. When you're settled, I'll skedaddle over to the Mc-Coy's spread for help. With five children, they should be well versed in delivering babies."

She bobbed her head in a distracted nod, pressing her knuckles into the small of her back with a grimace.

He scooted to her side. "Don't hold your breath through the pains. Just let 'em come."

"Is that what you tell the cows?" she snapped.

"I heard the midwife say that to my sister-in-law. I tell the cows to moo through the pain."

A reluctant smile appeared through her scowl.

"That's better." He'd paced the floor with his brothers through enough births to know Elizabeth was going to need all the humor she could muster. "You've got about six to eight minutes before the next pain. I'll be back lickety-split."

A feather-light touch on his sleeve stilled his retreat. "When you return from the Mc-Coy's, you can bunk down in the barn until the weather clears." She swallowed, glancing away. "But that's all. I expect you to clear out at first light."

Jack tipped his head in agreement. The widow was still a might skittish about his intentions. Considering their less-than-cordial introduction, he couldn't blame her. "Don't worry, Elizabeth. Everything is going to be all right."

"Easy for you to say, mister. You're not the one having a baby."

Jack couldn't help a dry chuckle. There was nothing like a crisis to reveal a man's true character, and he was encouraged by her fortitude. "You'll manage. You faced down an armed intruder, after all."

She cut him a sidelong glance full of wry skepticism before turning her back. Inexplicably annoyed with her cool response, he toyed with the wick on the lantern to cover his confusion. When had his social skills slipped? Usually a few charming words and a friendly smile were enough to put most people at ease.

With a shrug he closed the door to allow her privacy, then crossed through the kitchen. He loped out the splintered rear exit, snatching his hat on the way.

Driving snow pelted his face, stinging his bare cheeks. He tucked his scratchy wool collar beneath his chin as he fought through needle-sharp wind to his disgruntled horse. The gelding snorted a smoky breath, tossing its head. Icicles had already matted in the horse's thick mane and tail.

Jack tugged on the reins. "Sorry, Midnight. I'm just as frustrated by the delay as you are. I should have known that potbel-

26

lied old sheriff in town couldn't tell a homestead from a hideout."

The gelding nuzzled his shoulder.

"If I'd known the weather was going to change faster than a sinner on Sunday, I never would've risked the journey. Almost makes a fellow believe in divine providence." He tipped his head to the sky. "Mrs. Cole needs us to fetch help, even if she doesn't want to admit it yet. I know as much about the surface of the moon as I do about childbirth, and that ain't saying much."

The quicker he found help for the widow, the quicker he could continue on his journey. The more time passed, the colder the trail out of Cimarron Springs grew. Jack couldn't afford any additional dead ends and delays. If an innocent man was hanged because of his mistake, he'd never forgive himself.

His thoughts dark, he fought through growing snow drifts, sinking to his calves with each step. A flurry of movement caught the corner of his eye. Jack drew his pistol, searching the blowing snow. Wouldn't that just be the bee's knees if the outlaw was squatting right under his nose?

When no one sprang from the shadows, he tucked his gun away. He'd most likely seen one of the farm animals searching for shelter. The sheriff's mistake was troubling him, making him jumpy. He'd take a gander at the horses inside the barn before he returned to the main house. The outlaw he was searching for always rode a distinctive bay mustang. Men around these parts knew horseflesh better than humans, which might explain the sheriff's confusion.

Another thought sent him stumbling. A curtain of snow slid off his hat.

He'd forgotten the Colt sitting on the worktable.

"Well, Midnight," he muttered to the horse, "I hope Mrs. Cole has given up the idea of shooting me."

Jack swung up the bulky T-bar latching the barn door, then heaved the sliding panel to one side. The hayloft hook twirled in the wind above his head, banging forlornly against the loft door. Even before Midnight whinnied, shying to one side, Jack sensed a trap.

Elizabeth pressed the heels of her hands to her eyes, holding back the painful burn of tears. She panted through another sharp pain, her heart still thumping uncomfortably against her ribs.

She'd almost shot a Texas Ranger.

When the oilcloth over the window had

flipped up during a wind gust, she'd nearly fainted to see a stranger's dark form lurking outside. She'd grabbed her gun and waited, expecting the worst.

She wasn't expecting a lawman.

With his easy charm and fancy silver buttons, Jack Elder reminded her of her late husband. That charming behavior was bound to wear off, and she hoped he was long gone when it did. Aside from his useless good looks, she didn't need him returning to town with tales destined to send the gossip's tongues wagging.

A familiar sorrow weighed her down. She'd had enough of interfering busybodies as a child, and enough of autocratic lawmen as an adult. If the Ranger wanted to make trouble, there was nothing she could do to stop him. She'd fought the sheriff to stay in her home after Will's death, and she'd fight anyone else who threatened her tenuous security.

Recalling the scene in the kitchen, her blood pounded, and her face grew hot with humiliation. Thank heaven he'd be gone by morning.

Elizabeth cradled her belly, hesitant to offer up another prayer. She'd prayed for a husband, and God had sent her a smooth charmer named Will. She'd prayed for a

29

child, and Will had deserted her rather than care for his growing family. She'd prayed for Will's return, and God had sent her his body to bury.

Hurting and desperate, she'd prayed for help, and God had sent her a lawman. She let out a reluctant sigh. While he wasn't what she'd prayed for, at least he was willing to fetch help.

Elizabeth choked back a desperate laugh. She'd been hoping for a break in the weather, or more time to prepare before the baby arrived — anything but a great bear of a man treating her like a half-wit. *Delivering cows, indeed.* Thank heaven he wouldn't be delivering this baby. After hearing him talk, he'd most likely try to sweet-talk the infant through the process with a rakish grin, or expect her to moo through the contractions.

Overwhelmed by the day's events, she tucked her worn Bible beneath a stack of neatly folded cotton shirtwaists, fearful of praying for anything else lest she inadvertently unleash a plague with her clumsy words.

The only person she could truly count on was herself.

A violent cramp twisted around her middle. Shouting, she slid down the wall, crumpling to the floor. Her vision blurred.

A great weight pressed on her stomach, like a full-grown bull sitting on her belly. The torturous spasm kept building stronger and stronger. The urgent need to push overwhelmed her.

"Mr. Elder," Elizabeth called, her faint voice no match for the brutal prairie winds.

That flashy lawman was wrong — this baby was coming. *Now.*

CHAPTER TWO

The pain let up just as quickly as it had begun. Stunned by the intensity of the last contraction, Elizabeth panted. Each time she assumed the agony had peaked, another violent spasm proved her wrong.

A hopeless sob caught in her throat. She wiped the sweat from her brow with the back of her hand, amazed at how quickly her body swung between chilling cold and suffocating heat.

She needed help. She needed to stop blubbering and pull herself off the floor. Mostly though, she needed her mother to be alive, holding her hand and easing this devastating fear.

Elizabeth struggled to form a plan, but her brain refused to function properly. Her thoughts flitted from subject to subject until the torturous pain demanded her undivided attention.

Through the haze of her agitation, the rear

door banged open. Surprised Mr. Elder had returned so soon, Elizabeth craned her neck to peer around the corner. She'd seen the panicky look in his eyes at her condition earlier. Once he realized the increasing gravity of the situation, he'd saddle his horse and ride away as if a pack of wolves was nipping at his heels.

She shifted to press her palms against the floor. Her brief marriage had taught her one thing about men — they had a tendency to stay when they should go, and go when they should stay. Her arms collapsed like wet noodles beneath her weight.

Rallying her strength, she stretched to brace her hand against the dresser. This inability to force her body to respond frightened her as much as the pending birth. She had to be stronger. After all, she didn't need a man's dubious help. She'd survived for months without any assistance. She'd survive another day. The eminent desertion of one Texas Ranger was the least of her worries. The weak attempt to comfort herself failed miserably.

"Mrs. Cole," a familiar voice shouted.

Relief swept over Elizabeth like the first warm breeze of spring. "Jo," she called back. Here was the help she had prayed for. "I'm in the bedroom."

The young McCoy daughter burst into the room with her usual boisterous energy. Her frantic gaze swept across the bed. Elizabeth waved a limp hand from her wilted position near the dresser to catch the girl's attention. Jo's eyes widened at the sight of her employer slumped at her feet.

"What happened?" Jo demanded. "Did that man hurt you?" The girl knelt, whipping off her scruffy hat to reveal two long, serviceable braids. "Don't you worry none. I locked him in the barn."

"Oh, dear." Elizabeth struggled to sit up straighter. A band of steel wrapped around her abdomen like a vice. The pressure consumed her, blocking out all thoughts of the trapped Ranger. "It's the baby," she gasped.

"Is that all?" Jo flashed a crooked grin. "Don't you worry, Mrs. Cole. I told you at least a hundred times that I've helped my ma deliver plenty of babies. You don't understand 'cuz you're from back East, but most folks around these parts don't cotton to no doctor."

Elizabeth bore down on the pain, clenching her jaw against the agony. Jo checked her progress, then squeezed her hand. "The baby's dropped, Mrs. Cole, but I'm pretty sure you still have a ways to go."

"Are you certain?" Elizabeth choked out.

"Pretty sure."

The contraction eased, releasing the aching tightness around Elizabeth's belly. She drew in a shaky breath. "I guess we'll have to muddle through this together for a bit."

"I knew there was something wrong earlier." Jo shot her a black look. "Why didn't you say you were hurting?"

"I didn't know —" Elizabeth stopped herself before she told a lie. Of course she'd realized something was wrong. Knowing Jo would sense her distress, Elizabeth had fought to hide her growing discomfort. The girl was more perceptive than most people twice her age. "I didn't want to worry your mother. You said she wasn't feeling well."

A shadow darkened Jo's bright green eyes. At fourteen, Jo was the oldest of five children, and the only girl. Awash in a sea of males, she'd taken to dressing and acting like a boy herself. She'd been helping Elizabeth with the chores since Will's death six months ago.

Elizabeth trusted the girl's ability to help until they unlocked Mr. Elder and sent him to fetch Jo's mother. "That man you —"

"I couldn't go home, anyway," Jo interrupted, her voice thick with emotion. "Pa shooed me away at the gate. There's influenza in the house. The town's had five deaths already. If Ma dies, I'm all Pa's got to take care of the little ones."

A sound of distress caught in Elizabeth's throat. Concern for the McCoys overshadowed her own worries. "Your family will be fine, Jo. I'm sure. Your mother is a strong woman."

Elizabeth wanted to offer more words of comfort, but another contraction robbed her of speech. An eternity later she gasped, "Oh, my, that hurts."

"I know." Jo patted her hand. "It's going to get worse before it gets better. Mrs. Parker hollered so loud, my ears rang for a week. 'Bout squeezed my hand off, too."

Horrifying images of Mrs. Parker's suffering flooded Elizabeth's thoughts. They were alone. With the storm raging, and the nearest farm quarantined, no help was coming. "Perhaps we could save these stories for another time?"

"Oh, right." Jo flicked her head in a quick nod. "What is it Ma's always saying?" She snapped her fingers. "I remember now. She distracts 'em by talking, and telling 'em to concentrate on that beautiful baby they're bringing into the world."

"That's better."

"Hey, remember all those clothes we

sewed this fall?"

Elizabeth rolled her eyes. "You're the worst seamstress in the county. I sewed all those clothes while you complained you were dying from boredom. You'd rather be out shooting game than threading a needle."

"See? You're doing better already." Jo sat back on her heels. "Now deliver this baby so we can decide what to do about that man I locked in the barn."

"I'm a Texas Ranger."

Jo gasped at the intrusion. Hands fisted, she twisted to block Elizabeth while keeping her defiant gaze fixed on the Ranger.

Slanting a glance upward, Elizabeth found Mr. Elder filling the doorway and looking madder than a wet hen. His coat was torn at the shoulder, and an angry scratch slashed across his cheek.

Gracious. This day just kept going from bad to worse.

"He's a lawman all right," Elizabeth replied, restraining Jo with a limp hand to her forearm.

The girl relaxed her stance. "How'd you get out of the barn?"

"Just you never mind, missy." He plucked a length of straw from his hair. "What's going on in here?"

"Are you touched in the head, Ranger?"

37

Jo flung out a hand. "Can't you see she's having a baby?"

"Imprisoning a lawman can get you the firing squad."

"You don't look imprisoned to me."

Elizabeth shouted as suffocating pressure bore down on her pelvis. The two combatants fell silent, their identical shamefaced expressions almost comical. She panted through the contraction, ignoring the accusatory glares they shot at each other over her head. Silent now, Jack knelt at her side, a concerned frown puckering his brow.

When the pain eased, Elizabeth flashed the younger girl a reassuring smile. "I hope this doesn't take much longer. I was hoping to start another batch of bread later."

Given the girl's pitying smile in return, her joke had fallen on deaf ears. Too exhausted to care, Elizabeth rested her head against the wall to stare at the ceiling.

She'd thought she was capable of delivering a child without collapsing like a fragile greenhorn, but the endless cycles of pain had sapped her strength. Recriminations for her own foolish behavior rattled her composure. Why hadn't she thought to send Jo into town earlier? Instead, she'd dawdled over her chores, thinking she had weeks to prepare. Without Mrs. McCoy or the doctor, she and the younger girl were going to have to deliver this child alone.

Elizabeth turned to Jack. Regrets were a luxury she couldn't afford. "You can go now. We'll be fine."

Jo's head snapped up. "Not on your life. I need a pan of water and linens. As long as we've got ourselves a real, live Texas Ranger, we might as well put him to good use."

Elizabeth held up her hand in protest. Lawmen asked too many questions.

Mr. Elder rose to his feet. "I've got whiskey in my saddle bags for the —"

"Wait." Fear pierced Elizabeth's heart. "You won't bring whiskey into this house."

"Ma says it keeps the baby from getting dysentery," Jo added softly. "I need it to clean my hands."

Elizabeth sensed pity in the girl's eyes, but she brushed aside the feeling. How could Jo know about Will? Elizabeth had confided in no one.

"Can we get Mrs. Cole onto the bed?" the Ranger asked.

"No!" Elizabeth cried.

Every nerve in her body bore down on the pain. Desperate for the agony to end, she didn't want to be jostled or moved. The contractions were coming closer together, giving her less and less time to recover before the next increasingly agonizing spasm.

Her energy waned with each pain. The months following Will's death had been filled with turmoil, leaving her little chance to concentrate on the pending birth. Her shock and grief, her fear, had drowned out all thoughts of the future.

When the nagging backache from this morning had grown worse, she'd refused to heed the signs. As if, with the baby growing in her womb, her dreams were still possible. She'd pictured her future with a loving husband and half a dozen children running underfoot. The hopeful plans for her new life and a growing family had dwindled. She was a widow, alone and vulnerable.

"Mrs. Cole." Jack touched her shoulder, his voice filled with compassion. "Your baby needs you to be strong."

Elizabeth grimaced against another contraction. A salty tear caught on the corner of her mouth. The weakness shamed her, but she was exhausted from maintaining her rigid composure. It was time she faced the harsh reality of her circumstances. Women died in childbirth all the time.

She'd never ducked away from a difficult choice and she wasn't about to start now. "Promise me something, Mr. Elder."

Apprehension widened his eyes.

Elizabeth didn't know anything about the Ranger, didn't know if she could trust him, but she sensed a quiet determination behind his wary gaze. Unlike the local sheriff, he appeared to be bound by a code of ethics. While most men were only interested in their own pleasure, Mr. Elder's job forced him to take the needs of others into consideration.

She clasped his hand, comforted by the hard calluses covering his palm. Will's hands had been soft and smooth. The disparity gave her hope. Perhaps this man was different from her late husband. "Mr. Elder, if something happens to me, you'll see that my baby is raised by a real family. Don't let my child grow up in an orphanage."

He blanched. His Adam's apple bobbed. "You're going to be fine, Mrs. Cole."

"Prom —"

The Ranger held up his free hand to quiet her protests. "There's nothing to worry about."

Jo scowled. "Never mind him. My ma can take the baby."

Elizabeth shook her head. Mrs. McCoy worked harder than ten men combined. She ran her household on a budget barely fit for a pauper. Heaven knew the overtaxed woman didn't need an additional burden. Not to mention the time and cost of rearing another child.

"JoBeth McCoy," Elizabeth scolded, "your mother has enough to worry about with five children at home. She doesn't need another mouth to feed."

Jo ducked her head, silently acknowledging the truth. Another violent cramp hardened Elizabeth's belly. She panted, clutching the Ranger's hand.

When the contraction eased, Mr. Elder refused to meet her pleading gaze.

She was pushing him, a stranger, to make a difficult promise. Even if he agreed, she would never know whether or not he had fulfilled his pledge. Despite the uncertainty, she needed him to say the words. She needed to clutch a glimmer of hope for her baby's future.

She wanted a better life for her child. "Promise me."

Jack turned. His hazel eyes shined in the dim light. "I promise."

His assurance released the floodgates of her emotions. She sobbed through another searing contraction, the most powerful yet. Black dots collected at the edges of her vision, growing larger. The room clouded. Voices came to her from a great distance, as if she were tumbling down a well. Down, down, down to a place where there was no pain, no loss, just darkness.

"Please, God," she whispered. "Save my baby."

Cold panic tore at Jack's insides. "Wake up, Elizabeth," he ordered.

He clasped her chin in his hand, humbled by the fragile bones. She was so delicate, so young to be facing this pain. Beneath his touch, her head rolled limply to one side. Her glazed eyes slowly cleared. His heart soared as dawning recognition focused her attention. She was still too pale, but a faint blush of color had infused the apples of her cheeks.

She drew in a breath, her shoulders rising and falling with the effort. Sweat beaded on her forehead, and her pale blue eyes had lost their luster.

"I can't do this," she sobbed.

"You're doing real good. It's almost over."

He said the words out loud, though he didn't fully believe them in his heart. There were no certainties for anyone. With only the two of them to assist her, if something went wrong, they were lost.

Alarmed to find his heart beating like a stampeding bull, he pressed the widow's hand to his chest, sharing his strength. His emotional reaction startled him. He'd paced the floor with his brothers, but not a one of his sister-in-laws' births had affected him this way.

Jack squared his shoulders. He was immune to suffering. He'd seen plenty of people die, men and women both. He'd buried children, marking their graves with rough wooden crosses or crude piles of stones. Nothing moved him anymore.

A shrill cry shocked him from his stupor. He swiped at his forehead with the back of his hand. He'd never felt so helpless. He was sweating as much as the widow now. All the comforting words he'd spoken to his brothers while their wives were in labor came back to haunt him. He blinked the perspiration from his eyes. What a bunch of inadequate nonsense.

Humiliated to be at the mercy of a prickly girl who couldn't be more than fourteen, he gave Jo a pleading look.

She met his gaze, her face revealing nothing. "The baby's head is crowning. I'll need a pan of water and some fresh linens."

He hesitated to leave the women alone.

"Sometime today, Ranger!"

Jack stumbled to his feet, clumsy and out of his element. He rushed to gather the supplies, grateful for something to do besides worry.

He fled to the kitchen and gingerly tossed the contents of a sturdy creamware bowl out the back door. His fellow Rangers often chided him on his cool, collected demeanor, saying icicles ran through his veins instead of blood. They'd eat their words to see him now. Returning to the sink, he pumped the lever arm to prime the well, his hands stiff and uncoordinated.

After filling the bowl, he pawed through his saddle bags, searching for the whiskey. Fear strummed through his body with each of Elizabeth's jagged cries. He yanked a handful of linens from the side cupboard, sending the rest of the neat stack tumbling to the floor. His arms full, he returned to the bedroom, then knelt beside the perspiring widow.

Jo glanced up. "Scoot in behind her and help her brace when she pushes. This baby's a might stubborn."

Beseeching him with her eyes, Elizabeth jerked her head in a nod. Her silent plea humbled him. She looked on him as if he might actually soothe her pain — as if he was something more than a giant lump of useless male. For a moment, he wanted to be everything she needed.

45

Jack snorted softly to himself.

Who was he fooling? He was about as much use in this situation as a handbrake on a canoe. He rubbed his damp palms against his pants' legs, wishing he'd never followed those bank robbers out of Texas. Wishing he'd stayed in town. Wishing that potbellied sheriff had directed him anywhere but here. Even as the traitorous thoughts filled his brain, he helped Elizabeth sit up, his work-roughened hand dwarfing her slim shoulder. He slid one leg behind her back, bracing his boot against the dresser as he hunkered down.

The pungent smell of alcohol stung his nostrils. Jo rubbed the whiskey on her hands, then wiped them clean with a dry cloth. The girl's fingers trembled, but she managed a wobbly smile. "When the next pain comes, I want you to push as hard as you can."

For a moment Jack didn't know who was more frightened — the widow, the kid or him. Like a battalion of warriors mustering for war, the three of them nodded in unison.

Elizabeth clasped his hand in a now-familiar gesture. He cradled her against his chest, willing his strength to infuse her exhausted body. Her blond hair had tumbled loose from its bun, catching on his coat buttons. He carefully untangled the strands, then brushed the silky locks aside.

"You know how to pray, Ranger?" Jo asked.

This time he didn't hesitate. "Dear Lord, if you're looking down on us, now would be a good time for some help."

"Amen," JoBeth murmured.

Elizabeth's body stiffened.

"You're almost there," he soothed. "You can do this, Elizabeth. You're almost done."

Curling forward, she squeezed his hand, her whole body straining with effort. Her agonizing shout of pain ripped through him like a bullet.

"Oh, my goodness," Jo cried. "It's a girl. It's a girl, Mrs. Cole! You have a beautiful girl."

Following her announcement, a heavy silence filled the room. Jack waited, hearing nothing but the sound of his own heartbeat thundering in his ears. Jo carefully wiped the child dry with a towel. Her worried gaze met his over Elizabeth's head. At the stricken message in her eyes, his heart seized.

The bundle squirmed. A lusty squall exploded from the infant, startling them all into relieved laughter.

Jo carefully placed the baby on Elizabeth's

chest. The widow cradled her bellowing child, laughing and crying at the same time. "She's so beautiful." Elizabeth glanced over her shoulder, catching his gaze. "Isn't she beautiful?"

His eyes stung. He cleared his throat, recalling all the times he'd teased his older brothers for their weeping and wailing every time a niece or nephew was born. He'd never understood the vulnerable emotions those wet, froglike creatures inspired. Seeing Elizabeth's joy, her newborn, the miracle of life where there once was none, something in his chest shifted.

"Yes," he said, his voice husky. "She's beautiful."

While the two women laughed, awkwardly hugging each other over the baby, the walls crowded in around him. The air in the room turned dank and suffocating. His nerves tingled, warning him of an attack. He needed to escape.

This time, though, he feared the danger rested within his own heart.

Chapter Three

Elizabeth awoke in darkness to the clang of pots and pans and the mouth-watering aroma of frying bacon. Stiff and sore, she gingerly rolled to her side to check on the baby. The surge of energy she'd experienced immediately following the birth had plummeted soon after. A rare fatigue had overcome her, sapping her of strength and leaving her weak and listless.

Barely able to keep her eyes open, she'd mustered just enough energy to change out of her ruined dress with Jo's assistance. Her legs had proven too weak to hold her weight, so Mr. Elder had assisted her onto the bed. Silent and flushed red from his neck to his ears, he'd lifted her with treasured care.

He'd lingered to help Jo change the linens and tidy up the room, both of them waging a hushed, muttering war on the proper way to accomplish even the most minuscule task. Each time the Ranger had chanced a glance at Elizabeth, his cheeks had darkened to such a deep crimson, she'd feared he would burst into flames.

After ensuring the newborn was settled, a gown lovingly drawn over her body and crocheted yellow booties covering her feet, Elizabeth's two helpers had left mother and daughter alone in the hushed glow and hiss of kerosene lamps.

The infant had nursed voraciously, then stretched and yawned before falling into the peaceful slumber afforded only the very young, and the very old. Cocooned in a blanket of serene contentment, Elizabeth had been reluctant to surrender her gift from God. She'd dozed off with the infant cradled in her arms, her daughter's gentle breath whispering against her neck.

Swaddled tightly, the baby now rested beside the bed in a drawer Jo had extracted from the dresser and lined with blankets. Sighing, Elizabeth extended her hand over the edge of the mattress. She brushed the backs of her fingers over the supple, downy softness of the baby's cheek, then buried them in the shock of dark hair covering her head.

"How did I create something so perfect? So beautiful?" she whispered. "Thank you, Lord, for this is Your work."

Her heart swelled. Now more than ever, she needed to be strong. The awesome burden of responsibility weighed upon Elizabeth alone. Her daughter's survival in this wild, untamed land was at the mercy of her mother's courage. The prairie was brutal, especially for women and children.

Elizabeth glanced toward the darkened window, the glass panes frosted over like sugared candy. A tangle of memories pulled her into the past.

Her first month in Kansas, she'd stumbled between a cow and her calf. The animal had butted her to the ground, knocking the wind from her lungs. Will had been angry at her carelessness, chastising her for coming between a mother and her offspring. Elizabeth finally understood his warning.

The changes in her life over such a short time threatened to overwhelm her. In one short year, she'd been a wife, a widow and a mother. Last November she'd married Will after a three-week-long whirlwind courtship in New York and moved West. Three months later she was pregnant and three months after that Will was dead. The entire year had brought her full circle to this new life.

She might not know anything about raising children, but she loved her daughter already, had loved her since that first moment she'd felt the baby stirring in her womb. She'd die to save her child.

A child who currently had no name.

Elizabeth pressed her numb hands against cheeks burning with shame. How could she have been so thoughtless? She'd fallen asleep without naming her baby.

A vague memory took shape, Mr. Elder leaning over the infant, running his index finger reverently over the baby's cheek. "We'll name you tomorrow," he'd said. "When your mother has rested."

Gracious. Not only had she failed to name her child, she'd abandoned poor Jo to deal with the Ranger, alone.

So much for courage and fortitude.

She'd abandoned those dearest to her to fend for themselves — while she *slept.*

A lump of regret clogged her throat. "Oh, baby," Elizabeth sighed. "What a mother you have."

She caught the sounds of someone puttering in the kitchen, whistling a merry tune. Perhaps she was being too hard on herself. Nothing awful could have happened for Jo to be so cheerful. With the baby nestled snuggly in her makeshift bed, and Jo busy in the kitchen, no one had suffered unduly for Elizabeth's absence. After all, she'd just delivered a baby. An exhausting task, to be sure.

As for their uninvited guest, considering the late hour, Mr. Elder was probably long gone. Once a man wanted to leave, no one could stop him. She wouldn't be surprised if he was halfway to Texas already.

A twinge of loss stirred up her turbulent emotions. She recalled the way he'd held her hand, the encouraging words he'd murmured. How odd to think she'd never see him again.

She pressed a fist against her mouth to stifle uncontrollable sobs, alarmed by her inability to hold back the tears. She never cried, ever. Not when her father had died, not when she'd been escorted to the orphanage by two somber nuns while her mother looked on, not even when Will had left her for good. Yet over the past few days she'd been nothing but a watering pot.

Determined to quell the flood of emotion, she swiped at her cheeks. Weak women did not survive. Her baby was depending on her. She'd had enough trouble after Will's death, she couldn't let down her guard.

Heavy footsteps approached the door. A tentative knock sounded. "Are you all right?" a male voice called.

Her heart flipped. She absently smoothed

her hair and tugged her heavy wrapper higher over her neck. Why was Mr. Elder still here? Had the weather changed for the worse? Had something happened to Jo?

She lifted the baby from her cozy nest, and cradled the bundle against her chest. "I'll be right out," she called, unable to disguise the quiver in her voice.

The infant's cupid-bow mouth opened and closed in a yawn, her tongue working. Elizabeth pressed her cheek against the baby's forehead, willing herself to be strong. Tears escaped her tightly clenched eyes, dripping down her cheeks. Frightened by her lack of control, she bit her lip. Another telling sob slipped out.

The doorknob rattled. "You don't sound all right."

A long pause followed while Elizabeth struggled to find her voice.

The door opened a crack. "I hope you're decent, because I'm coming in."

Mr. Elder swung the door wider, his gaze searching the room, his lips set in hard line.

"What's wrong?" he demanded.

"Nothing."

Elizabeth sniffled.

His fierce expression turned hesitant. He crossed his arms over his chest, then dropped them nervously to his sides before finally planting his burly fists on his hips. "I'll just be going then."

He reached for the exit, his feet still rooted to the floor.

She sniffled again.

One hand clinging to the doorknob, he sighed heavily. "If nothing's wrong, why are you crying?"

Tears dripped onto the baby's forehead, startling the infant. Sleepy eyes blinked open, catching Elizabeth's gaze. She stared into their depths, caught in the dark and mysterious vortex, fascinated. It was like looking at an old soul in a new body. "My baby doesn't have a name."

"Is that all? I thought something bad had happened."

"Well," she huffed. "I wouldn't expect a man to understand. A good mother would never fall asleep without seeing to her child first. I left Jo all alone with you and . . . and . . ." A fresh wave of tears spilled down her cheeks. "This poor child has been on this earth all afternoon, without a name."

His gaze swung between her and the baby as if he was puzzling out a great problem. "It's not like she understands the difference."

"Oh, you, you . . ." Elizabeth fumed. "I cannot say anything nice to you, so I am not going to say anything at all."

She clenched her teeth to prevent a torrent of angry words, so resentful, she wanted to lash out.

"No need to upset yourself." Mr. Elder hovered in the doorway like a wild-eyed buck poised for flight. "It shouldn't be too difficult to name a baby. Did you and your husband have any names picked out?"

Elizabeth choked back another sob. The only thing Will had ever called their child was a "nuisance." He'd ridden away the day after he'd discovered she was pregnant.

Her blood turned to ice. What if the child found out she was unloved by her father? Unwanted? Everyone deserved to be loved. All children deserved a name.

She cradled her daughter protectively against her chest. No one knew the truth about Will, and she'd keep it that way. Certainly plenty of people suspected her late husband of cheating at cards, and not a few had grown suspicious of his shallow, jovial smile. But no one knew his true character. He'd saved that part of himself for the people he no longer needed to impress. Like his wife.

Elizabeth had a safe, peaceful home now, and nothing else mattered. Not even an insensitive lawman. She canted a sideways glance at the baffled Ranger.

Mr. Elder hesitantly straddled the threshold — one foot in the room, one foot in the kitchen — as if he couldn't quite commit to his escape.

He pinched the bridge of his nose. "There are some beautiful names in the Bible. Rebecca, Mary. And, uh, some more I can't think of right now."

The infant stretched out a single, tiny hand. Her five perfect fingers opened to the world. Love shimmered in Elizabeth's chest. Instantly calmed, she stared in wonder, awed by this exquisite, fragile human being God had entrusted to her. This miracle of life.

"There's Rachel," Mr. Elder continued. "And —"

"Wait," Elizabeth cut into his mumbled list. "Rachel." She liked the way it sounded, the way the syllables rolled off her tongue. "This is my daughter, Rachel."

The name fit.

Peace settled over Elizabeth like a down comforter on a cold winter's night. "Thank you."

"You're welcome." He leaned forward to peer at the baby, still keeping his body half in, half out of the room. "You can always settle on a middle name later."

Her heart sank.

His stricken gaze darted to her face. "You don't need to make a decision now."

"I guess not."

"Okay." He nodded. "Glad that's settled."

"Don't let me keep you," Elizabeth muttered.

Mr. Elder groaned. Pulling his foot into the room, he leaned one elbow on the chest of drawers, then rested his chin on his fisted hand. "What was your mother's name?"

Elizabeth conjured up the one hazy memory she had clung to all these years. She pictured a blond-haired woman with kind, sad eyes. For ten years Elizabeth had clung to her anger and betrayal. Why had her mother relinquished her only child to an orphanage? Why hadn't she fought harder for Elizabeth? Perhaps it was time for forgiveness. How proud her mother would have been of her first grandchild. Right then, Elizabeth felt as if she could forgive anything. Even Will.

"Rose," she said. "My mother's name was Rose."

"Rachel Rose." He smiled, his teeth even and white against rugged, wind-chapped skin. "That sounds like the perfect name for a little girl." He turned on his heel to leave, then paused. "Are you hungry?"

Her stomach rumbled. In all the confusion she hadn't eaten all day. "Starving."

He chuckled, threading his fingers through his dark wavy hair, ruffling the neatly cut strands.

A sense of foreboding wiped the half grin from her lips. She'd never again trust a man who spent more time at the barber than he did with his own family. She'd learned that lesson the hard way with Will.

The Ranger smoothed his hair back into place. "I thought you'd be hungry. I'll fix you a plate."

"I'll help you." Scooting her legs to the side of the bed, she winced as her tender muscles screamed in protest.

"Don't get up," he admonished. "I'll bring supper to you."

His casual declaration kept her frozen for a long moment. Her eyes narrowed on his face. Was he sincere? Save for a hint of beard shadowing his jaw, Mr. Elder appeared as fresh and crisp as a spring crocus. He wore his dark gray shirt tucked into his trousers, his leather vest neatly buttoned, the gun holster conspicuously absent. Before she could protest, he ducked back into the kitchen.

"Wait," Elizabeth called. "Where's Jo?"

"She's in the barn, doing chores." He

stuck his head around the corner. "That's one tough young'un.' "

"I didn't think you two were getting along so well."

"She's awfully opinionated for a youngster. But I'll let it pass since she took such good care of you. A lot of grown men don't have that kind of grit." He fisted his hand on the door frame, his head bent, his gaze fastened on the toe of his boot. "Are you sure you're all right? It's been a rough day."

A hint of blush tinged his handsome face, the scratch on his cheek from his barn escape barely visible. Elizabeth suppressed a grin. She found his awkward attempt to inquire about her health painfully endearing.

"I'm fine," she said. "I'd like to think it's been a day full of blessings."

He exhaled a pent-up breath. "Yes, it has."

With a parting nod he disappeared again, taking with him the strange tension she felt in his presence. Bemused, she stared at the empty space he'd occupied. Though a large man, he carried himself with an easy grace. His gestures were spare and clipped, but he managed to speak volumes with his brief answers.

Her stomach rumbled into her musings.

She brushed her nose against Rachel's.

"This should be a novel experience. Most men aren't interested in fetching and carrying for a lady unless they're courting. And we certainly aren't courting."

Elizabeth wanted to be annoyed with her frailty — she'd just declared her independence, after all — but the hunger gnawing at her stomach silenced her protests.

After pressing her cheek against Rachel's smooth forehead, she laid the baby on the bed. Twisting, Elizabeth fluffed the pillows behind her, sank her hands into the mattress and shimmied backward until she sat up straight.

She cradled her daughter in her palms. Rachel cooed, the sound no louder than the purr of a kitten. Tiny fingers worked in the air. Elizabeth kissed all ten tips, captivated by the miniature oval nails. She'd never seen anything so small, so absolutely flawless.

She inhaled Rachel's sweet essence, her heart swelling until she was sure it would burst right out of her chest. She'd been adrift for months, unsure of the future, and afraid to face the past. With Rachel, everything felt right. The way God had intended.

Mr. Elder returned a moment later with a steaming mug of coffee in one hand and a platter overflowing with food in the other.

"I can't eat all that!" Elizabeth laughed.

"You might be surprised."

Despite her protest, her gaze searched the plate, her mouth watering. He'd heaped a great mound of eggs next to a hearty slab of bacon. An enormous hunk of generously buttered bread balanced on the edge.

Worry dampened her enthusiasm. If this was what he had prepared for Elizabeth, how much had he eaten already? "Have you and Jo had supper?"

Purchasing more supplies didn't worry her. She had plenty of cash. Following Will's death, the somber undertaker had marched up to the house in his navy blue suit, his bushy salt-and-pepper eyebrows drawn into a fierce scowl. He'd slapped a fat wad of bills he'd discovered in Will's saddle bags into her limp hands. As if begrudging her the virtue of his honorable gesture, the disagreeable man had whirled and stomped away.

Money definitely wasn't the problem. It was the trip to town that had her stomach in knots. Traveling to Cimarron Springs meant facing the people who resented Will, even after his death. The people whose money and property he'd won in card games. The people who thought Will was a cheat. She'd felt the hot sting of their accusations as she'd run her errands on previous visits. The way the ladies had sniffed and swept their skirts aside when she passed, as if afraid of being tainted by association, was painfully burned into her memory.

Even the sheriff, a man who'd shared more than one raucous evening with Will, had accused her husband of being a cheat. He'd even threatened to seize her homestead if he discovered proof.

"I had a tin of beans earlier," Mr. Elder said, startling her from her gloomy thoughts.

Elizabeth blinked. "Wherever did you find those?"

"I packed them from town. I didn't want to deplete your food supply," he spoke matter-of-factly. "The weather has let up, but you never can tell in this part of the country. You've got enough to worry about without a full-grown man eating your winter supply. Might be a long season."

"Oh, yes, of course. I didn't think. . . ."

Confounded by Mr. Elder's kindness, Elizabeth placed Rachel in the makeshift crib while he patiently held her supper. She accepted the plate from his outstretched hand. Their fingers brushed together. The dark hairs on the backs of his knuckles felt rough and foreign against her calloused fingers.

He set the mug on the nightstand. "Anything else you need?"

Surprised to note her quickened pulse, Elizabeth shook her head.

He gestured in Rachel's direction. "She appears to be healthy and all. No worse for wear."

"She's perfect." That same warm light shimmered around Elizabeth's heart. "Would you like to hold her?"

He shook his head, backing up so quickly his hip slammed against the dresser. "I'll pass."

With a curt nod at Rachel, he strode out of the room.

Elizabeth glanced around the room. Was something burning? Certainly a big, strong man like Mr. Elder wasn't frightened of a *baby*. Something else must have spooked him.

She shrugged off the Ranger's odd behavior and returned her attention to supper. The nutty aroma of fresh-brewed coffee wafted from the night table, mingling perfectly with the scent of freshly toasted bread. She speared a hearty chunk of bacon, her taste buds dancing in anticipation. Chewing slowly, she savored the spicy, salt-cured meat.

An unexpected stab of guilt dampened her

enthusiasm. She felt as if she should apologize to Mr. Elder. But for what? For assuming he'd eat her food? It wasn't as if she'd actually accused him of anything. Still, no matter the circumstances, her lack of tolerance was unacceptable. So far, he'd been nothing but kind.

Her thoughts drifted back to the only other man who'd ever showed her the least hint of kindness. Hadn't Will started out in a similar fashion? She'd been sweeping snow from the walk outside the bakery where she worked in New York when he'd tipped his hat at her while strolling by. The gesture had stunned her. She couldn't recall a time when anyone had actually noticed her, much less acknowledged her with a greeting.

When he came back the following day, he'd called her "ma'am" and smiled so wide she'd blushed. By day three, she found herself jumping each time the bell chimed over the door, hoping he'd return. All day she waited, only to be disappointed. When she'd turned the closed sign for the evening, she found him lounging against the lamppost, his thumbs hooked in his pockets. Three weeks later they were married and on a train bound for Kansas.

He'd cared for her in the beginning,

showering her with gifts and attention as if she were a shiny new toy. But after the novelty had worn off, he'd changed. Elizabeth was certain that the Ranger was no different. He'd reveal his true colors soon enough, and this time she wouldn't be taken by surprise.

Elizabeth attacked her food with a new vigor. Considering her appalling display of blubbering this afternoon, she must work harder than ever to prove her independence. In order to survive, she had to be strong. More than just blizzards and Indians threatened her home, and she had to be prepared.

Jack sucked in a lungful of frosty air, then kicked another enormous stump into place. Two days had passed during his self-imposed exile on the widow's homestead. Two days of letting the outlaw's trail grow colder. He stepped back, swinging the ancient ax he'd found rusting near the wood pile high over his head.

Exhaling a vaporous breath, he swung the tool in a neat arc, burying the blade three-inches deep into the dry wood. Repeating the motion, he circled the stump, kicking fallen pieces back into place until he had a satisfying jumble of split wood. His shoulder aching, he rolled another stump into position.

The physical labor, the satisfying crack of the blade, cleared his thoughts. The pile grew taller, but he didn't slow his pace. Driven by a need to accomplish a useful task, he forged ahead. Someone had already cut the smaller branches. The pie-shaped pieces were neatly stacked in a long, sturdy wall covered in oilcloth and mounded over with snow. But the unwieldy stumps had been heaped together to rot, wasted.

Jack didn't like waste.

The work put him in control, gave him a sense of pride and accomplishment. He swung the ax until his biceps burned and sweat trickled down his collar, until Elizabeth's screams of pain during childbirth stopped ringing in his ears.

He knew she was fine, but he couldn't shake his impotent rage at his own helplessness. He'd borne that same weight on his shoulders staring down at his sister-in-law's prone body. Doreen had done nothing wrong. She'd been running her errands when she'd arrived at the bank on the wrong day, at the wrong time. She'd walked right into an armed robbery, and the outlaws had shot her. The senselessness of the act had shaken Jack's faith, making him question God's plan. Why Doreen?

The dark-haired beauty had married his older brother when Jack was barely sixteen. When he'd decided to join the Texas Rangers instead of working the ranch like his older brothers, she'd been the only member of the family to support his decision.

After the shooting, he'd let his emotions overtake his good sense. When an enraged posse had tracked down a man named Bud Shaw and declared him guilty, Jack had gone along for the ride. Even when every instinct in his body told him the man was innocent. During the following weeks, he'd split his time between the family ranch and a Paris, Texas, jail. Questioning the imprisoned man at length had only cemented his doubts. There were two Bud Shaws roaming the central plains, and the man rotting in jail, waiting for his own hanging, was innocent.

Jack had pulled every favor owed to him by the local judge to buy the wrongly convicted man half a year's clemency. Three long months had passed since then. Every day without locating the real outlaw weighed heavy on his conscience.

His nieces and nephews deserved justice — but so did the innocent man sitting in jail. The one decent lead Jack had followed had led him to this isolated homestead in the middle of nowhere. Dawdling here wasn't going to bring justice for anyone. Jack had lingered over the widow and her newborn long enough. He was party to a grave injustice, and he couldn't rest until he set it straight.

He slid the last stump into place. Squinting at the horizon, he wiped the sweat from his brow with his leather-clad hand. The day looked to be overcast, but clear and calm all the same. If he left in the next hour, he'd be back in Cimarron Springs by lunch. His hands tingled with expectation. The familiar anticipation of embarking on another journey focused him, chasing away his lingering unrest. He had a goal, a purpose.

The widow and her child were none of his concern. Jo's family, the McCoys, would see to her well-being. Besides, a pretty woman was never alone for long in this part of the country.

The ax missed its target.

Jack windmilled his free hand, managing to right himself just before he tumbled into the woodpile. Straightening, he darted his gaze to the house. No mocking faces appeared in the square windowpanes. Satisfied his gaff had gone unnoticed, he slung the blade over his shoulder.

"Guess that about does it," he muttered to himself.

With his thoughts focused on the multitude of tasks to accomplish before his journey, he barely noticed the frigid, knee-deep snow on his trek to the barn. He'd saddle up Midnight, say his goodbyes and be gone. Simple as that.

A rare thread of regret tugged at his heart. He forcibly pushed aside the nagging concern. Mrs. Cole had survived this long on her own, there was no need to think she needed his assistance. He was a lawman, not a nursemaid. He had a job to do.

Jack slid open the barn door, relieved to find the cavernous space empty. He inhaled the pungent aroma of hay and feed. The scent reminded him of home, of his youth. He'd grown up mucking out barns, working from dawn till dusk on his family's cattle ranch. The familiar sights and sounds released an unwelcome longing to work with hands, to build something lasting, to recapture the camaraderie he'd once shared with his brothers.

Chickens clucked and a cow lowed. Midnight, one of two horses in the four stalls, whinnied.

A sound outside the usual barnyard racket

caught his attention. Jack paused, tilting his head to one side as he heard it again. He recognized that sound all right.

His jubilant mood fled. Someone was crying. Not the pained howling of a body in agony, but a quiet whimper of despair.

Jack groaned. There was only one person on the homestead who'd hide in a stall rather than cry out in the open. Determined to slink away before he got sucked into another emotional conversation, he backed to the door. He'd already dealt with one weeping female this week. His problem-solving skills were limited to things he could shoot or arrest.

He had one hand on the door when another faint sniffle doused his annoyance. Compassion for Jo dragged his feet to a halt. The code of honor ingrained in him as a child reared its ugly head. He pressed two fingers to the bridge of his nose. He'd tackle this one last obstacle, and *then* he'd leave. After all, he'd comforted Elizabeth.

He was practically an expert on women now.

CHAPTER FOUR

Jack had an idea where to find the weeping girl. He crept through the barn, his boots silenced by the hay strewn over the floor. He should be saddling Midnight instead of chasing down the source of those muffled sobs, but his conscience drove him forward against his good sense.

Dust motes stirred in the shaft of light sluicing through the hayloft. The wind had blown the door open almost half a foot. No wonder he'd nearly frozen to death these past two nights. In his haste to escape Jo's trap, he hadn't fully latched the hayloft. He'd been so cold he'd almost hunkered down next to the milk cow for warmth.

He added another chore to his growing list. Better for him to climb that rickety ladder than risk having one of the women break a leg. The third rung from the top was nearly rotted through. Unfortunately, sealing his impromptu exit had to wait until he dealt with his current problem.

Stalling, Jack lifted his shoulders and stretched, easing the cramps from sleeping on the hard-packed floor. He tugged his gloves over his exposed wrists. The barn had given him shelter and little else. A feather bed in town called to him like a prayer.

He peered into the first stall, his gaze meeting the sloe-eyed stare of the caramel-colored milk cow. He inched his way to the second stall, glancing over the half door. Jo huddled in the corner, her thin arms wrapped around her legs, her forehead pressed against her bent knees. Two long braids brushed against the tops of her boots.

Midnight whinnied, stretching a velvety nose out the last enclosure. Jack saluted his companion with a finger to his brow. "Soon, I promise."

The girl jerked upright, her face averted.

Jack rested his elbows on the half door, chafing at the delay. He adjusted his hat forward before reminding himself this wasn't an interrogation, then set the brim back on his head in the "I'm friendly and approachable" position.

He didn't even know what was wrong, let alone how to fix the problem. Once again he cursed the mistake that had led him here. Why hadn't this homestead been teeming with hardened outlaws instead of weeping women?

He recalled Jo's mention of influenza. She was probably just concerned over her ailing family. Jack added the sheriff's failure to inform him of the influenza outbreak to his growing list of gripes against the incompetent lawman.

Sucking in a breath of a chill air to fortify himself, he contemplated his strategy. "Something bothering you?"

"Nope."

Jack bit back a curse. Didn't women love to talk? That's what all the fellows complained about, anyway.

As much as he'd like to turn tail and run, his feet refused to move. Frustrated, he reached into the stall, yanked a length of straw from a tightly cinched bale and twirled it between his fingers. "Seems like there's something bothering you."

She swiped her nose with an exaggerated sniffle. "You're touched in the head, Ranger."

The spark in her voice encouraged him. Rage was an emotion he understood, and inspiring anger in a touchy female was easier than shooting tin cans off a flat stump. "Then why are you crying?"

She threw him a withering glare. "I ain't

no weeping female, so why don't you do something useful, like ride on out of here?"

"Maybe I will."

Undaunted by her harsh words, he continued to twirl the hay between his fingers. A chicken flapped through the barn, pecking at the dirt around Jack's feet. He let the oppressive silence hang between them. People generally didn't like silence. Most folks would rather fill up an empty space, even if that space was better left empty.

Jo kept quiet, a trait that won Jack's increasing admiration. At least she wasn't crying anymore, another positive sign. If she didn't want to talk, then he sure wasn't going to force the situation. Looked as if he was going to make it to town before lunch, after all.

She bumped her hand down the length of one dark braid, her gaze focused on the hay beneath her feet. "Mrs. Cole says you were chasing bank robbers when you barged in." She shot him a sideways glance. "What if you make another mistake? What if someone gets hurt?"

His fingers stilled. He had the uneasy sensation this conversation had nothing to do with bank robbers. "You make a mistake, you make amends. That's all the good Lord asks of us."

"How do you make amends for lying?"

He busted the straw in two pieces. *Everybody lied,* he reminded himself. *Just not for the same reasons.* "You make up for lying by telling the truth. You wanna start now?"

"I told Mrs. Cole I could deliver that baby. But I couldn't." Her chin quivered. "I was so scared I wanted to run away."

Relief shuddered through him. He'd been expecting to hear something much worse. She was barely more than a child herself, no wonder she'd been terrified. He was making a fast slide past his thirtieth year, and he'd considered running away himself. "You delivered a baby. That's a grave responsibility. Being scared doesn't mean you lied, just means you're human."

"You ever get scared?"

"Every day." He barked out a laugh. "You wanna know a secret?"

She scrambled to her feet, brushing at the baggy wool trousers tucked into the tops of her sturdy boots. A voluminous coat in a dusty shade of gray completed the tomboy uniform. She flipped the braid she'd been worrying over one shoulder.

Her clear, green eyes searched his face. "What secret?"

"Truth is, I might have beaten you to the door. I wanted to hightail it out of that room faster than a jackrabbit out of a wolf den."

"Truly?"

He chuckled. How many times had he done the same? Judged someone's face, watching for subtle hints to test the sincerity of their answers? "I was terrified."

Midnight butted against the neighboring stall, reminding Jack of his purpose, of the unfinished business weighing on his conscience.

As Jo absorbed his confession, her shoulders relaxed.

He mentally patted himself on the back for his inspired handling of the situation. A few more words of assurance to wrap things up, and he could leave. He'd have to regroup in Cimarron Springs and interview the sheriff once more. Judging by the lawman's lazy work habits, the task of gathering information was going to take all afternoon, further postponing his trip.

He'd decided to visit Wichita earlier that morning. Every two-bit thief in Kansas wound up there at some point or another. The frontier city was the key to locating the outlaw, Bud Shaw.

"You're a brave girl for sticking it out," he encouraged.

He'd settled Jo's fears. He'd be in Cimarron Springs by this afternoon.

Jo looked him up and down. "You still chasing them outlaws?"

"*Outlaw.* There's only one left."

"What happened to the rest? How many were there all together? Do you always chase outlaws?"

Jack held up a hand, halting the deluge of questions. "There were three all together. They shot a . . . they shot a woman during a robbery in Texas. On their way out of town, the sheriff gut shot one of them, a man named Slim Joe."

"Did he die?" she asked eagerly.

"That kind of wound doesn't kill a person right off. Slim Joe had a lot of time to talk. He turned over his partners, Pencil Pete and Bud Shaw. We caught up with Pencil Pete right off and threw him in jail. Then we found Bud Shaw. Except, well, I think we made a mistake."

"Then Bud Shaw isn't one of the outlaws?"

"I think there are two men named Bud Shaw. I think the outlaw decided to take advantage of a man with the same name, and frame him."

Jack didn't want to expand, he'd already said more than he intended. Unease itched beneath his skin. There were two Bud Shaws, of that much he was certain. He'd

78

discovered too much evidence to refute the fact in his own mind. Just not enough to convince the judge.

Jo glanced at him, her expression skeptical. "But what if something else *does* go wrong?"

"I'll cross that bridge when I get there." Jack threw up his hands. "Why are you worrying about something that hasn't happened yet?"

"What if you can't find him? What then?"

"Standing around here talking about the future ain't gonna change anything. Why solve a problem before it happens?"

"Don't get all riled up, Ranger. You're spooking the animals."

Jack pressed the brim of his hat tighter to his head with both hands. Women confounded him. He had one female concerned about naming a baby that was too young to answer, and another looking for a solution to a problem that hadn't yet occurred. What was a man to do?

Gritting his teeth, he forced a smile. "Well, you did real good delivering that baby."

"Better than you. I thought you were going to throw up."

"So did I," he retorted, his voice more forceful than necessary.

She tossed back her head and laughed at

his shouted confession. Jack scowled and crossed his arms over his chest. Her infectious laugh soon had him chuckling. The sound rumbled low in his chest, rusty and neglected, then bubbled to the surface. He couldn't recall the last time he'd truly laughed, especially at himself.

He used to laugh with his brothers all the time — when they weren't beating the tar out of each other. They'd roll around in the dirt and blood, bent on killing each other, until one of them said something smart-alecky and the whole group erupted into raucous laughter. He missed that. Missed the camaraderie of his family.

Things had changed after their pa's death. His older brothers had ceased brawling, and started slicking back their hair. Weddings had followed, and then a new niece or nephew every year after. His mother had reveled in her role as grandmother before she'd died. Lord knew they'd all been lost without her. Jack was too young to take over the ranch by himself, and too old to be ordered around by his brothers.

He'd joined the Texas Rangers instead, and Doreen had supported his decision. Jack pictured his sister-in-law the last time he'd seen her. How the white-linen pillow had framed her ashen face, the growing pool of red seeping through the bandages.

His smile waned. Three months, and he wasn't any closer to catching the real Bud Shaw than the day he'd ridden out of town. He'd failed the one person who had always believed in him.

"You okay, Ranger?" Jo asked.

"Yeah, sure."

"You look like someone just walked over your grave."

"Not mine," he growled.

He'd crushed all the joy from their exchange, but he didn't care. "How far does a man have to go to find some peace around here?"

He pivoted on his heel, stalking out of the barn. The sooner he brought the right man to justice, the better.

Elizabeth hoisted the empty laundry basket onto the bed. Her weakened body protested the exertion. The past two days had been so chaotic, so full of change, she craved a task to ground her. A mindless chore. Something familiar and comforting.

She turned, catching her disheveled reflection in the looking glass above the dresser.

"Oh, my," she groaned.

Her hair hung in a tangled mess down her back. Her cheeks were flushed a bright pink in stark contrast to her pale face. Dark circles rimmed her eyes. She looked no better than one of the beggars she used to pass on her way to work in the city. She lifted her brush from the dresser. Tugging the bristles through the snarls, she worked the knots loose. The heavy mass soon smoothed and shined.

Elizabeth didn't approve of vanity, but even she had to admit her hair was pretty. She had the same blond hair as her mother, thick and long. Wispy tendrils usually framed her face, falling in soft curls around her cheeks. The past days' toil had left her forlorn ringlets drooping and lifeless. She'd love nothing more than another thorough washing and a decadent soak in the galvanized tub, but that would have to wait.

She braided her long strands with practiced fingers, twisting the coil over the top of her head and securing the thick rope with pins. She rubbed her lips together to add a flush of color, unsure why she bothered. There was no one here to care about her appearance, least of all her sleepy daughter.

The extra effort buoyed her spirits, though, and she needed all her mustered strength to face the mess the Ranger had surely made while she'd been laid up.

She reached behind her for the basket,

her gaze drawn to Will's trunk. The domed black chest sat just where he'd left it six months ago. He'd always been possessive of the battered piece of luggage. He never opened the lid in her presence, and he kept the hinge securely locked when he was away.

In the early days of their marriage she'd been obsessed with the contents, curious as to why he kept secrets from her. When the undertaker had delivered Will's personal belongings in a wooden crate, she'd expected to find a key.

Instead, the grim-faced undertaker had ignobly presented her with his grim bounty. An enormous sum of cash carelessly wadded together and secured with a band. The funds for Will's escape from domestic responsibilities.

Later, at the funeral, the undertaker had looked her up and down, suspicion in his lifeless gray eyes. The amount of money had been too excessive for a humble railroad worker, especially given Will's propensity for spending his paychecks before the ink had dried on the paper. Only a cheat could have acquired that much money, the undertaker's eyes seemed to accuse.

She'd decided then and there that what she didn't know couldn't hurt her. From that moment on, she lost all desire to peer into the trunk. The more details she discovered about Will's hazy past, the less certain she became of herself, of her judgment. By opening the trunk, she risked opening wounds that had only just begun to heal. Later, when she wasn't feeling so fragile, she'd delve into the skeletons he'd left behind during his hasty exit.

While Rachel dozed, she lined the laundry basket with another patchwork quilt she'd sewed especially for the baby, then laid the swaddled infant snuggly inside.

"A basket and a drawer." Elizabeth clicked her tongue. "We should have named you Laundry Day instead of Rachel Rose."

The baby blinked, her somber gaze trusting and innocent. A disarming tide of emotion rolled over Elizabeth. The awesome responsibility of shepherding this new life into the harsh world stunned her once again. She didn't know anything about babies. The years before her job at the bakery and then her marriage had been spent in an orphanage where the children were segregated by age.

While most of the older girls had chosen to work with the infants, Elizabeth had taken a job in the kitchens. Seeing those helpless babies, abandoned and alone, had been unbearable. She shuddered at the memory of sparse iron beds lined up against cold, bleak walls. The endless rules and constant chores. Thank heaven Rachel Rose would never have to suffer that life.

Elizabeth tipped her head to the timbered ceiling. "I think I know what you were trying to tell me. I was praying for myself when I should have been praying for others."

God had never been a presence in her life. Maybe that's why He hadn't answered her prayers. Mrs. Peabody from the orphanage had marched them to church on Sundays, their smocks pressed and their hair brushed smooth, but the service had been in Latin. Though Elizabeth had been entranced by the sheer beauty of the church, she'd never understood the words.

She'd been anxious to attend a service in Cimarron. Unfortunately, despite his earlier pious claims, Will had harbored an aversion to churches. They'd even been married by a justice of the peace. A ceremony so rushed, she'd barely registered the event before Will had whisked her to the train depot and settled them on a Pullman car bound for Kansas.

Elizabeth shook off the unsettling memories. Living in the past was a dull and lonely business. One thing was for certain, she'd never trust another man until she had seen a true test of his character.

She lifted Rachel's basket, then marched to the kitchen, her weary body braced for a full day of scrubbing. She raised her head, jerking to a halt. Every surface shined. Even the copper kettle gleamed in a shaft of light streaming through the clear glass window-panes freed from the dimming oilcloth.

Her eyes wide, Elizabeth glanced around the room. Jo must have been up all night to have accomplished such a feat. The brightly polished tin pots and pans hanging against the wall had been neatly arranged by size.

Setting Rachel on the worktable before the stove, Elizabeth made a note to give the girl extra wages this week. Will's money might as well benefit someone deserving of the blessing.

While she admired the spotless kitchen, Mr. Elder shouldered his way through the back door, his arms full of split wood, his hat set low on his head. A gust of frosty air swept a dusting of snow in his wake.

"I thought you'd be gone by now," Elizabeth blurted, astonished to find her heart thumping against her ribs. Certainly she wasn't afraid of him any longer. He'd shown himself to be honorable, if a tad overbearing. Heaven knew he'd had more than ample opportunity to take advantage of them.

His silver star caught the sun, reflecting light. The sight of the lawman's badge caused the memory of the sheriff's threats to explode in her head. There was more than one person in Cimarron Springs who'd like to recoup their losses with the sale of her belongings. Will had been a gambler, and everyone in town had lost money or property to him at one time or another. Yet despite the sheriff's threat to confiscate her property, he'd been too lazy to prove his suspicions.

She didn't need him spurred into action by another lawman.

Jack wiped his feet on the rag rug before stepping into the room. He jostled the wood in his hands for a better grip. "I didn't mean to startle you. I had some chores left." He jerked his head in the direction of the splintered hinges.

"That's very kind of you, but there's really no need. . . ."

Their eyes met and held for a long moment. She'd thought Will handsome, but her late husband paled in comparison to Mr. Elder. While Will had been fair with washed-out blue eyes, the Ranger's features were bold, exaggerated, not at all perfect.

His crooked nose indicated he'd broken it, more than once judging by the flattened bone. A faded scar ran the length of his strong jaw, visible through the stubble shadowing his chin. Deep lines creased his forehead between the dark slash of his eyebrows.

Taken separately, the imperfections should have lessened his attraction, but each one of those minor flaws worked together to lend him a rugged, earthy appearance. His scars revealed a man who had been tested and lived to tell the tale. The realization sent a tingle of apprehension down her spine. She sensed the Ranger's restless need to leave, his barely leashed discontent, even while he lingered, making minor repairs he might have abandoned with impunity. The discrepancy confused her.

Unsure what else to say, she tore her gaze away. She opened the oven door, and stoked the scarlet embers before setting a pan on the stove and pouring in a measure of fresh milk to warm.

Mr. Elder trudged through the kitchen three more times while she arranged her workspace, his arms heaped with a new batch of wood on each trip. She dusted her hands together and shook her head. At this rate, she wouldn't need to refill the woodpile until next fall.

Grasping a tin scoop, she heaped flour along with two generous pinches of salt into an enormous creamware bowl, then pressed her fingers into the mound, digging a hole. After brushing her hands on her apron, she reached into the pie safe and pinched off a corner of yeast, crumbling the moist leaven into the center of the flour. With the milk properly scalded, she added a dollop of bacon grease, stirring until the ingredients melted together.

While the mixture cooled, she wiped down the table with a damp rag. Once she'd gingerly tapped the side of the pan to ensure a lukewarm temperature, she poured the thickened milk into the well of flour. Waiting for the yeast to dissolve, she gradually added a generous handful of sugar.

The Texas Ranger pounded on the back door as she worked. Elizabeth winced at the hammering. Rachel barely stirred.

He paused his work at one point, stepping into the snug kitchen with his hat in his hands. "Is the noise too much? Am I disturbing your daughter?"

Her heart jolted. Hearing someone else call Rachel her daughter made the whole experience real. *This is my family.* Something no one could take away. "Looks like this child would sleep through dynamite."

He gestured toward her face. "You've got a bit of, umm, flour on your . . ."

Elizabeth's hand flew to her warm cheek. She scrubbed at the mark. "I didn't notice."

His own cheeks red and chapped with cold, he cleared his throat with a curt nod, then backed away to resume his work inside. She took in his appearance, smiling at the way his expensive wool coat with a fresh tear in the shoulder stretched over his broad shoulders. He was a large man with an enormous chest tapering down to a lean waist, but he kept a respectful distance, never using his size to intimidate.

He glanced over his shoulder on his way out, catching her curious regard.

Confused by the fluttering in the pit of her stomach, she ducked her head to tighten the apron around her waist. With the Ranger gone, she focused her attention on the liquid mixture foaming merrily in the center of the flour. Satisfied she'd waited long enough for the yeast to develop, she folded in the dry ingredients, invigorated by the familiar process. Making bread was her favorite chore.

She loved the silky texture of the flour, the way the dough gradually came together beneath the heels of her hands to form a smooth, elastic ball. The way the yeast smelled like a summer's day, warm and comforting.

Mr. Elder returned again, his saddlebags slung over his left shoulder. He'd packed to leave. To her chagrin, that curious fluttering resumed.

He snatched off his hat. "I replaced the hinges. You shouldn't have any problems."

"I appreciate that."

"I cut the stumps for kindling."

"Thank you."

An emotion she couldn't quite read flitted across his face. "Well, then. I filled the woodpile in the parlor."

The barren room was hardly a parlor, but she appreciated his concern. "I saw. Was there any room left to sit?"

He flashed a lopsided grin. Not the charming smirk he'd plastered on his face that first night to put her at ease, but a genuine smile. "Just enough."

She was struck by how young he looked without his usual scowl. His abashed expression softened the lines of his face, smoothing the customary crease of worry between his eyebrows. His hair wasn't black, as she'd supposed that first night, but more of a deep chocolate. His hazel eyes sparkled with flecks of gold around the irises, lightening the somber effect of his austere demeanor.

She was unaccustomed to such relaxed behavior in a man. Though he'd been delayed on his journey, he didn't prowl around the house like a caged animal, or burst into action with unleashed energy. He held himself straight and tall. Even when he feigned casual indifference, she sensed a stiffness in his spine, a certain resolve in his stance.

A sudden need to capture this moment overwhelmed her. She wanted to remember the way he circled the brim of his hat in his hands, the way he kept peeking at Rachel when he thought she wasn't looking.

There had been so few moments in her life she had tucked away, saving like price-less treasurers. Why this one? She glanced at Rachel Rose, swaddled in peaceful slumber. This unfamiliar emotion bubbling to the surface, this sensation of warmth and safety wrapping around her like a velvet cloak must be attached to the infant.

Elizabeth floundered for something to say, anxious to avoid the troublesome feelings Mr. Elder aroused. It was best he left now, before she was disillusioned, before time and familiarity revealed the cracks in his facade.

He stuck his hat on his head, lowering the

brim to shield his eyes. "I should be going."

Elizabeth busied herself with separating the dough. "Thank you for everything you've done. Someday I'll tell Rachel the story of her birth. How you thought I was a bank robber."

They both chuckled, her own forced laugh hollow and strained.

When the awkward silence fell once more, he peered at her from beneath the brim of his hat. "When I tell the boys this story, I'll be painting a more heroic picture of myself."

"You did just fine, Mr. Elder."

"After all we've been through, I think you can call me Jack."

Suddenly shy, she met his sheepish gaze. The name suited him. It was strong and solid. Elizabeth let her gaze skitter away from those compassionate, hazel eyes. "Goodbye, Jack."

"Goodbye," he replied. "I'll just be going."

Neither of them moved.

A sharp sorrow robbed her of breath. She attacked her kneading with renewed vigor.

"Jack," she spoke, prolonging the moment, "can you check on Jo? I don't know what's taking her so long with chores."

"I saw her in the barn earlier." His boots scuffed the floor.

Elizabeth suppressed a grin. He probably didn't even notice his own nervous fidget, the boot scuffing that reminded her of a young boy, but she found the gesture charming.

Her somber mood lightened like a leavened pastry. "Tell Jo I'm making bread."

She squelched the urge to slap her forehead. Of course she was making bread. Why had she said such a silly thing? What was wrong with her? She was behaving like a giddy schoolgirl.

Jack cleared his throat. "I will."

"Where will you go after this?"

She didn't even know why she'd asked, except that talking meant he wasn't leaving just yet, and she missed the company of another adult.

"I've got to see the sheriff."

Her effervescent mood plummeted. Clearing her throat, she stood up straighter. "Tell him we're doing fine. Just fine."

He nodded.

Another moment laden with unspoken words passed between them. She grasped for an elusive farewell, a way to thank him that encompassed her diverse emotions, but no words came. Jack pinched the brim of his hat between two fingers, tipping his head in a parting gesture before the door closed quietly behind him.

She pressed the back of her hand to her brow. The temperature in the room seemed to drop. Those pesky, annoying, infuriating tears were clogging her throat once more. What on earth was wrong with her?

A lank strand of hair had fallen across her forehead, and she shook it away with a sigh. She was tired, that was all. Rachel had awakened three times last evening to be fed and changed. All this weeping must be due to her exhaustion.

The growing fatigue pulled her to slump on the stool before the worktable. She didn't need a man around the house.

Rachel's face pinched up a like a dried apple, her lips trembling in distress. The infant's faint mewling reverberated in Elizabeth's chest.

Better that Jack left now. Keeping this home meant keeping her family together, and a wandering lawman asking questions about her past didn't bode well. She was glad he was gone. For good. She was doing *just fine* on her own.

Just fine.

If she repeated the mantra often enough, maybe she'd even believe her own lies.

CHAPTER FIVE

If Jack hadn't been so furious, he might have seen the humor in his current situation. First off, he'd never seen a man so partial to drab brown — the exact color of the hindquarters of a bay mare. Dressed head to toe in the unflattering hue, Cimarron Spring's sheriff resembled a great mound of lumpy, oozing mud.

The older man's dirty-blond hair was saturated with gray, and his eyes mirrored the washed-out beige of his stained and wrinkled shirt. An extra-long pair of suspenders stretched over his shoulders. A leather belt hooked on a freshly notched hole, perilously near the ragged tip, strained to cinch his spreading waist. Ferretlike eyes took Jack's measure.

The sheriff smacked his flabby lips together. "You shoulda told me you was lookin' for a *live* horse," he cackled, his enormous belly undulating with laughter.

"Now, that's a different story."

Clenching his teeth, Jack let his molten anger cool into hardened steel. He failed to see the humor in sending a fellow lawman on a wild-goose chase. "I'm looking for a *live* horse and a *live* man. A man who murdered a woman during a bank robbery."

Jack had been in Cimarron Springs for several days, waiting for a meeting. Both the sheriff and the town doc had been unavailable. While Jack understood the doc's busy schedule causing a delay, he'd yet to discern the cause of the sheriff's stalling. As far as Jack could tell, the only pressing item on that man's schedule was his next meal.

Under Jack's unyielding scowl, the jovial smile on the sheriff's face gradually dissolved into a blank stare. "Don't get all uppity on me, Ranger," the man spoke, his tone defensive. "I've got a lot going on here. There's a flu epidemic crippling the town. We've had six deaths already. The undertaker had to pile the bodies in the lean-to. Good thing it's winter or we'd a had a putrid smell."

The sheriff thoughtfully rubbed at his drink-reddened cheeks. No doubt concerned about the effect of such a noxious odor on his appetite.

"I'm sorry for the town's losses," Jack

replied, though nothing in the sheriff's demeanor suggested he had suffered unduly. "But you knew I was searching for outlaws, and you sent me to a homestead."

Jack kept out the part where he'd aimed his gun at a woman in labor — for Mrs. Cole's privacy, and his own credibility. He might have lived an uncommitted life, never staying long enough in one place to let the gossips sink their teeth into his hide, but Elizabeth didn't have the luxury of escaping a scandal generated by his stay on her property.

"You asked about a horse," the sheriff pointed out. "I told you the truth. Will Cole was partial to a distinctive bay mustang." The older man snorted. " 'Course, they're both dead now."

Jack reigned in his growing frustration. Incompetence was no excuse, and the sheriff's feigned ignorance had his teeth on edge. Elizabeth's husband certainly wasn't a bank robber. Enough money had been stolen during the Wells Fargo job to leave a man set like a king. Jack had yet to meet a thief capable of restraining his natural desire to immediately spend his ill-gotten gains. A fellow with that much money didn't live on an isolated homestead with only one milk cow and a bunch of scrawny chickens.

This trip to town had been a waste, and the trail out of Cimarron Springs had dried up, yet he found himself loitering in the sheriff's stale office, surrounded by walls yellowed with cigar smoke, as his growing defeat warred with his burgeoning curiosity. Jack had discovered long ago that if he let people talk long enough, they let down their guard. That's when his job got interesting.

He kicked back in his chair, forcing himself to link his hands behind his head. Gossip was a good lead into more important matters — like outlaws and stolen money. Of course his renewed interest in interrogating the sheriff had nothing to do with the widow and her newborn. This exercise was strictly related to the Wells Fargo job.

"What happened to Mr. Cole?" Jack asked.

"I miss that Will."

Jack's sudden consternation at the mention of Elizabeth's husband startled him. Before now, he hadn't actually thought of her late husband as an actual flesh-and-blood man with friends and family. Will Cole had been a shadow figure, undefined, relegated to the past. Talking with the sheriff about Will made him real. Jack had a sickening realization he wasn't going to shake the dead man's presence any time soon.

"You miss Will?" Jack asked noncommittally.

"He was a man who appreciated a good joke." The sheriff shot Jack a telling look, as if sending a fellow lawman into a snowstorm was some sort of great lark, and Jack was a spoilsport for not appreciating the humor.

Jack forced himself to concentrate on the droning conversation while the sheriff touched on a multitude of subjects with the mentions of Will Cole spread out sparsely in between. The way the sheriff carried on about everything from the weather to the lack of tasty licorice at the dry goods store, Jack figured he'd see the spring thaw before an insightful piece of information spilled.

The sheriff spat a wad of tobacco juice into the spittoon at his feet. "That Will Cole sure was a charmer. Came into town every night when he wasn't traveling. Had a job with the railroad, ya know."

"The railroad, huh?" Jack encouraged. So far, the sheriff had bragged about all of Will's dubious attributes — his gambling, his drinking, his roving eye. The last transgression bothered Jack most. He wondered if Elizabeth knew, and prayed that she didn't. What kind of man dishonored his wife that way? If Jack had a woman like Elizabeth waiting for him, he wouldn't be hang-

100

ing around rancid saloons.

He recalled the humor in Elizabeth's clear blue eyes as she'd thanked him for his help. She had a way of looking at him, really looking, as if nothing was more important than listening to what he had to say. When she'd smiled at Rachel, her face had lit up like the sun rising over the Rockies. He'd never seen anything like it.

The sheriff scratched at his domed belly. The unwelcome grating of his overly long fingernails against coarse cotton interrupted Jack's fond recollections of Elizabeth.

The potbellied man wiggled his upper lip to adjust the wad of chew tucked between his cheek and gum. "That Will sure had a lot of luck with gambling. Real generous, though. Always bought a round of drinks before he left."

Elizabeth's fearful words echoed through Jack's head. *You won't bring whiskey into this house.*

She might not have known every disreputable detail about her late husband, but she knew plenty. Did she know that her husband had most likely supplemented his income as a card cheat? Professional sharps often gave away just enough of their winnings to keep the other players from growing suspicious.

Jack stared at a spot of cracked plaster

scarring the wall above the sheriff's head. "What happened to Mr. Cole?"

The sheriff's expression grew somber. "Will and his horse slid down a gully sometime early summer. Must have been the end of May or the first part of June. Can't rightly remember. We had a real bad rain. Just kept pouring down for over a week. I was about to build an ark myself." The sheriff cackled at his own joke.

Jack forced a grin to keep the sheriff talking. He'd rather be anywhere than listening to the painful details of Elizabeth's troublesome past, but shying away from cold, hard facts never solved a problem.

"Anyway," the sheriff continued, "Will was riding over by Hackberry Creek. His horse slid down an embankment, broke its neck. Landed right on Will's leg. The poor guy must of drowned when the creek water rose." The sheriff leaned forward. His overburdened chair groaned in protest. "We kept that part about his suffering from his missus. I told her he died right off. She's one of those greenhorns from back East. Real weak little thing. I figured she'd die within a year. Most of those city folk don't survive long out here."

The sheriff's remarks had Jack's hands curling into fists. He recalled Elizabeth's accent, the slight lilt in her voice that gave her words a lyrical quality.

"She from Boston or something? She's got a particular way of talking."

"New York, maybe. Leastways, that's where Will found her. Real whirlwind courtship from the way he told it. She was some sort of orphan working for scraps in a bakery, when Will saved her. His job with the railroad took him all over the country. I think maybe her parents came over from England. Can't say for certain. She wasn't much for talking. Hardly came to town at all. Not even for church."

Jack muffled his snort of disgust. From what the sheriff had just said, her husband came to town often enough for the both of them, and his activities weren't conducive to attending services on Sundays.

What kind of a fellow left his wife all alone for weeks on end, this close to Indian territory, then took off again to gamble just as soon as he'd arrived home? Life on the plains was too dangerous for that kind of self-centered idiocy.

Jack adjusted in his chair. "Mrs. Cole shouldn't be out on that homestead all alone."

"I talked to her after Will died. Told her she was a fool to stay." The sheriff lowered his voice to a conspiratorial whisper, "I even offered to marry her myself."

Jack's heart skidded to a halt. "You what?"

"Offered to marry her. Women around these parts are harder to find than an Irishman at work. Not that I care to raise another man's brat, but sometimes you gotta take the wheat with the chaff."

"I see."

Jack gritted his teeth at the insult to Elizabeth. He wasn't a man who liked violence; most problems could be solved amicably with subtle negotiation, but some people were just too pigheaded to listen. That's when a man had to use force.

The sheriff brought his hand to his cauliflower-shaped ear and buried one finger up to his grimy knuckle. "Never could figure out why a man with that much to live for would be down by the creek that day. Doesn't make any sense."

His casual declaration finally piqued Jack's interest. "What doesn't make any sense?"

The older man continued working his finger back and forth in his ear. He scratched so deep, Jack figured his brain must itch.

"Will was awful fussy about his appearance. He wasn't much for dirt or mud. Kept his hat dry and his boots clean. His buttons shined so bright, they'd darn near blind a man."

Jack felt himself flush. Hadn't his own brothers mocked him for his fussy way of dressing? He'd ignored their ridicule because they didn't understand life outside a cattle ranch. A Texas Ranger mingled with people from every walk of life. Jack had discovered early on that men respected appearance before they respected words. His dress wasn't vanity, it was survival.

Elizabeth's sweeping assessment of him that first day flashed in his mind. Her gaze had lingered on his coat. Had she been thinking of Will? Was the disappointment blazing in her pale blue eyes directed at Jack, or at her late husband?

His mind lost in thoughts of Elizabeth, Jack snapped back to the present when he realized the sheriff had spoken.

"You touched in the head, Ranger?" the sheriff all but shouted.

Beginning to wonder himself, Jack bit back a sharp reply.

"I said, where are you going from here?"

"Thought I'd make my way to Wichita," Jack said.

"Yep. If I was a bank robber, I'd travel on up to Wichita." Spittle ricocheted into the spittoon. "There's more money to be had in the big cities."

"If you were a bank robber, my job would be a whole lot easier."

The sheriff started to laugh, then thought better of it and stuttered to a halt. "You mean something by that, mister?"

"Not at all," Jack soothed. "Just means you're a lot handier, being as you're sitting right in front of me and all."

"That's what I thought you meant," the sheriff replied, mollified for the moment.

Jack assumed the "hey, we're all friends here" smile he used when gathering information. "You've been real helpful, Sheriff . . ."

"Stanton."

"Sheriff Stanton. Don't suppose I'll ever forget that name."

Jack forced his hands to unclench. Pushing off from the arms of his sturdy wooden chair, he stood. "It's been real nice to meet you, Sheriff Stanton. I've got to visit the doctor before I leave. If you think of anything else that might be useful, that's where you'll find me."

The sheriff struggled out of his chair, his lumbering rise to his feet accompanied by the crackle and pop of his joints. Straightening, he hoisted his muddy brown trousers over his potbelly, then shook them back down into place.

Jack had never been so grateful for the double security of a belt and suspenders.

The sheriff picked at his yellowed teeth. "Think I'll head over to the saloon. Get something to eat, maybe something to drink, then call it a day."

Jack added gluttony to the sheriff's growing list of sins. The clock hadn't even struck the noon hour, and here the man was ready to start drinking. Spending only twenty minutes a day on the job didn't leave much time for work. The next time Jack needed a lawman in Cimarron Springs, he'd know better than to count on Sheriff Stanton.

Too dense to pick up on Jack's disgust, Stanton droned on about how much the community paid him to play cards. Jack cut short the pleasantries and stepped into the gray afternoon.

A young couple bumped past him, bundled against the cold. The gentleman took his companion's hand as they traversed an icy patch. The woman smiled shyly.

A flurry of memories drew Jack to a halt. He hadn't thought of his parents in years, but something about the couple brought them to mind. How many times had his own father displayed the same courtly manners with his mother? Held her elbow to cross a rocky patch of ground, or stepped forward to hold open a door? Jack recalled their private looks over the dinner table, their shared jokes.

He'd never thought of his parents as anything but two ordinary, middle-aged folks raising a family. But a newer, more mature understanding dawned on him. His parents had been young once, like the couple he'd just seen. Young and courting. The novel idea kept him rooted to the spot.

"Someone nail your feet to the boardwalk, Ranger?" The sheriff nudged him out of the way. "Looks like the doc's heading for his office. There's another sawbones farther down the road, but I wouldn't recommend him. Takes a little too much of his own tonic." The sheriff held his pinky in the air and touched his thumb to his lower lip. "If you get my meaning."

Jack gave a curt nod. With every other person in this town drunk or loafing, he wondered how any work got done.

Focusing his attention on the tall, slender man the sheriff had indicated, he crossed the snow-packed road. Crystalline flakes caught on Jack's eyelashes and stood out like dandruff on his wool coat.

He squinted at the ominous sky. *Great.* Just what this day needed, more snow.

Brushing the flakes from his shoulders, he stalked toward the gentleman sporting a black bowler and clutching a crisp, leather satchel.

"You the doc?" Jack asked abruptly.

The man glanced up, his sharp gaze annoyed at the interruption. "Yeah, that's me, Doc Johnsen."

The fair-haired doctor was younger than Jack had expected, with translucent blue eyes indicative of the Norwegian populations farther north. Blond hair curled beneath the brim of the doc's bowler. While Jack sized up the man, two well-dressed young women paused on the boardwalk. One of the women pointed a gloved finger at Doc Johnsen, whispering to her companion. They both giggled, holding hands to their mouths before scurrying away.

Jack tugged his hat lower over his dark hair. You never could tell what women found attractive. What did looks matter when there was work to be done? A head full of curly golden locks never stopped a bullet. Besides, the doc still had the "wet behind the ears" appearance of a body too young to be seasoned by life.

Then again, something in the way the younger man sized Jack up with one long sweeping gaze told him he'd be able to survive the West with his wits intact. Glancing down the street, Jack sighed. What other choice did he have? The doc might be young, but at least this fellow wasn't imbibing his own tonic.

Jack stuck out his hand, his faultless instincts urging him to trust the man. "You're just the person I wanted to see. I'm Jack Elder. I was wondering if you could check on Mrs. Cole. She delivered her baby on Sunday. I'll pay you double your usual fee to check on the widow and her baby."

"I'll be." Doc Johnsen gave Jack's hand a brisk, solid pump. "I just checked on the McCoy family a few days ago. I planned on visiting Mrs. Cole on my way back, but the weather changed, and I didn't want to risk the trip. I hope she was able to get help. It pains me to think of her out there all alone."

Jack had been so focused on locating the doc, he hadn't thought of how he would explain his own involvement. "Well, Jo — uh — Jo McCoy was with Mrs. Cole last I knew."

Those translucent blue eyes narrowed with curiosity. "You don't say."

Forced to elaborate on his role, Jack paused, searching for an answer that wouldn't incite more questions. The emotions attached to those events were still too raw, too slippery to share with a stranger. "I, ah, passed by on the way to town." That was the truth. Not as if he was lying or anything. "Jo was there with Mrs. Cole. The baby seemed healthy."

"Well, then. I'm sure everything is fine. Mrs. McCoy is about the closest thing we have to a midwife around here, and Jo often assists her. If need be, Jo's smart enough to send for help."

Jack's stomach contracted into a tight ball. How would Jo send for help? The widow's swayback mare probably scraped the snow drifts with its distended belly. What kind of fool lived on the prairie without a decent horse and wagon? He gave himself a mental shake. The same kind of fool woman who stayed on a homestead, alone, when she was nine months pregnant. That's who.

His heart rate quickened with anger before he hardened his resolve. The widow was someone else's problem now. "How are the McCoys?"

"There's a whole lot of McCoys leaning over chamber pots." The doc chuckled. "They're a strong lot, though. The fever has gone through two of the older boys. Should take another week or so before everyone is healthy again."

"Is that the worst of it?"

The younger man gave him a knowing look. "We've had deaths in town, to be sure, but mostly the elderly and the infirm." He switched his satchel from one gloved hand to the other. "There's not an elderly or infirm McCoy in fifty miles. They'll need some time to recover, but I'm confident of the outcome. I'm sure they'll be out to see Mrs. Cole soon enough."

"Confident, are you?" Here was another person with a total disregard for the dangers Elizabeth and her newborn faced. Almost everyone he'd talked to so far acted like a lone woman with an infant, living on the plains, was just a matter of course.

"Mrs. Cole shouldn't be living out there by herself," Jack snapped. "Someone ought to talk some sense into her."

The blond man shrugged. "It distresses me, too, to think of Mrs. Cole doing all that work, especially with a baby to care for. Don't see how we can stop her, though." Doc Johnsen stood up straighter, his neck flushed. "I offered to marry her myself after Will died. She turned me down so politely, I almost felt bad for asking."

Something hot and ugly rolled in Jack's stomach. "Really? Seems like I heard something similar from someone else."

The snow must have covered the divots

left in the road by the town's bachelors in their treks to and from the widow's door after Will's funeral. While it wasn't unheard for a woman living out West to marry within weeks after her husband's death, Elizabeth had turned them all down flat. She'd chosen to remain a widow, rather than remarry. Had she loved her husband that much?

The logical conclusion nearly bowled him over. She'd wasted her love on that fool, and Jack didn't like waste. He also didn't like the way his own emotions had tipped upside down. Instead of anger at her refusal of the handsome doctor's perfectly reasonable offer, the only feeling he could muster was cold relief.

Lack of sleep must be driving him mad. The boarding house in town had played host to a crowd of rowdy cowboys until the wee hours of the morning. Whatever the cause of his unrest, he vowed to leave all thoughts of the widow behind and concentrate on the present. Jack reached into his pocket for payment, but the doc waved away the proffered bills.

"No payment necessary. I was heading in that direction, anyway. I'd best be going, the day's half over already. Nice to meet you, Mr. Elder."

The doc continued his brisk walk in the

opposite direction. Jack turned on his heel to follow, drawn to say something more, to send a message. He slowed his pace. His job was not to babysit the woman, his job was to pick up on the outlaw's trail.

He'd heard from another man in town that a foot of snow had fallen up north. With any luck, the killer was holed up in Wichita because of the weather. Jack's brothers were counting on him, and he never let family down — not for anything, or anyone. Not even a pretty little widow with laughing blue eyes.

After all, she'd been fine on her own up to now.

She was a failure. In six short weeks, her life had descended into bedlam.

Elizabeth glanced around the chaotic room, taking in the overwhelming mess. Recently laundered rags set to dry littered every available surface. Tin plates and cups overflowed the sink. Dirt tracked in by muddy shoes streaked the floor in spokes away from the back door. A pan of fragrant winter-vegetable stew bubbled on the stove.

She laid Rachel against her shoulder, patting the infant's back. The baby had been crying for almost twenty minutes. Not the sweet mewling sounds from previous weeks, but great squalling sobs that had Elizabeth's stomach churning. What if something was wrong with her daughter?

The firewood Jack had left for the stove, the supply she'd thought would never end, had dwindled. She needed to gather more kindling to keep the house warm enough for Rachel, but each time she began a task, a fresh crisis distracted her.

The doc had stopped by several weeks before, giving Rachel a clean bill of health. He'd also hinted that a certain Texas Ranger had been asking the sheriff a lot of questions about Elizabeth's late husband and her living situation. She'd spent the days after Doc Johnsen's visit on pins and needles, terrified the sheriff would start threatening her ownership of the property again.

As if sensing her tension, the infant wailed louder. Elizabeth gently rocked the baby. "Shh, shh, shh," she cooed.

She bent to set down Rachel, determined to remove the boiling stew from the stove before dinner burned. While she suspected the sheriff was using his threats as leverage to marry her, she still feared his retribution at her continued refusal.

Alarmed to note Rachel's face turning a

brilliant shade of red, Elizabeth paused mid-air.

What in heaven's name did that mean? Had the infant taken ill? Gracious, fourteen-year-old Jo knew more about babies. But with all the young McCoy boys full of unleashed energy from their forced confinement and causing mischief, Jo had been too busy at home to tutor Elizabeth on child rearing.

At least the younger girl had managed to slip over this afternoon to help with chores. The assistance was invaluable, and the company kept Elizabeth sane.

She rose wearily to her feet, doing the only thing that seemed to work to quiet Rachel. Back and forth she paced, patting and shushing. Her steps chewed up the distance between the kitchen and the parlor. No amount of soothing comforted the infant.

Exhausted, she slumped onto a chair and attempted to feed the baby, but Rachel wouldn't latch on. Elizabeth set to pacing again, tears of frustration gathering in her eyes.

Jo stepped through the back door, an armload of kindling in her hands.

"I was going to do that," Elizabeth grumbled over Rachel's howling cries.

"That baby sure is squawking. What's

wrong with her?"

"I was hoping you would know. I've tried everything, but nothing soothes her."

"She might be colicky." Jo raised her voice to be heard over the wailing infant.

"What's colic?"

"It's when their stomach gets upset."

Certainly if the problem had a name, there was also a solution. "Is there a cure?"

Distracted by their conversation, the baby's sobs relaxed into snuffled hiccups.

Jo shrugged, not pausing on her way to the parlor. "I can't rightly remember. I'll ask my ma when I go home tonight."

Rachel burped. The baby brought her fist to her mouth with a contented coo, and snuggled into Elizabeth's shoulder.

Elizabeth blew out a sigh of relief. Who knew there was more air in that tiny body? She'd already been burped before. Elizabeth did everything on a schedule. Unfortunately, her daughter didn't seem to like schedules. Everything Elizabeth knew about child rearing would fit into a thimble, and she'd exhausted her limited knowledge weeks ago. She hadn't realized raising an infant was so intense, so grueling. She had to learn faster. Rachel Rose was depending on her.

A pungent odor teased Elizabeth's nostrils.

She glanced up to find a haze of smoke floating near the ceiling. Something in the kitchen hissed and popped.

The stew!

She dashed to the stove and found dinner bubbling over. Dark brown blobs streaked down the sides of the pan, igniting in the grate.

Elizabeth whirled, colliding with Jo.

The girl rolled her eyes. "I'll take care of it."

Jo snatched a flour sack off a loaf of bread, then wrapped the cloth around her hand before reaching for the pot. Grasping the handle, she scooted to the exit. Elizabeth balanced Rachel on one shoulder, holding open the door with her free hand.

Jo crossed the threshold, searching for a place to drop the scalding pan. She stepped off the landing to her left. Her toe skidded along a patch of ice. Her feet slipped out beneath her. Limbs flailing, Jo struggled to right herself. The pan flew into the air. Vegetable stew rained down, splotching into the snow like blobs of mud.

A sickening thud accompanied Jo's shriek of pain.

CHAPTER SIX

The forlorn town of Cimarron Springs huddled in the distance beneath dismal clouds signaling yet another snowstorm. Jack reined Midnight to a halt on a ridge overlooking the Arkansas River. The horse's muscles bunched beneath him as the animal stomped and snorted.

Thoughts of the pretty widow buzzed relentlessly in his head like fireflies trapped in a Mason jar.

Nervous anticipation scratched beneath Jack's skin the closer he traveled to Cimarron Springs. More than a month had passed, and he had nothing to show for his time. Plenty of the locals around Wichita knew of Bud Shaw in passing, but no one had seen the outlaw in months.

He teetered infuriatingly close to a capture, yet the killer eluded him. Compounding his difficulties, only a few hundred dollars had been recovered from the Wells

Fargo robbery. If Bud Shaw maintained control of the balance, there was no telling how far and how fast the outlaw had run.

With the threat of snow hanging heavily in the air, he couldn't afford any delays. Even if he wanted to linger in Kansas, an innocent man faced certain death if Jack dawdled over a blue-eyed widow and her infant like a lovelorn fool.

"Lord," he spoke, his voice lost in the blustery wind. "If you're looking down on me, now would be a good time for some help."

Midnight stumbled over a slick patch of ice. Jack tugged on the reigns, struggling to regain his balance in the saddle. "Don't worry, old boy. My ma always used to say, 'God doesn't mind if your prayers are long or short, He hears them all.' "

The horse snorted a vaporous breath as it skittered over slick, packed snow, jerking to a halt where the wagon tracks split. One road stretched west, to Cimarron Springs. The other meandered south, over the border into Indian territory. Jack urged the horse forward. Midnight shied, dancing to one side.

Reaching back, Jack slapped the obstinate animal's hindquarters. "No more stubbornness. We have a long way to go before there's rest for either of us."

Midnight pawed at the frozen ground. Jack sighed. At least the delay gave him another opportunity to study Cimarron Springs. Black smoke drifted from the multitude of chimneys burning coal and wood against frigid north winds.

An elusive thought teased his brain. A piece of the puzzle that didn't quite fit. What was he missing? Rubbing at his eyes, Jack sucked in a deep, icy breath. He'd seen the gaudy innards of so many seedy saloons, the stench of rancid cigar smoke still clung to his coat.

He needed something — anything: a name, a rumor, even another sighting of that bay mustang. The next best thing to Bud Shaw was someone who knew the outlaw well — someone who knew where the killer had holed up. Outlaws weren't known for their honor.

According to Sheriff Stanton, Elizabeth's husband had run with coarse company, and a lot of it. Gamblers were bound to cross paths. Perhaps Will Cole had mentioned his card-playing buddies to Elizabeth.

The hairs on the back of Jack's neck stirred.

She hadn't recognized Bud's name all those weeks ago, but she'd been awfully distracted. It was a long shot, but what did he have to lose? At this point, he was desperate for another lead. Anything but these infuriating dead ends and false starts.

Jack studied the cluster of buildings.

There had to be a reason why every clue led to this sleepy little town. His plan wasn't totally without merit. Cimarron Springs was the last place Bud Shaw had been spotted, and where the trail had grown cold. And if Jack was wrong, Kansas was as good a place as any to rest. After sending out a few telegrams, he'd pay a visit to Rachel Rose and her mother.

A new plan formed in his mind, the steps laid out like a bricked path in his brain.

His plan served two purposes. Inquiring about the widow's late husband gave him a legitimate reason to check on her and the baby. If her husband had played cards with Bud Shaw, she was a link to the killers and their stolen loot. She might even be in danger.

The outlaw was a braggart, and there was no telling who else was looking for that money — or who else was following the same leads.

Jack's gut twisted. The face of every victim he'd ever buried, every child whose grave he'd marked with piles of stones flashed in his mind. A sudden image filled his brain. He pictured the smudge of flour on Elizabeth's cheek, and a new urgency drove him forward. Kicking Midnight into a canter, he gave in to his growing impatience.

This surge of anticipation had everything to do with finding Bud Shaw, and nothing to do with his rampant worry for a tiny infant girl and her beguiling mother.

Elizabeth bent her head against the ferocious wind. How long had she been walking? Over an hour at least. The deep wagon ruts she usually followed to the McCoys had been whipped smooth with snowdrifts, forcing her to search for familiar landmarks, instead. Only the spindly cottonwood trees lining the creek bed kept her from straying completely off track.

She pressed her mittened hands to her face. At least the painful stinging in her cheeks had faded into a dull ache. No matter the discomfort, she had to keep moving. Thoughts of Jo and Rachel drove her forward. They were depending on her, and time was running out. Elizabeth concentrated on lifting her numb feet, placing one foot in front of the other in a relentless march through white oblivion.

A flash of light caught her attention. Rubbing her eyes, she squinted, then glanced behind her. Nothing appeared on the horizon. Probably just the wind playing tricks on her. She yanked her hat closer over her ears, forcing herself to focus on moving from one landmark to the next, rather than crossing the whole overwhelming distance.

Rippling hills of relentless snow and ice stretched on forever. Studying the flat terrain kept her thoughts from wandering into all the frightening consequences of her perilous journey.

Her scattered thoughts drifted back to her journey West only a year ago. This was how the prairie had looked when she'd first arrived from New York — the grasses flattened and windblown. After the bustling crowds of the city, the barren landscape had overwhelmed her with its lonely visage.

When the golden mantle of spring had finally settled over the desolate prairie, she'd practically wept with relief. By mid-summer, stalks of wheat grasses had rippled in the wind, moving like golden waves on the ocean.

Spring seemed an eternity away. No matter how far she walked, the distance to the next rise refused to shrink. She longed to sit and rest, just for a moment. Time had become her enemy.

A low rumble vibrated beneath her feet. Thoughts of Indians and outlaws robbed her of breath. Heart pounding, she jerked around to find a great black horse charging across the plains. Elizabeth froze. The apparition galloped over the white snow, chewing up the distance. Her brain told her to move, but her feet refused to obey.

At the last moment she stumbled to one side. Covering her face, she braced for a blow from those enormous, coal-black hooves. The horse skidded to a halt, kicking up a shower of snow. A great bear of a man in a familiar dark wool coat leaped down, stalking toward her as if he'd materialized straight out of the blowing storm.

Elizabeth backed away, terrified by the low menace in his approach. He raised his arms. Her hands flew to her face in a protective gesture.

"Fool woman," Jack shouted over the wind.

Something heavy wrapped around her shoulders. She peeked with one eye to find her shoulders swathed in a tartan fabric. He'd covered her with a wool blanket. Her apprehension waned a notch.

"What are you doing?" Jack demanded.

Fear, relief and annoyance jumbled together in a confusing churn of emotions.

"Getting help," Elizabeth snapped back through chattering teeth. "Jo fell. She's hurt her foot and her ribs. I think she's broken her ankle."

Tightening the comforting blanket around her shoulders, she noted how the cold had seeped through her coat. With the Ranger's sudden appearance, all of her physical discomforts came rushing back.

Jack grunted. Only his eyes showed between his hat and his muffler, but those hazel orbs sparked with exasperation. "You were fool enough to walk out in this weather?"

"It wasn't snowing when I started."

"You left an injured kid to mind your baby. What were you thinking?"

The obvious censure in his question sent her stumbling back a step. "R-Rachel was sleeping. I wasn't going to be gone that long."

Her first instinct had been correct. He wasn't annoyed, he was furious. Anger radiated from his enormous body like steam rising from a hot spring. For the first time since he'd barged into her life, she feared him.

He looped the reins around his leather-clad hand with a scowl. "You're going home."

Afraid or not, he had no right to order her around.

"I'll do what I please." Elizabeth ducked away from his outstretched arm. "You go back to town and fetch the doctor. I can walk home on my own."

"You'll ride with me." His expression dared her to disobey his order. "Then we'll decide if Jo needs a doctor."

"You're not in charge of me."

"As long as you're behaving like a lunatic, I am."

Trembling with the accumulated tensions of the past days, Elizabeth knotted her fists at her sides. "What did you just call me?"

"You heard me. You left an infant and an injured kid alone so you could freeze to death in a snowstorm. That's a lunatic decision if ever I heard one."

"How dare you question my decisions? What else was I supposed to do? Send the milk cow?"

He hooked one finger into his woolen muffler, tugging the material down to reveal the full force of his disapproving glower. "Look, lady. If you die, Rachel is an orphan, and we both know how you feel about that option. You coming or not?"

A stubborn denial sat on the tip of her tongue. Swirling flakes battered her face.

Searching the distance, she was shocked to discover the group of trees she'd been aiming for completely obscured by churning snow.

She pictured her daughter's wise, trusting eyes and Elizabeth's stomach sank. The Ranger was correct, her life was no longer her own to gamble. Pride clogged the words in her throat.

"Let's go," Jack declared, softening his demand to a brisk instruction. "I've already checked on the house, and Jo and the baby are fine."

"You what?"

"How do you think I found you? I stopped for a visit on my way out of Cimarron Springs. By the looks of the place, I assumed something awful had happened."

Elizabeth huffed. Of course he'd already been to the house. Hadn't he mentioned that Jo was minding the baby? Nettled, she refused to dignify his remark with an answer. The condition of her home was none of his affair. He wasn't exhausted from raising an infant. She'd like to see how well he'd fare after taking care of a baby all alone with only a few squandered hours of sleep each night.

He hoisted himself onto the horse, holding out a hand. Floundering in the gathering snow, she shook her head. The thought of climbing atop that enormous animal terrified her almost as much as the man sitting astride it.

He beckoned impatiently. "Put your foot in the stirrup and I'll pull you up."

"I don't need your help."

" 'When pride cometh, then cometh shame. But with the lowly is wisdom.' "

"Are you mocking me?"

"The Bible isn't meant to mock you, Elizabeth."

Once again, her own ignorance condemned her. She'd opened her Bible plenty of times. The worn copy had been bestowed upon her by Mrs. Peabody from the orphanage. Banished to find work in the city at sixteen, all the girls had received a Bible and two dollars. The orphanage had given her plenty of training in working hard, and little else. Elizabeth had treasured the book, one of her few possessions, but she hadn't studied the scriptures as much as she would have liked. Sure of her unworthiness, she'd been humbled by the wisdom the book contained.

There hadn't been much time to learn, anyway. The hours at the bakery had been from dawn till dusk. The family who owned the shop had insisted she stay behind on

Sundays in order to prepare the kitchen for busy Monday mornings. During her three-week courtship, Will had promised to accompany her to services. He'd broken that promise along with so many others.

Jack reined his horse to a halt before her, effectively blocking her flight. "If you won't think of yourself, at least think of Jo. She was sick with worry when I left to find you."

"How dare you judge me." Her voice broke. "I did the best I could while you were gone."

Suddenly another man stood before her. Another man who had left her, again and again, until at last he'd been so disappointed, he'd left for good.

"I'm here now."

Jack nudged the horse closer. A cutting wind brought moisture to her eyes. Numbing cold penetrated the tartan blanket around her shoulders. Uncontrollable shivers racked her body.

If she refused, he'd know she couldn't ride. Drained of fight, she focused on a glimpse of the scrollwork design stamped into the pommel of his leather saddle.

Constantly living in fear was exhausting. From the moment her mother had abandoned her at the orphanage, the grueling emotion had ruled her life. Even her marriage had been fraught with fear — fear that Will might never return from one of his many trips — and fear that he would.

She didn't want to be afraid anymore. She didn't want to be a disappointment to anyone, especially herself.

Elizabeth grasped the Ranger's hand. The coarse threads of her woolen mittens dug into her fingers as he squeezed. Gathering her courage, she lifted her booted foot. The leather stirrup loomed impossibly high.

"The other foot," Jack grumbled.

Fuming, she shifted her weight. Her skirts stretched over her knee as she drew her leg higher, finally sinking her toe into the narrow loop.

He effortlessly tugged on her arm. She managed to swing her leg over the back of the animal. Matted snow clumped wetly to her hem as her skirts flapped over her calf. Seated precariously, Elizabeth wrapped her arms around Jack's waist and hung on for dear life. His large body sheltered her from the worst of the buffeting wind.

Glancing over his shoulder, Jack caught her gaze. "You set?"

Her heartbeat raced. She nodded, not trusting herself to speak. His face loomed so close she noted the flecks of gold surrounding his irises. Heat emanated from his body, enveloping her in warmth. Her bone-rattling shudders stilled.

"We'd best get back home, then," he muttered brusquely. Despite the urgency in his voice, he gently nudged the horse at a sedate, slow ramble.

Elizabeth glanced down, quickly pinching her eyes shut again. The hard ground rushed by a great distance away. She fisted her hands in his coat, hugging Jack closer. The rough wool abraded her cheek with the horse's uneven gate.

The muscle along his strong jaw clenched and unclenched, as if he was biting back his fury. With every step that brought them closer to home, her initial annoyance at his high-handed behavior blossomed into outright resentment. She didn't want to be afraid, but she didn't want to be ordered about or subjected to this seething resentment.

The horse stumbled, sending her teetering to one side. Shrieking, she fumbled to regain her balance.

Jack pressed his leather-clad hand over her woolen mittens to hold her steady. "I've got you."

His protective gesture acted like a bucket of ice water on her smoldering anger. Elizabeth sighed. The lawman was simply a convenient target for her irritation. In truth, she wasn't angry with Jack. She was disappointed in herself. Once again, an impulsive decision had proven disastrous. Going for help had been the wrong choice. She hadn't known it was going to snow.

A sharp wind kicked up, tearing at the tartan blanket. Jack leaned forward, urging the horse to a quicker pace while still keeping a firm hold on her arm.

The faint outline of her homestead appeared in the distance. Three modest buildings clustered beneath the branches of red oak, sugar maple and linden trees planted by settlers long since gone. The protective copse of trees stood guard against the maddening winds that drove across the plains from season to season.

The bunkhouse appeared first, with the barn set farther back and to the left. The one-story main house with its covered porch sat closest to the road to town. Those buildings represented everything she owned, every piece of her desolate history. Her only hope for the future.

Here was the one piece of security she'd managed to cling to despite the relentless forces buffeting her safe, ordered world. Here was the only property she'd ever owned, the only home that had ever truly belonged to her. Her heart had soared the first time she laid eyes on the modest spread. Now she waited for the familiar surge of possessive emotion.

Nothing.

Her stomach plummeted. She clawed for purchase on a slope of conflicting emotions, but the drab structures failed to inspire anything but apathy. There was no life in the wood, mortar, brick or glass. The absence of her usual giddy pleasure unsettled her. Instead, she felt trapped. Without those steadying markers, what did she have?

Rocked by the loss, she clung to Jack, letting his body shield her from the driving snow while she absorbed his comforting warmth. She could pretend, just for a moment, that she wasn't alone any longer. Rachel's birth had driven home how desperately she needed someone to confide in, to lean on.

Her cranky rescuer veered away from the barn, continuing on a path toward the house. He reined the horse to a halt before the front porch. Jack turned his head, bringing his profile into view.

Without speaking he held out his hand. Elizabeth grasped the offering, swinging to the ground. When her feet hit the solid earth, she feared her legs would buckle. As if sensing her distress, Jack held her mittened fingers until she steadied herself.

Glancing up, she recalled how he'd looked the night Rachel Rose was born. Her pulse quickened. What a blessing that evening had brought. The memory had her heart opening like the first crocus of spring, new and reborn.

Finally, here were the feelings she'd been searching for.

Anxious to ensure Jo and Rachel's safety, she whirled, racing up the shallow, slippery steps to yank open the door.

She dashed to the bedroom and discovered them both sleeping peacefully. Jo with the blanket tucked beneath her chin, Rachel in her makeshift crib. Elizabeth pressed a hand to her chest. *Thank the Lord.* No one had suffered for her impetuous dash for help. She took several deep breaths as her thundering heartbeat gradually slowed. Backing out of the room, she crossed to the pantry. Embers sparked in the stove's grate. The fire's warmth chased away the last of her frosty chill.

With her fear for Jo and Rachel eased, the Ranger's sudden appearance in her life troubled her. What did he want? Why had he returned? If she was truthful with herself, she was just as disturbed by her flustered reaction to him. She'd best guard her heart against softening to him. For all she knew, he'd come to check on her at the sheriff's bidding.

Preparing for a long talk, she reached for the tin coffee kettle. She didn't know why Jack had wandered back into her life, but she was going to find out. One thing she did know for certain.

His return meant trouble.

"You can't handle an injured girl and newborn baby all by yourself," Jack spoke, dizzy from talking in circles with the mule-headed widow for the past twenty minutes.

Upon his return from the barn, Elizabeth had laid out coffee and pulled peach-filled kolaches sprinkled with crystallized sugar from the oven warmer.

He surreptitiously reached for another pastry. "There's too much work to be done."

"And what do you suggest I do?" Elizabeth countered. "Jo can't be moved."

He licked a spot of jam from his thumb. Problem was, he kept getting distracted when he should be trying to outwit her. Not that his distraction was entirely his fault. She was even prettier than the last time he'd seen her. Her lustrous hair was braided into an elaborate knot at the base of her neck, highlighting her slender throat. Her pale blue eyes had grown more vibrant, a charming hue that reminded him of a clear summer's day. Only the faint circles of exhaustion darkening her eyes like bruises indicated her exhaustion.

She wore a crisp white shirtwaist tucked into the wide band of her blue gingham skirt. Looking at her, he could hardly believe this was the same round woman he'd burst in on weeks ago.

A woman that pretty shouldn't be risking her life. "If you're in trouble, send for help."

She grasped the baking sheet with one hand, slipping her spatula beneath two more kolaches.

She slid the pastries onto his plate with a scowl belying her thoughtful act. "I believe that's what I was doing when you referred to me as a lunatic."

Abashed, Jack studied his calloused hands. He absently flicked a crumb from his palm. "I apologize for that remark. I was, um, concerned, and might have let some emotion leach into the situation."

"Gracious, I don't believe I've ever heard you string so many words together into a sentence." She wiped her hands on the crisp, white apron knotted around her waist. "That was an articulate, almost heartfelt apology."

He scowled, not knowing if all those showy words added up to a good thing or a bad thing. To cover his confusion, he bit into another luscious pastry, then groaned in delight as peach filling enveloped his upper lip. Right then he didn't care if she was praising him or insulting him. As long as he was eating her tasty baking, nothing else mattered.

"Your apology is accepted," Elizabeth grudgingly offered. "You may stay for supper."

"That's mighty kind of you." Where did she think he was going, anyway? "You didn't happen to look outside recently? It's a whiteout. You and I are going to be sharing more than supper together."

Watching her cheeks flush a becoming shade of pink, he immediately regretted his words. "I meant to say, this snow is forcing me to hole up here for a few days until the weather clears."

She crossed her arms over her chest and glared at him. "You might as well be truthful. Did Sheriff Stanton send you out here?"

"What's that supposed to mean?"

"You —"

Rachel let out a shrill wail. Jack started, surprised to hear such a robust noise from such a tiny package. The widow's face clouded with worry as she lifted the crying baby from her woven laundry basket. To his astonishment, the child appeared to have doubled in size in the weeks he'd been gone.

"Mrs. Cole," Jo called from the other room.

Elizabeth's attention swung between the red-faced baby and the bedroom, torn between the two demands. "I need to check on Jo."

Quickly wiping his sticky hands on his pant legs, Jack rose to his feet. "Let me hold Rachel."

Elizabeth hesitated.

He quirked an eyebrow. He'd been present for the delivery, certainly she trusted him to hold the infant for a few minutes? "She's already crying. I'm not going to make it any worse."

As she cautiously handed over the baby, the widow caught her lower lip between her teeth. The impossibly light bundle fit perfectly into Jack's outstretched arms. Adjusting the blankets, he tucked Rachel close to his chest. The baby's distraught howling ceased. Peaceful silence filled the room.

Elizabeth's jaw dropped. "What did you do?"

"Nothing." He shrugged, secretly pleased

with his success. "Check on Jo. This isn't the first baby I've ever held, you know."

Her eyes narrowed.

"I have nieces and nephews, remember?"

Another crimson flush spread over the apples of her cheeks. "Of course."

She spun away from his mocking regard, tugging her apron strings loose on her way to check on Jo.

Jack blew out a long, relieved breath. "I'm not much good at talking with the ladies."

He studied the baby, her perfect Cupid's bow mouth, her dark, solemn eyes. An unfamiliar contentment seeped through his veins like warm molasses. He'd spent the last decade of his life immersed in the filth and human muck littering every dark corner of the American West. He'd grown so accustomed to dishonesty, he expected most men to tell a lie even when the truth would suit them better. Yet here in his arms rested an innocent human life, completely reliant and trusting.

His chest tightened. He felt as if he'd betrayed the child by leaving, though his guilt made no sense. This rag-tag group was none of his concern. He'd done far more than most men in his position would have.

He caressed Rachel's cheek reverently with his finger. Her mouth worked, rooting toward his touch. A protective instinct banded around his heart. One minuscule hand stirred beneath the blankets, a seeking arm struggled free. Five pudgy fingers wrapped around his knuckle.

Rachel's mouth spread into a wide, toothless grin. His heart brimmed with awe. They were connected. He didn't know how or why, but his fate was irrevocably linked to this child and her impossible, beautiful, infuriating mother.

And he didn't like it.

He didn't like it one bit. Caring meant risking loss. He'd seen too much in his career as a Ranger to convince himself otherwise. He'd witnessed enough of other people's suffering to know he never wanted to risk such sorrow in his own life. He never wanted to suffer the way his brother had after Doreen's death.

If the Lord had brought him to this place and time for a reason, he had to trust the Lord to guide him still.

" 'Great is our Lord, and of great power,' " he whispered to the infant cradled in his arms. " 'His understanding is infinite.' "

Jack prayed he was worthy of that understanding.

CHAPTER SEVEN

Jack rubbed his eyes, appearing as unbearably weary as Elizabeth felt.

"Have you ever fired a gun before?" he asked.

"Once," she replied.

If you could call Will grabbing her hand and pulling the trigger actually firing a gun. Then, yes, she had. It wasn't an event she liked to recall. Will had been unsympathetic to her bruised shoulder, even belly-laughing at her pain.

"You can't live on the prairie without knowing how to shoot a gun."

Elizabeth scowled.

Jack paused in his lecture.

They stood in a clearing several hundred yards from the main house. Jack had scoured the barren landscape before deciding on the safest area to test fire her shotgun. While snow had mounded in six-foot drifts along the gentle dips in the ground, this section had been swept smooth by fierce winds. Tufts of grass spiked through the white frost as if Mother Nature had given the whole prairie a bad haircut.

Jack had instructed her on how to clean and load the unwieldy firearm earlier. Now the moment she'd been dreading all morning loomed before her.

She sucked in a fortifying breath. "I'm ready."

Gripping the cold metal barrel, she clamped her jaw shut. She loathed guns, the noise and the violence. Despite her fear, she steeled her resolve. Her fledging independence required her to learn, no matter how repugnant the task.

"You've got only one chance with this particular shotgun," Jack said. "So you have to make your shot count."

Elizabeth chanced a sidelong glance at her reluctant instructor. His double-breasted coat stretched taut over his broad shoulders. His dark hat sat low on his head. Her cheeks warmed. He stuck his left foot slightly forward and angled his body.

His woolen overcoat with its wide lapels resembled the pea jackets she'd seen on dock workers near the harbor. She pictured Jack on the bow of a ship, strong and sure, the wind whipping through his hair.

"Here's how you stand." His deep-timbered voice intruded on her musing.

Shaking away the fanciful thoughts of rolling waves and unfurled masts billowing in the breeze, Elizabeth mirrored his stance, inordinately pleased at his curt nod of approval.

"Raise the barrel like this." He lifted both hands as if he held a phantom gun, his left eye squinting into the distance.

Once again she mimicked him, raising Will's ancient shotgun to level the sight at a stray line of brush on the horizon.

"That's not quite right," Jack murmured, rubbing his chin in thoughtful consideration as his gaze swept over her stiff form.

He circled to stand behind her. Elizabeth tensed. He wrapped his arms around her upper body, not quite touching the nap of her coat. He leaned forward. His breath fluttered against her cheek. His right hand covered hers, their skin separated by layers of leather and the thin cotton gloves she'd donned this morning in anticipation of the firing lesson. Gently nudging, he adjusted the barrel to rest more firmly in the crook of her shoulder.

"Like this," he said.

Her stomach performed an unexpected flip. Elizabeth jerked her head in a nod.

His left arm came around her body, guiding her with surprising gentleness to rest her stiff fingers on the smooth, mahogany forestock. "That's better," he said. The vibration from his baritone voice tickled her ear. "You're shivering. Are you cold?"

"A bit," Elizabeth gasped, hoping her quivering voice hadn't betrayed her.

This uncontrollable trembling had everything to do with the large, warm male cradling her in his arms, and nothing to do with the weather. To her shame, she ached to close her eyes and rest her head in the hollow of his shoulder. To feel safe — just for a moment. To forget that he might very well be here at the sheriff's bidding, ready to snatch the rug from beneath her fragile security. After all, why else would he have returned?

Elizabeth straightened her spine. "What next?"

"Squint your left eye, and focus your right eye on that shrub in the distance. You've got a near sight on the barrel, and a far sight on the muzzle. Line them up against your target."

She concentrated on his instructions, willing her thudding heart to slow. The wind kicked up again, ruffling her skirts around her ankles. Focusing her attention on the target, she ran the tip of her tongue over her parched lips. The arm holding her steady stiffened.

Jack audibly cleared his throat. "That's it. Now bring your cheek to rest on the stock and line up the sights."

His scent enticed her — a distracting combination of wood smoke, shaving lather and something musky.

"There's going to be a kick when you pull the trigger. Keep the stock tight against your shoulder, or it's going to hurt."

"Okay," she replied, blinking against the wind.

Her courage drained away as the memory of her last experience returned with startling clarity. How her ears had rung from the thunderous report. The way her shoulder had stung for a week. Elizabeth pinched her eyes open and shut a few times to release the tension, then shifted her feet.

"Take your time," Jack murmured.

He waited patiently while she gathered her nerve. When she nodded, he released his hold on the gun, letting her steady the weight while still maintaining his comforting position behind her. She felt his chest move with his deep, even breathing. Her sporadic heartbeat grew more even. She concentrated on the present, clearing her thoughts to focus on the target.

Anticipating the kick, she tightened her grip, then slowly squeezed the trigger as Jack had instructed. Buckshot roared from the barrel with a thunder-clap burst. Fire exploded in her shoulder, launching her backward. She stumbled hard against Jack's chest.

He steadied her with a hand to her hip, then reached around to pull the smoking barrel from her limp hands.

Elizabeth pressed icy fingers to her ears. How she loathed loud noises. Jack appeared before her, propping the gun against his leg before tugging her stiff hands away from her head.

"That's enough for today." He rubbed warmth into her raw fingers. "You need better gloves."

"I thought these would make it easier to pull the trigger." Her teeth chattered. "I've got my m-mittens in my pocket."

She drew back her hands, but he held firm, cupping them in his palms. He tipped his head forward, blowing a warm burst of air over her tightly clenched fists. A shudder coursed through her body.

"Is that better?"

His tender voice slipped over her like a caress. She jerked her head in a nod.

He nudged her chin up with his gloved hand. "You did well."

She had to pull her lower lip between her teeth to keep it from trembling.

Her heart pounding, she met his steady gaze. His eyes fascinated her. In the dim light of the cabin, they appeared dark and mysterious. A vague brown. In the hazy afternoon, his irises flared over the brown-and-gold flecks, highlighting the green edges. Whiskers already darkened his cheek, though a blot of red dotting his chin indicated he'd nicked himself shaving that morning. How quickly his beard must grow.

Elizabeth tilted her head to shake the spell. "The prairie is fascinating, isn't it? In the city, I never noticed how the clouds roll in for a thunderstorm like black smoke puffing from a train engine. Out here, you can see a storm coming for miles." The nervous words tumbled off her lips.

"I don't know." Jack shook his head with a sigh that sounded suspiciously like self-reproach. "Sometimes a downpour sneaks up when you least expect it."

His eyes filled with a curious sorrow, Jack stepped away to crack the shotgun and rest it over his horse's saddle. He returned to stand before her, his arms crossed over his chest.

A peaceful calm settled over Elizabeth. For the first time in a long while, she *was* all right. She was shaken, but proud. Proud of herself for taking aim and firing. Proud of herself for overcoming her fear. Giddy exhilaration stirred in her chest. "I did it!"

"You did real good." He smiled, the corners of his eyes crinkling. "You killed that bush dead."

Suddenly jubilant, she raised up on her tiptoes and quickly bussed him on the cheek. That might have been the end of it, except he turned his head at the last moment, and instead of finding the rough stubble of his cheek, their lips collided. His mouth was firm, but surprisingly soft. Shock held her immobile for a beat.

She leaped back, groaning in embarrassment as he blinked at her spontaneous gesture. "I'm so sorr —"

The intense look in his eyes silenced her apology. Jack caught her around the waist, splaying his hand over the small of her back. He gathered her close to him, gently, ignoring what was only a halfhearted resistance. A muscle in his jaw ticked, the fisted hand at her back tightened.

Blood roared in her ears. She tipped her head back, craving the comfort of his embrace. Her lips parted.

With an abrupt grimace, he thrust her away. "We should get back."

His gaze didn't quite meet hers.

"Yes." His rejection stabbed her heart, hurting more than the throb in her shoulder from the gun's kick. "Of course."

What on earth had come over her? No longer cold, her flaming cheeks could melt the frozen tundra. Kissing Jack had felt like the most natural thing in the world, as if she'd been anticipating this moment her whole life. Knowing he didn't share her feelings sent a hard knot forming in her chest.

She'd been tempted to kiss two men in her twenty-three years, and neither of them had truly wanted her affection. The realization stung.

Desultory small talk accompanied their return to the house, each of them attempting to cover the embarrassment of Elizabeth's spontaneous, foolish behavior. Knowing the day couldn't get any worse, she removed Will's revolver from its place in the empty lard tin and held the stock with two fingers, the barrel dangling to the floor.

"Will you help me load this, too?"

"Careful with that." He accepted the gun, flipped out the cylinder, then gave it a spin. "This gun has never been fired. There's not even a speck of grease on the cylinder. Still, you have to remember the first rule of gun safety. Treat every gun as if it's loaded."

Elizabeth rolled her eyes. That was the whole problem in a nutshell. "Not this one."

His expression grew thunderous. He rested the gun on the table with a grim twist of his lips. "You have a child in the house now. Every gun is loaded. Period. You treat every weapon you pick up, put down or point at someone as loaded."

Cords of tension formed in her neck. She willed herself not to shrink away from his censure. "Fine. It's loaded."

"Excellent." His gaze slid over her face. "I didn't mean to snap at you, but with a baby in the house we can't be too careful." He nodded to the back bedroom where Jo rested and Rachel napped. "Where are the bullets?"

"I — uh — I don't know."

Frowning, he flattened both palms against the table. "I thought you wanted me to load this?"

Elizabeth immediately regretted her impetuous decision to request his help. No matter how hard she tried to forget, every corner of the house was fraught with reminders. Even searching for bullets stirred up recollections of a past she'd rather forget. Will had always been so possessive about his property.

Though he'd been gone for more than eight months, longer even than they'd been married, she still felt his disapproving presence each time she searched his belongings. Her time with Will had been blessedly short, but the echoes lingered. Folding her arm across her stomach, she unconsciously touched the arrowhead scar on her arm over her sleeve.

Will was gone, she reminded herself. He had hurt her for the last time.

If she wanted to maintain control of her home and her property, she had to learn how to defend herself. Considering Jack's dramatic entrance all those weeks ago, she had to force herself to learn a new skill, even if she was mocked for her ignorance. The next stranger who visited might not be a Texas Ranger with chocolate-brown hair and hazel eyes. She had her daughter to think of now. If it took her all winter, she'd perfect the skill.

Memories or not, it was time to face her future. "I think the bullets are in here."

Heart thumping, she crossed to the pantry, then let her hand linger on the knob. Taking a deep steadying breath, she pushed open the door. Neat rows of mason jars lined the shelves; apples, peaches, pickles and a rainbow selection of various other preserves. She took down the heavy galvanized bathing tub that hung on a hook on the outside wall.

"Odd time to take a bath."

Shrieking, her hand flew to her chest. The tub banged to the floor with a metallic clang. "You startled me."

"I see that." He quirked an eyebrow, reaching for the tub. "You want me to put this some place for you?"

"No, no." Elizabeth shook her head. "I need to stand on it. I think the bullets are up there." She indicated a crude wooden crate teetering on the top shelf.

He easily reached over her head, dwarfing her with his superior height. Crowded together in the confined space, his unique male scent enveloped her once again. Without his coat she caught a clean, crisp scent like freshly washed sheets. A lock of hair fell across his forehead, lending him a rakish appearance. She envisioned him as Mr. Darcy in the Jane Austen novel her mother had loved. Yet she couldn't picture Jack sipping tea in an ornate parlor. He belonged on the open range, herding cattle, not confined indoors. He exuded a strength and assurance at odds with his cautious gentleness.

Her breath quickened. She was hot and cold at the same time, the sensations nothing like fear. An anxious anticipation stirred in her limbs. She needed something, wanted something from him, but the yearning was elusive, ethereal.

He grasped the box, turning on his heel in one swift motion to exit the room. She blew out a long breath, shocked at the way her blood surged through her veins. By the time she'd gathered herself enough to follow him out, he'd set the box on the sturdy worktable.

The forlorn sight of Will's legacy robbed her of breath.

Here was an emotion she understood. Sorrow. The color of the leather had leached away, giving Will's saddlebags a dull, lifeless appearance. How quickly the vibrant material had faded.

Jack cleared his throat, startling her back to the present. Her numb fingers tugged the buckles loose.

Hooking his thumbs into his belt loops, Jack lowered his head. "How long has your husband been gone?"

Her mind slid over the memories. "Just over eight months."

"I'm sorry for your loss."

She couldn't force her gaze higher than

154

the mother-of-pearl buttons at his chest. "Thank you," she replied simply.

How did she explain this confusing whirl of emotions to Jack when she didn't even understand the feelings herself? "We were married for only six months. It's strange to think he's been gone longer than we were together."

Avoiding Jack's sympathetic gaze, she lifted out each item, a dismal accounting of Will's life — a knife, matches, the hollow swish of liquid from his engraved flask, a deck of cards and finally the paper-wrapped bullets. What must the Texas Ranger think of the telling assortment?

The second bag bulged with a large object. Feeling safe in the Ranger's presence, she checked inside to discover a Bible. She paused, her hands trembling. She'd never thought of Will as a man to carry around a Bible. He'd never gone to church once in the entire time she'd known him. She recalled all his promises during their whirl-wind courtship. He'd talked of God and church, but his words had been brisk and shallow. She'd thought he would guide her on her faith journey, but his wisdom had proved false.

Jack rested a warm hand on her drooping shoulder. "I didn't mean to bring up sad memories."

Tears burned behind her eyes. "They're not sad, so much. Not like you'd think. In some ways, it's like he's on another trip."

Jack let his hand drop back to his side. "He traveled a lot?"

"For his job with the railroad. Even after he died, I felt like I was waiting for him to come home after another long absence."

Crushing guilt erased her prepared speech. The one she'd murmured to the few kind ladies from town who'd braved their husbands' censure and brought her cakes and condolences after Will's death. She'd been so alone for so long, that all her dammed up conversation jostled to be unleashed.

She cleared her throat, driven to talk to someone, anyone. "I had to get used to him being gone, you see. I must have gotten too good at forgetting."

"I think I understand."

Elizabeth started at his revelation. She'd expected his censure, his disgust at her admission. "You do?"

"I felt that way when I first left my family's cattle ranch. When you're away from the people you love, you have to lock away those feelings, or the memories eat away at your joy until you're not happy any place."

His deep voice soothed her battered

156

senses. His quiet understanding drove her to speak of the long buried memories. "Once I forgot to set a place for him at supper. It was a habit, you know? One bowl, one plate, one spoon. I didn't even realize what I'd done until he came in to wash up."

Jack scuffed the toe of his boot along the braided edge of the rag rug beneath the worktable. "What did your husband do when he realized he didn't have a plate?"

"He didn't even notice. He just sat down to eat. I guess he thought I wasn't hungry." She glanced up, quickly ducking away from the pity shimmering in the Ranger's eyes. "You can teach me how to load the gun another time."

In truth, even when Will had been home, he'd never truly been there. He was always off to town, always making grand plans for the next adventure. She'd told him time and again that she was satisfied with their little slice of the prairie, but she hadn't been paying attention to his unspoken replies, his restless need to escape her. She'd thought she'd done everything to be the perfect wife, but she hadn't done nearly enough. Will was never going to be satisfied. Especially not with her.

Jack donned the fake smile she had begun to think of as his Texas Ranger grin.

Her confession had obviously made him uncomfortable.

"I really should teach you how to load this gun," he said. "No time like the present."

A yeasty smell teased her nostrils, providing her with a much-needed distraction. "I need to check my baking."

Brushing past Jack, she plucked a fragrant loaf from the warm oven. Carefully holding it in a towel, she tapped the golden-brown crust, satisfied with the hollow report. "It's perfect."

Jack's face lit up at the sight. "Ma'am, I don't think I've ever eaten so well, and I've traveled all over the country."

His praise ignited a warm glow in her chest. She couldn't remember anyone actually complimenting her. "I should bake well. I must have baked thousands of these when I apprenticed in New York."

"Mind if I have a slice?"

"Buttered?"

"Is there any other way?"

She laughed at his horrified expression. "I guess not."

Leaning one hip against the worktable, he crossed his arms over his chest. "What's it like, New York?"

"Crowded." A delicate shudder sent the serrated knife in her hand trembling. "You can't believe all those people live in one place. The noise and commotion never stop."

"Must have been quite a way to live."

"In some ways, it was more lonely than living out here. When you see people together, families and married couples, friends, it reminds you of what you don't have."

She'd thought she'd conquered the loneliness, making do with Jo's company and the occasional visit to town or a trip to the McCoys.

But she missed this, talking to someone. Just talking. "All I ever wanted was a family. Something to call my own that couldn't be taken away. But nothing lasts forever, right?"

His eyes darkened. "You have to hold on to the memories. The Bible says, 'All go unto one place, all are of the dust, and all turn to dust again.' "

"I like that." She considered his solemn visage. "That's all we really have, isn't it? Our memories."

The corner of his mouth tipped up. "The good and the bad. Seems the longer I stay away from home, the more I cleave to the fond memories. The bad ones seem to fade away in their place."

"I wish I could say the same." She sighed.

Exchanging this easy banter unleashed a yearning for human companionship. She wanted to immerse herself, to hang on to the light and never let go.

"Where are you from?" he asked. "Originally, that is. You still have an accent."

"My father would be proud to know that I still carry a piece of his homeland." She thought back to her own fond memories. "My family is originally from Bucklebury, England. We lived with my uncle just outside the village. My father was a baker, but as the youngest son, there wasn't much room for him in the family business. We traveled to America when I was five so he could open his own store."

She hadn't thought of England in years, but images came flooding back like pictures behind a scrim, hazy and diluted. She envisioned the rolling green hills, the misty fog that hung over the fields at first light.

She slathered butter onto the steaming, soft bread. "My father started a pastry shop in New York. For a few years he worked from dawn to dusk. When I was nine, a fire burned down the whole block. We lost everything. My — uh — my father went to work for someone else after that." She let her voice trail off.

Better to end the story there. She had

been too young to understand. Too young to realize that her whole life was about to change, forever.

Jack accepted the slice of bread, studying the melted butter as it pooled into the fluffy air pockets. "Why don't you move back to New York? Live with your parents? Raising Rachel Rose with your family would be better than living out here all alone."

She pondered her answer, wondering how much to reveal. "My parents are both dead. After my father died, my mother was sick, and then . . . and then she died, too. I spent several years in an orphanage." She skirted around the truth. Not quite lying, but not telling the whole of it, either. "All of the girls had to have jobs and I, well, I chose to work in the kitchens. The task helped me feel closer to my family, to my roots. When I was too old for the orphanage, I even took a job at a bakery. That's where I met Will."

She glanced up, startled by the stricken look on his face.

"I'm sorry," he muttered. "I didn't realize."

There was more to her story, but she couldn't bear to reveal her pain. Not when he appeared so horrified to learn she'd spent half of her life in an orphanage.

"Other people have suffered far worse than I."

He made a noncommittal sound in his throat. "Why don't you at least move to town, open your own bakery? I'm sure there are plenty of people who'd devour your cooking."

"I couldn't," she protested with a nervous laugh.

"Why not?"

"Well, I, uh —" She paused. "I guess I never thought about it before. I don't know if I could handle the work alone."

"Hire someone to help out. There's always a body in need of work. 'The hand of the diligent man maketh rich.' "

A bakery. Elizabeth pictured a warm kitchen, a bell tinkling over the door to indicate a customer. A place of her own where people gathered. A place where people knew her. How well would the people in Cimarron Springs greet Will Cole's widow? The warm image dissolved. If the scathing stares they shot at her on her rare trips to the mercantile were any indication, not very well. Even after Will's death, his legacy haunted her. Memories were long, and she'd always be Will Cole's widow. Elizabeth's heart sank. The homestead that had saved her, trapped her at the same time.

She briskly chafed her hands together, rubbing off the last bit of flour dust. "It's time to prepare supper. Do you mind keeping Jo company while I work? She's getting real antsy being cooped up in there."

"After another fortifying slice of bread."

Running a bakery sounded heavenly compared to running the homestead. She'd barely survived the autumn, working eighteen hours a day to prepare for winter. The long cold months had given her a brief reprieve, but spring loomed just around the corner. With the change in weather came planting the kitchen garden and all the other repairs neglected over the winter.

Elizabeth pressed the heels of her palms against her eyes. The rare glimpse of hope at a new future had left her longing for things that could never be.

How did one pray for an answer, when the question remained elusive? "Are there any Bible verses on hope?"

He chewed thoughtfully. "I don't know. I seem to recall something about 'in His word do I hope.' "

" 'In His word do I hope,' " she repeated. "Amen."

Hope was a dangerous thing. A luxury she couldn't afford.

■ ■ ■ ■

Jo winked at Jack. "You're a real charmer, aren't you?"

He cradled his forehead, warding off the stinging pain that pierced his brain each time Jo spoke. Her constant jabs wore on him. "I thought you broke your ribs, not your lips. Why am I sitting here reading to you, when reading is probably the only thing you *can* do?"

"Because Mrs. Cole told you to keep me company." She smirked. "Now, let's see, was that before or after you brought up her late husband and her life in the orphanage?"

"If you minded your own business as well as you mind mine, you wouldn't have two cracked ribs and a sprained ankle."

"You're getting sloppy with your insults."

Jack blew out a frustrated breath. He was still kicking himself for his awkward handling of the situation earlier. Jo's probing questions delved too deeply into his wounded dignity. "*Pride and Prejudice* is an odd name for a book."

"Mrs. Cole said her mother brought it over from England. It's one of her favorites."

"I don't see why. Nothing happens." Unless you counted people doing an awful lot of talking about their feelings, and not doing a whole lot of action concerning those feelings.

"It's very romantic."

Jack turned over the book to check the back. "Am I missing something?"

So far, the main character had insulted the heroine, and the heroine had insulted him right back. Where on earth was the romance in that?

"It's about a cranky fellow who can't seem to get along with anyone." A sly grin coasted across Jo's face. "Should be right up your alley, Ranger."

The barb struck home with deadly accuracy. "You sure you wouldn't rather take a nap?"

"I've been sleeping all day." She plucked restlessly at the quilted comforter, clutching her side as the movement jostled her sore ribs. "Why did you come back?"

"It was on my way home." He flipped open the book to a random page. "Now, where were we? I'm sure Mr. Darcy is about to do something romantic like tossing Miss Bennett into the river."

"Where do you live, Ranger? This place isn't on the way to anywhere."

His temper flared. Trust Jo not to let a sleeping dog lie. It was none of her business why he'd decided to check on the widow. "Do you want to flap your lips, or do you want me to read?"

"You're crankier than usual." She appeared almost gleeful in her assessment. "Guess you didn't catch that outlaw."

"No." He snapped shut the book. "I didn't."

Rachel stirred restlessly at the commotion. Jack lifted her from the cozy nest of blankets, and tucked the infant into the crook of his arm. She cooed. His chest expanded with pride. No matter how upset the baby was, she always calmed in his arms.

"That day in the barn," Jo continued. "You told me you were chasing a bank robber, right?"

"Yep."

"I been thinking about what you said, but I still can't figure out why you ended up here. How did you stumble onto this homestead? This place ain't on the way to nowhere."

Jack hesitated, but talking about his case was a whole lot better than reading Elizabeth's "romantic" book. "The man I was chasing —"

"Bud Shaw?"

"Yeah, that's him. He disappeared along the train route, but his horse didn't. People remembered the mustang. That animal caused a lot of trouble along the way. When I arrived in Cimarron Springs, the sheriff said a fellow living out here had a feisty bay mustang. The whole thing seemed logical. Made sense that the fellow got off the train at Cimarron Springs and headed home."

"Didn't the sheriff tell you that mustang belonged to Will Cole, not that fellow you were looking for, Bud Shaw?"

"Could have been a lot of explanations for that. Maybe Bud Shaw had a partner we didn't know about. Maybe he was using another name to throw us off the trail. Criminals aren't exactly known for making things easy."

Jo snorted. "Still, if you thought a light-weight like Will Cole was a bank robber, I'd hate to see what kind of other fellows you've chased in your career."

Jack glanced furtively over his shoulder. "Keep your voice down. Mrs. Cole has dealt with enough painful reminders today."

"Don't worry. She's off to feed the animals while you're in a nice warm house loafing around and playing nursemaid, remember?"

This time the barb bounced off his thick hide. Jo was hiding her pain with her sharp words. Jack smoothed the blanket over the infant, using the distraction to sneak a look at Jo's exhausted face. Her two braids hung listlessly over her shoulders. Lines of fatigue showed at the corners her mouth. Her green eyes stood out against her ashen face. She was putting on a good show, but he could tell she was hurting. What was wrong with him, snapping at an injured girl?

"I'm telling you, Ranger," she continued. "Mr. Cole could hardly pluck a chicken let alone rob a bank. He reminded me of this snake-oil salesman that came to town last spring. He talked up a real storm, but once you got past all the hot air blowing through his lips, there was nothing to him."

"Really?" The question slipped out.

"Yeah. Maybe that snake-oil man is your bank robber. Maybe his secret ingredient is stolen money. That's about as good of a theory as Will Cole."

She chuckled at her own joke while Jack remained thoughtful. He'd heard enough gossip about the widow's late husband to last him a lifetime. He was growing heartily sick of how the conversation kept circling back around to the man. Will Cole might as well be standing in the room, not six feet under. "It's not appropriate to talk about Mr. Cole."

"I'd say it's more appropriate than kicking down a dead man's door, isn't it?"

The shooting pain in his temple intensified. "We've gone over this already. I was looking for Bud Shaw." He braced his free hand on the seat of his chair, the book pressing painfully into his palm. "If you don't want me to read to you, maybe I can pull out one of Mrs. Cole's samplers and you can stitch us a pretty flower hanky."

"I'd rather poke my eye with a stick."

"That's what I thought."

Pleasant sounds from the kitchen indicated Elizabeth's return. She stepped into the room, her eyes sparkling with health.

Rushing to his side, she reached out to run her knuckle along Rachel's cheek. "Good morning, beautiful."

His breath snagged in his throat. He caught a tantalizing hint of sweetened vanilla and lavender. Tendrils of golden hair framed Elizabeth's face, curling along her cheek. Her hair wasn't simply blond, as it appeared at first, but a curious mixture of aged gold, flaxen and an alluring hint of bronze.

His blood pounded. He longed to reach out and loop one of those charming ringlets around his finger, just to see if it felt as soft as it looked.

Elizabeth's gaze swung between him and Jo as she flashed a hopeful grin. "Everything okay in here? Are you two getting along?"

"Couldn't be better."

"Like beans and ham."

"Excellent." Elizabeth brought her hands together with a clap. "It's so nice to see the two of you mending fences so well."

She smiled so wide he caught a rare glimpse of the place where her eyeteeth overlapped her front teeth ever so slightly. He found the modest imperfection delightful, especially since it was only visible when she smiled the widest.

She turned her radiant gaze on him. "Can you hold Rachel for a few more minutes? I'd like to start supper."

Swallowing hard, he nodded.

Heaven help him. She had him tongue-tied and tangled in knots. Returning to the homestead was a mistake, a mistake he'd soon remedy. The longer he remained, the more his emotions became entangled with the plight of this ragtag bunch. Tonight he'd complete the task he'd come here for in the first place. He'd show Elizabeth his newspaper clippings, and see if she recognized any of the wanted posters.

"Mrs. Cole?"

She raised an eyebrow.

His mind went blank. What was he supposed to say? *By the way, did your husband ever gamble with outlaws? Did he happen to mention their names?*

"Nothing. Never mind."

She shrugged and turned away.

Jack grunted. His entire plan was ridiculous. This whole delay had been an excuse to see Elizabeth again. And what was wrong with that? There was no harm in ensuring her health. After aiming a gun at the poor woman, and practically accusing her of lying, it was the least he could do.

Jo caught his attention, a mischievous glint in her green eyes. After Elizabeth rounded the corner, safely out of view, the little bugger had the audacity to stick out her tongue at him.

Jack rolled his eyes and prayed for a break in the weather. The sooner he found the real Bud Shaw, the better. Staying here was stirring up more problems than he could solve. Even as he itched to resume his journey, he couldn't shake the feeling that he'd been drawn here for a purpose.

Jack rubbed his chin while pots and pans clanged in the kitchen. The widow was too serious by far. She had a perpetual frown of worry between her eyes, and saved her smiles like precious coins. She needed to relax and let a little fun into her day. Maybe that's why the Lord had brought him here, to bring some laughter into her life.

But his time was running short. How did he distract from her rigid schedule, and self-imposed rules long enough to discover the joy still left in the world? He glanced out the window. A grin spread across his face. Staring at the snow gave him an idea.

CHAPTER EIGHT

"Gracious, what's that man doing?" Elizabeth stretched over the bed and scratched a hole in the frost-covered window.

"I don't know," Jo replied. "He pulled off the oilcloth earlier. He's mighty busy doing something, but I can't figure out what."

Elizabeth stood, knotted her muffler tighter around her throat, then tucked the fringed ends beneath the collar of her woolen coat. "Just like a man to fuss around when there's work to be done."

She knelt and adjusted Rachel's blanket. The infant's toothless grin filled her heart with wonder. "Did you get more precious last night? Did you? You sweet little thing."

Jo made a gagging sound in her throat.

Elizabeth rolled her eyes. "You'll feel differently when you have your own babies."

"Never. I'm not having any brats. Not after what you went through."

"It's all worth it."

"I don't plan on finding out."

Elizabeth ducked her head to hide her knowing grin. "I'm off to gather eggs for supper. If Rachel gets fussy, I'll be back shortly."

"We'll be fine. Now stop running yourself ragged."

"Don't be silly." Elizabeth pressed the back of her hand to Jo's forehead, relieved to find the skin cool and dry. The more days that passed without a fever, the more Elizabeth's relief grew. Jo was making a blessedly quick recovery. "Mr. Elder was able to get a message to your family. You'll be happy to know they're all praying for your health."

Elizabeth managed to keep her irritation hidden. What were the McCoys to think of a Texas Ranger hanging about? Mr. Elder hadn't shared how he'd explained his presence to the neighboring family. "Your brothers miss you. Once the weather warms a bit, I'm sure they'll be tracking over here to see you."

Jo snorted. "Not like I'm going anyplace."

"You'll be up and about in no time. Jack — Mr. Elder said your ankle isn't broken. Just a sprain and some cracked ribs."

Jo rubbed her leg and groaned. "This is one winter I'll never forget."

"You and I both."

Elizabeth chuckled dryly. With a last lingering glance at Jo and the baby, she stole from room.

Safely out of view, she scowled. Mr. Elder had taken word to the McCoys without even a by-your-leave to Elizabeth. She'd discovered him missing when she'd wandered into the barn half asleep, groggily attending her chores, only to discover his jet-black horse missing. After taking several deep, shuddering breaths, she'd set about her chores, determined to push him out of her thoughts.

Jack had returned hours later, casually relating his trip to the McCoys. As if rambling in and out of their lives had no consequences. Elizabeth expressed her frustration under her breath. At least Will had taken the time to say goodbye when he'd left.

She glanced out the window, annoyed to find the bunkhouse chimney billowing smoke. Jack had taken charge of a whole lot of things in the past forty-eight hours. After declaring the barn unfit for sleeping, he'd moved his belongings into the bunkhouse, setting up shop like he planned to stay all winter.

Elizabeth tugged on her woolen mittens. She vowed to speak with him that evening. If he could travel to the McCoys, he could travel to town. There was no need for him to stay any longer. A strange man shacked up in the bunkhouse was bound to draw attention.

Reaching for the doorknob, she considered the other reason he had to leave. She couldn't afford to let anyone know how accustomed she'd grown to his comforting presence — a reassurance that was as dangerous as it was foolish. The more she grew to depend on him, the more difficult her life would be when he was gone.

With a resolute huff, she pushed open the rear door, relieved to find the wind had calmed. The orange-ball sun had made a rare appearance through the clouds, turning the rolling prairie into a blinding, sparkling wonderland.

She had just reached the bottom step, when something wet and cold pelted her from the side.

"Just the person I wanted to see," Jack called from her left.

She turned. He stood there smiling, as though he was impervious to the frosty winter air.

Elizabeth dusted the white from her shoulder. "Did you just throw a snowball at me?"

"I need your help."

She searched his face for any sign of guilt. Not even a suspicious twinkle showed in his hazel eyes. She slanted a glance upward. Icicles hung like frosting from the eves above her head, turning the house into a gingerbread confection.

Perhaps a bit of snow had melted from the roof. "Why do you need my help? I'm fetching the eggs."

"Already done."

He jerked his head. A wire basket full of eggs rested in the snow near the corner of the house.

She ground her teeth together. She didn't like how he was taking over all the chores. He was disturbing her schedule once again.

"Stop fussing over your routine." He grinned. "Follow me."

The accusation stung. "I do not fuss. I have a certain way I like things done. A certain order to my chores that maximizes efficiency."

"You're definitely fussing now. Why don't you help me finish the snowman?"

Crossing her arms over her chest, she tapped her foot on the packed snow. "A what?"

"Haven't you ever built a snowman?"

Elizabeth gaped at the fool man. *No one built snowmen, did they?* While she pondered the question, Jack disappeared around the corner.

With a weary sigh, Elizabeth trudged in his wake. Since the eggs had been gathered, she *did* have a few extra minutes this morning. Perhaps if she indulged him for a moment, he'd leave her alone to finish her chores.

Perhaps she'd simply watch his antics. She hadn't managed more than a few hours of sleep at a stretch in months. For weeks she'd existed in a blurry fugue. This morning, in an exhausted haze, she'd stumbled right into the doorjamb. Frolicking around in the snow was not on her to-do list.

As she rounded the corner, another snowball hit her on the opposite shoulder. "What are you doing?" she sputtered.

"It's a snowball fight. You're supposed to hit me back."

"I will not." She knew full well how these games went. He'd use the opportunity to show off his superior strength and skill, humiliating her in the process. "Have you been drinking your *medicinal* whiskey?"

He shrugged. "I'm having fun."

Since when did he have fun? He was always frowning and serious. "Are you ill?"

He stared at her as if *she* were the one acting like a fool.

"Some of us have chores." Elizabeth glared at him, one hand shielding her eyes from sunlight sparking off the shimmering, white snow. "Enjoy your fun. I'm going back in the house."

She pivoted on her heel. A soft explosion shattered over the back of her head. Chilly blobs trickled down her neck. "You — why — you."

Fuming, she bent to gather a handful of snow. If he wanted a fight, she'd give him one. She packed the frozen material together, cocked back her arm and let the ball fly. White exploded over his face.

"You have good aim," he said with an ice-covered grin.

"And you called *me* a lunatic?" Gracious, the man didn't even have the good sense to be annoyed. The time for fun and games was over. "I don't have the energy for this. You and I need to have a conversation, Mr. Elder."

His jubilant expression fell. "So it's like that, is it?"

"Yes." She didn't care that her words had wiped the joy from his face. She didn't care at all. She didn't even know what he was insinuating with his cryptic declaration and hangdog expression. "It's like what?"

"Never mind." He brushed the snow from

his hands. "Let's have this talk."

She stole a furtive glance at the window. No doubt Jo was watching them with rapt attention. "Not in the house. I don't want Jo to overhear."

He quirked an eyebrow. "The bunkhouse, then?"

Warmth crept into her cheeks. His temporary quarters were closest to where they stood, but she shied away from his offer. "It's not proper. How about the barn?"

She waved in the opposite direction.

"What's more proper about the barn?"

A lump of snow had caught between her boot and her stocking. The ice was starting to melt, sending a stinging cold trail down her ankle. She shifted her feet. "There's more activity in the barn."

"I guess I see your point." He wiped the snow from his face with a bandanna he'd unfurled from his pocket. "But the pig isn't going to be much of a chaperone."

"Fine." She gritted her teeth. "We shall conduct our conversation in the bunkhouse." Straightening her collar, she assumed her most disapproving frown. "But only because I left my rosetta iron in the cupboard last summer."

"Your English is showing, Miss Prim and Proper," he teased.

"Well." The nerve of the man! One minute he was pelting her with the snowballs, and the next minute he was mocking her heritage. "The English are very fine people. I take that as a compliment."

He winked at her. "As intended."

"Oh," Elizabeth huffed. She really didn't have time for this foolishness. Tossing him off her property was going to be so much easier since he had reverted to this annoying behavior.

She marched to the bunkhouse and yanked open the door with too much force, then leaped out of the way as the heavy wood ricocheted, nearly taking off the end of her nose in the process.

Good heavens, this wouldn't do at all. She was accustomed to being in control. He had her huffing and grinding her teeth like a fishwife. Pausing for a long beat, she took a deep, fortifying breath. While her pulse slowed, she studied his temporary quarters, struck by how clean and tidy the space appeared.

The bunkhouse had replaced the original sod homestead years before Elizabeth and Will had arrived. The long narrow room had five empty cots lined up along either side of the center corridor. A sturdy pine box capped the end of each bed for the worker's storage. The previous owner had been a wealthy adventurer from back East with grand schemes for improving the land. His dreams had fizzled beneath the relentless prairie winds and his wife's discontent.

She rarely used the space except for cooking occasionally in the summer months to keep the heat out of the main house. An enormous cast-iron stove used for heat as well as cooking dominated the center of the room. Unbidden, images of the orphanage came rushing back. A familiar wash of loneliness clouded her vision. She recalled staring at the ceiling, night after night, praying for the loneliness to end.

She wanted to run to Rachel and cradle her baby, never letting go. What a tragic choice her mother had had to make, surrendering the care of her only child. Elizabeth curled her hands into fists. That would never happen to her. She'd fight a grizzly with her bare hands to keep her baby.

A gentle hand touched her sleeve. "Are you all right?"

"Of course."

She shook off the gloomy feeling along with the last of the melting snowflakes. Lingering in the past was a dull and lonely business.

Clearing her throat, Elizabeth squared her

shoulders. "You're going to have to leave. It isn't proper for you to be here. The Mc-Coys know you're back. They're a nice family, but I don't want word of a single . . . of a man . . . of *you* reaching Cimarron Springs."

Jack leaned one shoulder against a sturdy support pillar and crossed his arms. "Mrs. McCoy didn't strike me as the kind of woman to gossip."

"Be that as it may, gossip has a way of spreading like wildfire during a draught."

Chilled from her trip outside, she sidled down the narrow center aisle toward the cast-iron stove. She stole a discreet glance at Jack's belongings. He'd taken the bunk nearest the warming fire. His saddle bags and other paraphernalia were neatly laid out on a small side table. Each item had been carefully arranged — razor, mirror, pencil and paper. How different from what Will had carried, and yet how similar. They were both drifters, men who preferred to live their lives unencumbered.

Nothing encumbered a man more than a wife and child.

She'd already made one mistake concerning a man. She couldn't afford another. She wouldn't let the Ranger's laughing hazel eyes lure her into a false sense of security.

"Listen, Mrs. Cole," he spoke. "I'd like to leave. I have work to do. But I can't abandon you to care for Jo and Rachel all alone. It just isn't right."

"We managed quite well on our own."

"Yeah. That's why I found you half frozen in a blizzard." He raked his hand through his hair. "You're a greenhorn with no idea what you're up against. You haven't an inkling what you're risking."

He crossed the length of the room, crowding her until they stood inches apart.

A shiver of panic snaked down her spine. She refused to back away, even when she had to tip back her head to meet the raw fury glittering in his steady gaze. "What happens to us is none of your concern."

"You don't have enough wood cut to make it through the rest of the month, let alone the rest of winter. What are you going to do then?"

His accusation straightened her spine. She was all the more determined to prove him wrong. "I'll manage. I always do."

"Yes, but it's not just you anymore, is it?" His freshly shaven face flushed with anger. "You have your daughter to think of now."

She felt heat creep up her cheeks. "Are you insinuating something?"

"No, I'm telling you. Move to town. Be

184

near people. Then I'll leave. If you don't care enough to save yourself, at least have the decency to think of your child. She doesn't have a choice. You do."

He could question her skills all he wanted, but he'd better steer clear of her mothering. "How dare you question my devotion. I can protect my daughter. I can protect my home. This is where I belong."

"Prove your devotion. Sell the buildings. Move to town."

She swallowed around the lump in her throat. If only things were that easy. She didn't want Rachel to live under the townspeople's scorn, and she didn't know where else to go. Right then, the homestead was the safest place for them.

"It's not that simple."

" 'Course it is."

"This is none of your business."

Anger swelled in her chest. He was a threat. A threat to her home, a threat to her reputation, and a threat to her peace of mind. "What does a drifter know?"

Hurt flicked in eyes, passing so quickly she might have imagined the emotion if not for the agitated tic in his cheek. "I'm not a drifter, I'm a lawman. I have a purpose."

Suddenly, she wanted to hurt him as much as he'd hurt her. "Really. Then where

is your home? What is your purpose now —
besides threatening me?"

"*Threatening* you? I saved your hide.
Twice." His boots scraped the floor as he
pivoted away. "And this isn't about me. This
is about you living on a homestead without
even a rifle."

"I have the shotgun and Will's revolver,
remember?"

"You've fired the shotgun twice. And
you've never fired the revolver. How are you
going to react in an emergency? That's not
your only handicap, and you know it. You've
limped through half the winter, but once
spring comes, you'll never be able to keep
up. How are you going to climb on the roof
and clear the chimney? How are you going
to cut hay, chop wood and still care for Rachel? You can't handle all the work on your
own."

Elizabeth narrowed her eyes. She was well
and truly tired of being told what she could
and couldn't do. She'd done a fine job of
caring for the homestead while Will was
away, but he'd never once complimented
her abilities. Instead, he'd search until he
found something out of place, a frivolous
chore she'd failed to accomplish, then he'd
pounced. She didn't need a man to criticize
her efforts. Jack wasn't so perfect, either.

"It's not safe," he continued. "You don't have any idea what I've seen. You have no understanding of the dangers facing a woman." He stabbed his hand through his hair again, appearing to reconsider his tact. "And it's not practical. If you want me to leave, you'll have to prove you're capable."

He splayed his hands, pained frustration glittering in his eyes. "Don't you miss the company of other people?"

"That's none of your business," she spoke, her voice pinched. "I don't have to prove anything to you."

She'd never confess her insecurities, but his words eroded all her rationalizations. Her head ached at the thought of the insurmountable tasks awaiting her in the spring. She needed more time to think, to plan.

Rubbing her temples, she blew out a long breath. Those problems were months away. She'd figure something out, she always did. "Why do you care? You'll be gone. Back to Texas."

"I'm saving somebody else from the trouble of cleaning up your mess."

"I've never been a burden to anyone."

She'd love nothing more than to report him to the law for trespassing, but involving the sheriff risked drawing attention to herself.

"Say something," he demanded. "Defend yourself. Tell me how you're going to cut enough wood to keep the house warm for the next three months. Tell me what you're going to do if there's an Indian uprising."

"God will take care of us. 'Consider the ravens. For they neither sow nor reap. Which neither have storehouse nor barn. And God feeds them. How much better are we than the fowls?' "

"You're a naive fool who never should have left New York. This isn't a page from a penny tale, this is the real thing. Do you want to know what it's like out here? Really like? I once saw a man hanged for shooting his whole family. You want to know why he murdered them?"

His implacable expression unnerved her. "You're just trying to frighten me with these petty parlor tricks."

"He shot them because he couldn't stand to watch his family starve. Is that what you want? Do you want to watch Rachel starve? To see your own flesh and blood waste away in misery before your eyes?"

Elizabeth pressed her hands to her ears. "Be quiet. You don't think people starve to death in the city? They die in the gutter while people step over their bodies like so much garbage. No place is safe. You don't frighten me."

How dare he intimidate her. This was a home. Land. A roof over her head and the prairie stretching out to the horizon. If she lost this house, she had nothing. Here on the homestead she had shelter, a sustainable source of food and the possibility of a legacy for her daughter. She had a future.

He paced the narrow aisle. "I'm not going to quit until I talk some sense into you. If you keep on the way you're going, you'll end up a pile of stones on the prairie. Is that what you want for Rachel? No one will even remember your names."

She froze, numbed by the thought of the anonymous piles of stones littering the prairie. "This is pointless."

Drained by the frustrating conversation, not to mention more exhausted than she'd ever been in her whole life, Elizabeth spun on her heel for her dramatic exit.

Instead, she stubbed her toe. "Ouch."

With tears of frustration pricking behind her eyes, she rubbed her foot. "What else can go wrong today?"

Jack lifted the heavy metal box she'd collided with onto the bunk. "Since you're not going to take my advice, it looks like I'll be staying a few more days. At least until Jo is up and about."

Her annoyance suddenly felt like relief. That was absurd. Of course she was mad. She was furious.

"Where on earth did the box come from?" she asked to cover her confusion.

Certainly he hadn't dragged the heavy object around on the back of his horse.

He wrestled the box into position. "I found this in the bottom of one of the lockers. You might as well take it back to the main house."

Startled by the abrupt change in conversation, she touched the lid. "I don't recognize this."

"It's yours now. I found it on your property."

The metal shape was vaguely familiar. Had the box belonged to Will? She had a hazy recollection of a furtive trip to the bunkhouse last spring.

Jack stared at her expectantly. Her hands grew cold. Dare she open the box in the Ranger's presence? Certainly Will hadn't left behind anything of value. He'd cleared the house of valuables before he left.

She pinched off her mittens. If she didn't reveal the contents, Jack would only be more suspicious. She couldn't afford him asking any more questions, or worse yet, reporting back to the sheriff.

As she vacillated, Jack's expression stilled and grew serious. She sensed the return of the Texas Ranger in the speculative gleam of his eyes.

Her resolve crystallized. There was no reason to assume the box held anything worth worrying about. If Will had left anything valuable, he'd have left it in his trunk in the house.

She licked her lips, tentatively stretching out one hand. Flipping open the lid, she sucked in a breath. Jack loomed behind her. She glanced over the contents. Several crumpled bills, four gold watches, a money clip and a revolver nestled in the box. She poked around with one finger, brushing the bills aside to reveal two thin gold rings.

Inordinately relieved to find the box filled with harmless objects, Elizabeth sighed. "This must have belonged to the previous owners."

"These items don't belong to you?"

She shook her head. "I told you. They must belong to the previous owner. A man from Pennsylvania lived here for years. His wife never could adjust to the prairie, so they moved back East. They must have left these things behind."

"Why didn't someone discover the box sooner?"

"Will kept a few hired hands when we first moved, but they took off."

Much to her relief, they hadn't returned. She'd never been partial to the company Will kept, and she definitely didn't like being alone with them when Will traveled.

Jack frowned. "How many watches does one man own? It doesn't seem right."

From the corner of her eye, she studied the objects. Fear pooled in her stomach. Another explanation dawned on her, one that she didn't want to share. "I don't suppose we'll ever know for sure."

The more she thought about it, the more certain she become of the objects' origins. If Will had won the personal items on one of his many gambling binges, he wouldn't have told her. He'd known she didn't approve of his card playing. But like everything else in their brief marriage, her opinion hadn't mattered. He'd done as he pleased, no matter how much his actions hurt her.

Another worry pressed on her. She recalled how the sheriff had threatened to seize her land if he found out the property was purchased with illegal money. Gambling wasn't illegal, but cheating was — and most people in town were suspicious of Will's propensity for winning.

Before Will's death she'd gone to the mercantile and the clerk had refused to serve her. The man was angry because Will had won his best horse in a card game. Fearful of another tense encounter, she'd curbed her trips to town.

Jack lifted a watch. "If they don't belong to you, I'll turn them over to the sheriff. This looks mighty expensive. Someone is missing this fancy piece."

Elizabeth thrust out her hands. "No!"

This was proof, leverage to use against her. If she lost her home, the land, she lost everything.

Guilt and fury ground together in her stomach. She couldn't afford to have the Texas Ranger around any longer. He had to leave. Her decision made, she tugged on her mittens. She'd handle this on her own. She didn't care how much Jack's eyes reminded her of the flaxen and emerald grasses sweeping across the plains in spring.

She pointed a finger at him, the irritated gesture lost in her enveloping mittens. "I expect you to be gone in one hour."

"Why are you mad at *me?*" he asked, his tone placating. "Can't you see I'm trying to help you?"

"I don't need your help."

"You're too stubborn for your own good, Elizabeth Cole."

"Maybe I am, but it's my decision. And I'm asking you to leave."

"I have a job to do, and no one is going to stand in my way. Not even you."

"Your job has nothing to do with us. Coming here was an accident. A mistake."

"I'm not so sure anymore."

Fear swept over her like a chill wind. "All the more reason you should go."

She slammed the door behind her.

Jack rested his fisted hand on the bedrail while he inhaled the lingering scent of lavender and vanilla. Last night, he'd asked himself the same questions Elizabeth had demanded of him. What *was* his purpose? Were his suspicions founded in logic, or based on emotion? Why was he still here when the widow's problems were none of his concern? More than once he'd packed his bags, preparing to leave, only to find his footsteps dragging.

The truth, he'd finally admitted to himself, was that he didn't know why he was still here. He thought he'd conditioned himself to ignore petty human emotions, but all his conditioning had deserted him. The widow's needs had become his own.

Her fears had become his fears. Her fate had become his responsibility. He was torn between honor and affection.

He finally understood his purpose.

When a bank was robbed, the outlaws often took more than money. They stole from the patrons, as well. Valuables such as watches, rings and pocket change. Exactly the sort of items floating around in that box. He opened the lid and lifted out the four watches. The hairs on the back of his neck stood on end.

He'd tracked the outlaw to Cimarron Springs, and the trail had grown cold at the widow's front door. He'd tracked a bay mustang and a man with cold eyes and a charming smile from Colorado to Kansas. From one livery to another he'd relentlessly pursued his prey. His instincts had led him here for a reason, and Elizabeth had tripped right over that reason.

Jack flung open the heavy stove door and tossed another log onto the dwindling fire. The widow feared the sheriff, and Jack was starting to wonder why.

Like other men smelled trouble, Jack recognized the distinct odor of fear. He didn't think the widow knew the origin of the items, but she knew enough to be frightened.

Her late husband must have been involved with the outlaws. The question remained, how much did she know? Elizabeth didn't strike him as the kind of woman to condone that sort of activity. Then again, people did all sorts of things he'd never thought possible. Could he really trust her?

Had his emotions clouded his judgment? There was no such thing as being a little bit guilty. She was a party to a crime or she wasn't. Simple as that. Either way, she was hiding something. He hadn't looked any deeper, because he hadn't wanted to know the truth.

Unbearably weary, he pinched the bridge of his nose. If he ceased pursuing justice, if he let an innocent man hang, he lost everything that made him a man, everything he believed about himself.

He'd have to pressure her until he learned the truth. No matter what the personal cost, until he knew where the widow placed her loyalties, he had to treat her as a suspect.

Jack rubbed at his chest. Why did he feel as though someone was tearing out his heart?

CHAPTER NINE

Elizabeth eyed the loaded revolver on the worktable. Short of shooting the Ranger, she didn't know how else to get rid of the man. Tempted though she was, she'd never resort to violence. Too bad her options were appallingly limited. Involving the sheriff would only cause more problems, and asking Mr. McCoy for help was out of the question. What would she tell them, anyway, "There was a Texas Ranger on my property. He was cutting wood and taking care of chores, so I shot him?"

Elizabeth snorted.

Since their argument that morning, he'd holed up in the bunkhouse. Perhaps he'd simply leave on his own. She knew his food supply must be getting low. Better for her if he scampered off to town because he was starving. Better than having to admit that her husband was a card cheat. Better than risking her ownership of the homestead by revealing the truth. Jack was nothing if not a lawman, and he'd have to do the right thing. Even if the right thing left Elizabeth homeless and penniless. She'd expect him to do no less.

As if conjured from her thoughts, Jack appeared on the horizon, his rifle slung over one shoulder, an enormous turkey dangling behind him from a leather strap. *So much for starving him out.* He cut through the dry brush edging the creek bed with long strides, his broad shoulders grazing the barren tree limbs. A dark hat shadowed his eyes.

Her heart did a little flip, but she quickly squashed the emotion. Angry with her weakness, Elizabeth stomped to the barn, setting about her chores with angry vigor. She didn't even bother to look up from the grain bin when the heavy panel door creaked open. He had to leave, didn't he? He had a case to solve.

"Thought you'd like fresh meat for supper," Jack called.

She peered at his catch from the corner of her eye. Her mouth watered.

"I'll dress this," he declared, tossing the plump bird onto a worktable beside the sandstone sharpening wheel.

Ignoring his peace offering, she scooped a dipper of feed and dumped the contents into the burlap sack slung over the milk cow's stall. Unable to resist, she canted him another sideways glance. Jack flicked the pad of his thumb over a shiny silver knife, testing the edge.

His hands snagged her attention. They were sturdy and strong with a dusting of dark hair over the knuckles. Those hands could break a man's neck, yet she'd never seen them raised in anger. He held Rachel with an aching tenderness belying his superior size. She recalled clinging to his hand during Rachel's birth, the feel of his calloused palms, how his strength had been both alarming and comforting. She marveled at the combination of size and grace.

The milk cow bumped against the stall, startling Elizabeth from her reverie.

He was up to something. She'd starve before she accepted Jack's offering of dinner. "There you go, Betsy."

The cow snuffled in response.

Elizabeth noted the empty pan of milk she'd set out for the feral cat that had taken up residence in the barn. She splashed a few drops from the pail into the dish. The cat had proved useful in keeping rodents out of the grain bin. While the mangy thing was mean, ornery and ugly, the cat served a useful purpose and Elizabeth was content to keep her homely little mouser happy.

Setting down the pail, she wrinkled her nose against the pungent scent of manure. Time to clean out Betsy's stall. That chore meant climbing into the hayloft for bedding. While Elizabeth wasn't exactly afraid of heights, climbing the rickety ladder was not her favorite activity. Instead, she puttered around the barn, putting off the task as long as she could.

A half hour passed while she stalled, avoiding Jack as he efficiently divested the turkey of feathers. At last, chiding herself for being a frightened ninny, she grasped the rails and carefully set her booted foot on the first rung. The ladder creaked and groaned with her careful ascent. Hoisting herself over the ledge, she stood, then brushed her hands together with a relieved sigh. She'd survived the climb one more time.

Dust motes floated in the beams of light shafting through the loft door. The faulty latch never stayed shut. One strong wind was enough to blow the door open a crack. Elizabeth glanced over the ledge, catching sight of the top of Jack's head. She had a fair idea how he'd escaped the barn that first night. No wonder he'd been so grumpy. Even if he'd dangled his whole body out the loft door, he still had a good five foot plunge onto the snow below. The fall must have bruised his dignity *and* his hide.

Served him right for kicking down my door.

She crept forward, only to be yanked to a halt. She glanced down. Her hem had caught on a splinter. Tugging her skirts free, she continued on her way, her arms outstretched for balance as she tiptoed to the open door. Maintaining a safe distance from the ledge, she stretched one hand and heaved the door shut.

Blood pumping, she scurried away from the edge, then faced the dwindling stacks of hay bales. How different the space appeared from last spring when Will had hoisted the bales from Mr. McCoy's sturdy wagon and stacked them to the ceiling. Winter was only half finished, and she'd used her stores more rapidly than she had anticipated.

Another problem she'd have to deal with soon.

Discouraged by the thought, she yanked a heavy rectangle off the stack, then kicked the tightly bound straw bale over the side to the barn floor. Betsy snuffled at the disturbance.

"Oh, be quiet, you grumpy old thing," Elizabeth called.

Turning, she grasped the ladder rails and

stretched her left foot to the first rung. Adjusting her hold, she reached for the second rung and pressed the ball of her right foot onto the slat. A crack sounded. Her boot broke through the splintered wood. She lost her balance, flailing her leg to find a solid purchase. The jerky movement sent her left foot skidding off its rung. Clutching the rails, she arched backward, her feet dangling.

"Help!"

"Don't let go!" A deep voice called from behind her.

"I hadn't planned on it," she bit out through gritted teeth.

Boots scuffled, indicating Jack's hasty dash to assist her. Arms burning, she strained to hold herself aloft. A bead of sweat trickled down her cheek.

She felt the ladder strain, a telling creak sounded near her ear. She gasped in horror as one of the nails separated from its anchor. A hand snaked around her calf. The nail slid out another half inch.

"Don't come up!" she shouted. "The ladder won't hold us both."

She glanced down, quickly squeezing her eyes shut. Ten feet remained between her and the hard-packed dirt below. She'd surely break her leg if she let go now. "Pull that bail beneath me. I'll jump down."

"It's too far. You'll break your leg."

"Maybe I'll break my left leg," she gasped. "Together Jo and I will be one whole person."

Scrambling, she hoisted her leg to reach the first rung, but her booted heel caught in her petticoats. Jack clambered up behind her. The ladder sagged. Desperate to counter his weight, she tore through the cotton fabric to release her heel and leaned forward, pressing her forehead against the dry wood. "Get down."

A hand snaked around her waist. "I've got you."

"But who's got you?"

He chuckled, the vibration sending the nail sliding further from its mooring. "You can let go."

She gently shook her head so as not to agitate the overburdened ladder. Her fingers strained. "I don't know how much longer I can hang on."

"Let go."

She hadn't heard him use his brisk tone of voice since that first night so many weeks ago.

Fear surged through her veins, giving her strength.

Even if she had wanted to release her grip,

he was still too far below her. When she dropped down, the loss of balance would send them both plunging to the ground. "I can't let go."

The arm around her waist tightened. "You're going to have to trust me."

"No!"

He heaved back, yanking her with him. Her fingers wrenched from their hold. Her mittens snagged on the rough wood and slipped from her stiff hands. With a shriek she fell, pitching backward to the packed dirt below. Jack's feet hit the ground first. The force of their fall sent him stumbling backward.

Together they tumbled to the floor. Jack cushioned her landing, holding her tight against his chest. A cloud of dust billowed around them.

Too stunned to move, she stared at the timbered ceiling. His solid body protected her from the chill ground, warming her back. Adrenaline still rushing through her veins, she flipped over. A chicken flapped in the dust just behind Jack's head.

Realizing they were still intimately entangled on the floor, Elizabeth scrambled to one side. She ignored Jack's muffled grunt of pain when her knee dug into his thigh.

"Why did you do that?" she demanded.

"We could have both been killed."

With a casual grin, he pillowed his hands beneath his head. "Mighty sore maybe, but not killed."

"Oooh, you daft man."

He quirked an eyebrow. "Daft?"

"Yes, daft," she replied, the indignation leaching from her voice.

She cut a glance at the broken ladder. The *daft* man was correct. The distance had seemed much more dramatic when she was dangling from the ledge. She hung her head in her hands, willing her hammering heart to slow. The tension gradually drained from her body, replaced by a curious lethargy. When her breath ceased coming in sharp gasped, she chanced a peek at Jack. His gaze rested on her face, somber and concerned. She knew she should be angry, but his eyes captivated her. The way the color grew darker nearer the rims.

She pressed her palms against his chest to leverage herself upright, then paused. His heartbeat thumped solid and sure, but rapid all the same, against her outstretched fingers. He wasn't nearly as unaffected by their contact as he feigned.

He kept the half grin on his face, his hands firmly locked behind his head, but she sensed his coiled tension, a subtle shift in his attitude. Tilting her head, she considered his casual pose.

She sensed if she pulled away, he wouldn't stop her, but she had no desire to test her theory. There was something alluring about the way he never rushed a moment. Surrendering to the urge, she ran her thumb over the rough surface of his stubble-covered cheeks, letting her finger linger on the thin white scar barely visible along the length of his jaw. The slight disfigurement gave her a glimpse into his checkered past.

She savored the rare quiet moment. Even though he threatened to stay, eventually his case would force him to leave. She couldn't forget he'd rescued her. Three times. His hazel eyes evoked a warm longing. As if her soul had been searching for refuge, and Jack held the map. A rare impulse took hold of her. She wanted to know everything about him. His home, his past, his future.

Had he ever been in love before? Had he ever wanted to give up his job and settle down?

She grazed the scar with her finger. "How did this happen?"

He turned his face into her hand. "Mule kick."

His lips tickled her palm, sending shivers down her spine. She felt buoyant, brave and invincible. The stubborn tilt in his chin gave her the courage to tease him. "Was this mule an animal, or one of your brothers?"

He grinned, and she felt the movement all the way to her toes.

"You're a very perceptive woman. I come from a long line of stubborn men."

At the husky sound of his voice, her heart quivered.

Her feelings for Will had been bright and intense, like lightning bursting in the sky. But they'd faded just as quickly. She'd never been in love with Will, but at least she finally understood his draw. She'd been in love with the way he made her feel. For someone who had been alone most of her life, his attention had been intoxicating, and brief. If their courtship had been even a week longer, she'd have seen the chinks in his respectability.

By the time she'd noticed the signs of his cruelty, they'd boarded a train bound for Kansas. There was nothing for her to do but stay, and face the consequences of her rash behavior.

With Jack the sensations felt like a summer shower — unhurried, light and enduring. The juxtaposition of the two men was startling. Spring rain brought daffodils and crocus, while thunderstorms flattened the prairie grasses and uprooted trees.

Fighting his attraction taxed her resolve. Especially when he made her insides melt like warm butter. Why did Jack have to threaten everything she held dear? She didn't want her well-ordered existence to change any more than it already had. Whatever Will had done was in the past, but she didn't know if Jack would see it that way.

She'd carved out a life for herself and a future for her daughter, a carefully maintained, brittle sense of safety. But Jack chipped away at the foundations of her security with his lack of faith in her. No matter what happened, she didn't want to be wrong about a man again. She couldn't risk her own heart, and she definitely couldn't risk Rachel's affection.

"Why won't you just leave?" she whispered, blinking frantically against the sting of tears behind her eyes.

He studied her for a moment, then offered a tired smile. He tugged one hand from behind his head and gently brushed away the moisture from her cheek with the pad of his thumb. "I can't. You know why."

Her heart turned in response to his gentle caress. Being here like this wasn't proper. She should flee, but her limbs refused to budge. Jack was right again. The pig wasn't much of a chaperone.

"What about your case?" she asked, hoping to change the subject, to dissipate this frightening intimacy.

"For the first time in my career, I've failed." A shadow flitted across his eyes. "I've run out of leads."

His obvious distress struck a chord. He'd helped deliver Rachel, he'd chopped wood and shoveled snow. He'd even mucked stalls, and she had never once thanked him for his help. There was no way to repay him, unless . . .

An idea sprang into her head. "What if I help you? I'm good with puzzles. I've seen your newspaper clippings." The more she thought about the idea, the more enthused she became. "Perhaps I can discover a pattern."

He rolled his head from side to side in a negative motion. "There's nothing you can do. I've been looking at those clippings for months. What makes you think you can find a connection?"

She braced her hands on either side of his head, daring him to hold her gaze. "What makes you think I can't? I'm a fresh perspective and I don't have any emotions attached to the case."

His eyes narrowed in thoughtful consideration. Another emotion she couldn't define flitted across his face. "I guess it wouldn't hurt to let you try."

She grinned, pleased with the opportunity to prove her abilities. The idea was inspired. If she found a new lead in his case, he'd be forced to leave. Without his interference she and Rachel returned to their safe, orderly world.

After seeing the box, she feared he suspected the truth about Will's gambling. Perhaps if Jack solved his case, he'd forget all about the watches. "Bring your newspapers to the house this evening. We're having turkey for supper."

"My turkey?"

"*My* turkey. I'm assuming you shot it on my land."

Elizabeth's coat sleeve had torn during her ordeal, and the frayed material parted to her elbow. Jack caught her arm, turning her hand to reveal the arrow-shaped scar on her skin. She quickly brushed her sleeve down to cover the mark.

"How did you get such an odd scar?"

"It was a long time ago," Elizabeth mumbled.

The escaped chicken pecked at the ground near Jack's head.

"Myrtle," she called to the chicken, shoo-

210

ing the bird away with her outstretched hands. "Back to the henhouse with you."

She glanced down to discover her skirts draped intimately over Jack's legs. She quickly brushed them aside, but not before he quirked an eyebrow at the hasty motion.

Rolling to one side, Jack stood, then brushed the dust from his pant legs. "You name your chickens?"

He pulled her to her feet and quickly dropped his hand to his side. She noted how he flexed his fist a few times, as if disgusted with the contact. Her heart sank.

Elizabeth knelt before the brick of hay, tugging the bailing twine free. "That hen is very memorable. I call her Myrtle the Mouser because she's always escaping the chicken coop to chase down mice with the barn cat."

"Please tell me you're joking."

"I'm perfectly serious."

She scooped Myrtle into her arms, then whirled to face the Ranger. He towered above her, an incredulous grin on his handsome face. She had the distinct impression he was laughing at her and not the chicken.

"Here." She thrust the bird at his chest. "Make yourself useful and put Myrtle away. I'll get the turkey started." She patted the chicken's feather-soft head. "I'll clean your cage tomorrow."

"Not tomorrow." He juggled Myrtle in his hands. "It's the Sabbath."

"Of — of course," Elizabeth stuttered, not sure of the reference, but afraid of looking foolish. "I guess I just forgot."

Myrtle struggled, feathers flapping in the Ranger's face. Grimacing, he shrugged. "It's hard to keep track of the days."

"Yes, well, I'd best get back inside. I've left Rachel alone for too long already."

She paused, unable to tear her gaze away from the tall man. At his murmured assurance, Myrtle settled into his arms. Jack had an affinity with animals and children. A way of charming them with his amiable smile, though she knew a layer of steel rested beneath that friendly grin.

"Supper is at six," she said hastily. "And don't forget your newspapers."

She had stumbled upon the perfect solution. Reviving his interest in his case would surely focus his attention on something other than her. The sooner he moved on, the better.

Right?

Jack dunked his face into the bucket of ice-cold water, quickly straightened, then flung back his head, sending a shower of water droplets raining over the floor.

He ran his hands through his drenched hair, smoothing down the mass. Rubbing his face, he groaned at the stubble already covering his chin. Perhaps he should shave again. He shook his head. No, that was foolish. He wasn't attending a church social. Then again, this was the first invitation he'd received to dine in the house since his return, and his beard *was* a bit long.

Reaching for his shaving kit, he studied his face in the tiny mirror. The reflection showed a man in his early thirties, not handsome certainly, but not ugly, either. There was nothing fundamentally wrong with any of his features. Certainly no one would call him handsome, but women had fawned over his older brother, Robert, and people often said the two of them bore a passing resemblance. The comparisons had to mean something.

A glint of sliver caught his attention. He squinted, tilting his head farther to the right. Several gray strands stood out in stark relief. His fears realized, he whipped around to the left and studied the opposite side of his head. He was graying at the temples! When had that happened?

With one calloused finger, he smoothed down the offensive outcropping. Surely he wasn't old enough for gray hair. Thinking back, Jack mentally ticked off the years. His father had been forty-five with a full head of silver when he died.

But his father had been *old.* Not much older than Jack was now, though.

The realization stunned him. He arranged a hunk of hair over the gray spot, then brushed it back into place again. He wasn't old, he was seasoned. The look was distinguished. He squinted into the mirror. Besides, who wanted to be young and impulsive?

With that thought firmly in place, he reached for his shaving kit again. He lathered his face and carefully pulled the razor over his rough beard, idly wondering how the widow thought of him. Did she see him as mature? Or old? He stilled his hand. He'd never considered Elizabeth's age, but she was definitely younger than him. In her early twenties perhaps.

She had a brisk, efficient way about her, a maturity beyond her years. The thought of her living in an orphanage sent his stomach dipping. She had such a wide-eyed innocence about her. As if she refused to be broken by the evil she witnessed in the world.

A pot of water boiled merrily on the stove

to his left. The steam drifted over the shirt he'd hung from the center beam, smoothing out the wrinkles. Jack grunted at the sight. His fellow Rangers would have a heyday if they saw him now, primping like a debutante for her first dance.

He studied his face in the mirror again, checking every angle for missed whiskers. Satisfied with the results, he wiped the excess foam from his face. Of their own volition, his hands went to the minuscule vial of aftershave tucked in the corner of his bag. A gift from his sister-in-law, though he couldn't recall which one.

He did remember the gift had been accompanied by a whole lot of ribbing from his brothers, and not a few hints from his mother that she was ready for another daughter-in-law and a passel more grandchildren.

Embarrassed by his uncharacteristic vanity, he dropped the vial, snatched his shirt from its perch, then snapped out the last of the wrinkles. He swiped a drop of cologne on his pant legs. It was a turkey dinner, not an audience with Queen Victoria.

He had to stay focused. Elizabeth's offer of assistance had haunted him all afternoon. Why had she finally decided to help him? This dinner was about finding out how much she knew, and questioning her about her husband's activities. It wasn't as if he was going courting or anything. This was business.

He strode across the clearing to her door, not bothering to don his wool coat for the few steps to the widow's house. His gaze lingered on the shiny, unweathered hinges he'd replaced only weeks before. He knocked sharply. His job was to free an innocent man from the hangman's noose, not deliver babies.

The door swung open. A puff of warm air scented with roasting turkey sent his mouth watering. He glanced up. His heart jolted. All thoughts of outlaws and interrogations fled his brain. He'd just seen Elizabeth hours ago, yet she'd done something different with her hair, or maybe it was a new dress. She was so beautiful, she'd rooted his feet to the floor. Jack swallowed. Doing his job had just gotten a whole lot more difficult.

CHAPTER TEN

Elizabeth soon discovered one thing about the lawman — he sure knew how to eat. She heaped a third helping of apple pan Dowdy onto his scraped-clean plate while he looked on with rapt interest.

"I couldn't possibly have any more," Jack protested, drawing the plate closer to his chest, his fork poised in the air. "But since you've already served some up, I'd hate to see it go to waste. I've never eaten a finer meal, Mrs. Cole."

His formal address set her back a notch. "You're welcome."

He'd been different all evening, though pinpointing the exact difference eluded her. His manners remained impeccable, yet a hint of solemnity colored his actions. His conversation stayed smooth and rigidly correct — almost too correct. Perhaps that was the problem. On the one hand, his deference made her feel important, cherished.

On the other hand she felt as if he was holding something back, keeping a part of himself hidden.

The change in his attitude had her off balance, unsure how or why their relationship had altered. Instead of alleviating the tension between then, their encounter in the barn had heightened the strain.

She fussed with her apron, smoothing a nonexistent wrinkle from her skirt. "My mother always insisted on starting at the beginning whenever there was a problem. Let's review what we know for certain. You're looking for a man named Bud Shaw because he's a bank robber."

"There's more to it than that." Jack's knuckles whitened where he gripped his fork. "I put the wrong man in jail. If I don't find the real Bud Shaw, an innocent man will hang. I can't live with his death on my conscience."

Elizabeth's hand flew to her chest. His raw confession lent her a rare glimpse into his vulnerability. He sat stiffly, as if waiting for her to accuse or berate him. But for what? She certainly wasn't his judge and jury.

After a moment she asked, "How can Bud Shaw prove this man's innocence? I thought he was an outlaw."

"Because Bud Shaw is also in jail."

Elizabeth widened her eyes. "You're searching for Bud Shaw. And Bud Shaw is in jail?"

Jack pushed his empty plate forward, set his forearms on the table and clasped his hands together. His somber gaze fixed on a point just above her left shoulder. "I'll start at the beginning." He exhaled a heavy breath. "There was a string of bank robberies from Kansas through Colorado last year. They crossed into Texas sometime during the spring. My brother's wife was shot during one of the robberies."

"Is she all right?"

The stark agony in his exotic hazel eyes rocked her. He must have been close to the woman for such a reaction. An unexpected shaft of jealousy stabbed her. She pressed her hand tighter against her chest, quelling the hateful emotion. What kind of person was jealous of an injured woman? What was wrong with her?

Certainly she was no stranger to jealousy and envy. Growing up she'd watched other families with yearning in her heart. She'd even noticed how Will had paid particular attention whenever a pretty woman passed by, but she'd never experienced this sort of spite in her heart.

Jack seemed to gather himself, shrugging

his shoulders as if divesting himself of the somber memories. "No. She didn't make it." He cleared his throat. "Emotions got involved during the initial hunt for the outlaws. People wanted justice, and they wanted it fast." He finally met her sympathetic gaze. "In our rush to capture the outlaws, we made a mistake. There's an innocent man set to hang, and I can't save him."

As if physically weighted by the burden, his shoulders sagged. The gesture touched a place deep within Elizabeth's heart. She understood the wearing pressure of guilt.

She lowered herself to perch on the edge of her chair and leaned over the table. While she longed to reach out and press her hand over his, to absorb his pain, instead, she said, "Why do you think this man is innocent?"

"Instinct."

She dug her fingernails into her palms. How nice it must be, to trust in one's self. She'd lost that confidence the moment she agreed to marry a man who cared more for personal appearance than he did for his wife. She missed the sure knowledge of right and wrong, and her ability to judge the difference.

"Did you investigate the other robberies?"

He shook his head.

"Why not?"

"I only got involved because of my sister-in-law Doreen. My brothers are ranchers. I'm the only one in the family who had the background to investigate. Except that it's not really what I do. I'm more of a negotiator. I'm good at tracking." He stared at his hands. "At least I used to be. As for the other robberies, the Rangers had already done their job. Wasn't much more I could do."

He appeared reluctant to elaborate on his job duties. Though she didn't understand why, she decided not to pressure him. "Tell me what you think happened."

Jack cleared his throat. "We captured the wrong Bud Shaw."

"Two men and one name."

"Yes, but only one of them is a killer."

"It says here the Texas Rangers captured two outlaws." She glanced at his jotted notes. "Certainly they can identify each other."

"Pencil Pete says the man sitting in jail is Bud Shaw, all right. Says Bud is the one responsible for shooting a clerk up in Colorado Springs, too." Jack's eyes grew cloudy, distant. "But I don't buy it. Old Pencil Pete is too gleeful, too fired up about

221

selling out one of his own gang. I've put plenty of men away for doing crimes. I've watched them trample each other to cut a deal. But I've never seen a man so eager to identify one of his own with nothing in return. Something isn't right."

Heat from his simmering frustration washed over her in waves. She'd been around him long enough to see the subtle signs of his distress. The way he kept his palms flat on the table. The muscle that ticked along his jaw.

She forced her own tightly clenched hands to relax. "Then we'd best find the killer. I owe you that much."

Whether she wanted to admit it or not, he'd been a help around the farm. He'd cut wood and mucked stalls. He patiently instructed her on loading Will's gun, he'd even kept Jo company, distracting the younger girl from the crushing boredom of laying in bed all day.

Elizabeth hadn't asked for the Ranger to barge into her life, but he'd made himself useful none the less. Assisting him in discovering a new lead served two purposes — she'd repay her debt, and she'd remove his reason for staying.

She forcibly squelched the nagging doubts that sprang up each time she thought of Jack leaving. This was the right thing to do. He was a drifter and a loner. Men like that didn't change.

If her thoughts lingered over the way his voice gentled when he talked to Rachel, or the way the baby seemed to instantly calm in his presence, then she blamed the weather. The long winter had left her fatigued, and more prone to melancholy. Things would be better in the spring. There'd be more people around. Life on the homestead would be less lonely.

The longer Jack stayed, the less she'd want to let him go. "Let's start with the bank robbery."

She stood, crossed to the kitchen cupboard and swung open the door. For the first time in a long while, she had a concrete goal. A purpose. Her thoughts raced as she pulled down a lead pencil and one of her precious sheets of paper. "We'll start with the last robbery. How many outlaws were involved?"

"Three."

"How many people were injured?"

His lips drew into a thin, white line. "Just Doreen. She was reaching for her reticule. One of the men spooked at the movement. He shot her."

She gave his hand a quick squeeze. "I'm

so sorry about your sister-in-law."

"Thank you," he replied, his voice husky.

To ease the tension, Elizabeth jotted down several notes before flipping over the paper. "Sketch the inside of the bank and where everyone was standing. To the best of your knowledge at least."

"I don't see what —"

"Please," she implored. "I need to know everything. I need to get a picture in my mind of what happened."

Reluctantly complying, he concentrated on the sketch. With his head bent, he drew a remarkably detailed outline of each chair, desk and window. A lock of hair fell over his eyes, and he swatted it away. Her fingers itched to smooth the chocolate waves back into place.

His hair had grown. With his face cleanly shaven, he appeared even more dangerous than the first time she'd seen him. The impulsive side of her, the part that had led her to Kansas in the first place, was drawn to that danger. How tempting to rest her burdens on his strong shoulders, to share her fears and insecurities, to let the low rumble of his baritone voice soothe her.

Elizabeth started, ashamed of her wayward thoughts.

While she struggled to force her attention

back to the robberies, Jack indicated the locations of the three outlaws and the four civilians.

"What's that?" She indicated a box drawn near the edge of the picture.

"That's the safe."

Their fingers brushed together. The touch struck a vibrant chord within her. Their gazes locked. His hazel eyes sparked with an inscrutable emotion.

Her heart jolted and her pulse pounded. A plaintive cry from the bedroom sent Elizabeth stumbling to her feet. "While you're finishing that, I'll fetch the baby and check on Jo."

He jerked his head in an absentminded nod, his attention once again focused on the sketch. Elizabeth paused, wondering if she'd imaged the flare of emotion in his eyes. Another lusty cry from the baby yanked her from her contemplations.

She fed and changed Rachel while Jo twirled one mahogany braid and frowned over a dog-eared copy of *Pride and Prejudice*.

Elizabeth's chest constricted at the forlorn sight. "Would you like me to sit with you? Keep you company? You must be getting lonely."

The girl glanced up and smiled, dropping her braid to shoo away the interruption.

"This is a good part," she whispered. "I'm almost finished."

Elizabeth quirked an eyebrow. *So much for entertaining the invalid.*

Her guilt assuaged, she flashed a knowing smirk at the top of Jo's head. The very proper English romance certainly had her tomboy helper engrossed.

Rachel fussed in her drawer, kicking away her blankets to reveal her darling, stocking-clad feet. Elizabeth picked her up and cradled the baby to her chest. There was something grounding about holding Rachel to her heart, feeling her daughter's warm breath rustling against her neck. For a moment everything was possible, the future wild and free.

Elizabeth closed her eyes, letting herself imagine her life if Will had loved her even half as much as Jack loved his family. Tears pricked behind her eyes. She surreptitiously wiped them away, relieved to find Jo too engrossed in her book to notice. They'd love each other, she and Rachel, and that would be enough.

With the baby propped against one shoulder, Elizabeth returned to the dining table, then struggled to clear the plates with her free hand.

"I'll hold Rachel," Jack offered. "I've

finished with the drawing."

Elizabeth rested the infant in his outstretched arms. His enormous hands dwarfed the growing baby. He tucked Rachel into the crook of his elbow where she stared at his face in curious wonder. Lost in a private world, the two made faces at each other.

The stern Texas Ranger melted away, leaving in its place an affectionate, openhearted man with an affinity for fatherhood. The sight warmed Elizabeth's heart.

Jack touched the infant's nose, assuming a mock expression of stern disapproval. "I hope you haven't been giving your mother any trouble."

The infant's mouth worked, as if she were struggling to form a reply. A tender affection stirred in Elizabeth's chest, a glowing circle of light seemed to grow and expand around her heart. She had dreamed of this moment, in the deep recesses of her heart where the harsh light of truth failed to penetrate. She had imagined this event in her waking dreams. A home, a family, the soft haze of firelight chasing away the evening gloom. The fresh smell of baked apples wafting around her. Of course, she'd pictured the man to be her husband, not a Texas Ranger who'd burst into her life with his gun drawn.

"You're smiling," Jack said. "What are you thinking about?"

"Nothing. Nothing at all. Now where were we?"

His smile faltered. "The newspaper clippings are all here." He indicated a neat stack of folded papers. "I've circled the relevant articles."

"Excellent." She assumed a brisk efficiency. "First though, tell me about the man you captured. Tell me about the Bud Shaw you jailed."

Jack absently rocked the infant, his eyes thoughtful. "He's quiet, I guess. Just an ordinary fellow. He had some problems as a kid, rustling cattle with his father and the like, but nothing violent. He's just ordinary."

Elizabeth sighed at his frank reply. Jack didn't consider her questions silly or unimportant, he simply answered them with his usual straightforward, direct responses. As if they were equals. The cozy room took on a misty shimmer from the kerosene lanterns, softening the homestead's rough edges. For the second time in so many weeks, she wanted to stretch out time and capture this moment in her memory.

She sat up in her chair, pulling away from his magnetic draw. "Why do you keep saying he's ordinary?"

"Because the real Bud Shaw is larger than life. People describe him as handsome, gregarious, a gambler and a fellow all the ladies clustered around." Jack adjusted Rachel to the other arm. The baby kicked and cooed in delight. He dropped a kiss to her forehead. Elizabeth's heart stuttered at the unconscious gesture.

Unaware of the havoc he wreaked on her senses, Jack continued, "The fellow serving time in a Paris, Texas, jail doesn't strike me as that sort of man."

Elizabeth crossed her arms over her chest. She couldn't help but think of another man who fit the description of gregarious lady charmer. As far as she could tell, leopards did not change their spots. At least not for long.

"Did Bud Shaw do the shooting?"

He shrugged. "We believe so."

Elizabeth blew out a relieved breath. The description had been so similar to Will. Yet Will's gun had never been fired. He'd carried the flashy piece like a badge of honor, but even Jack had noted the gun's pristine condition. "How much time have you spent with the Bud Shaw in jail? Could he be acting?"

"I spent two weeks in Paris helping my

brother with the arrangements after Doreen's death. I didn't see any behavior to indicate the man was anything but a quiet, conscientious worker who'd run into some trouble in his youth."

Jack smoothed his thumb over Rachel's eyebrow. The infant captured his index finger, tugging it toward her mouth. He grinned, a dimple appearing on his left cheek. The baby explored his hand, even taking a tentative bite at his thumb. Jack held Rachel as if it were the most natural thing in the world. As if he were meant to serve the role.

Rubbing her hands over her eyes, Elizabeth dragged her attention back to the clippings. "What led you to this man in the first place?"

"Slim Joe was gut shot during the last escape. Before he died, he gave me the names of Pencil Pete and Bud Shaw. Slim even told me where Bud lived. His name and address matched a signature at the hotel the night before. We went to his spread and found part of the money hidden behind his woodshed."

"Sounds like Bud is guilty."

"To you and everyone else. Even the other witnesses aren't certain. He looks close enough to the description to be the man.

But something isn't right. He doesn't act like a criminal. He doesn't even seem the type."

Elizabeth suppressed a grin. The frustration in his voice was incongruent with the silly faces he kept flashing at the infant to make her gurgle in delight. "Does anybody else share your conviction?"

Jack barked out a laugh, startling Rachel. The baby's face pinched as if she might cry. He crossed his eyes and stuck out his tongue. A smile stretched across her round face. "Not hardly. Bud Shaw would be dead and buried already if it weren't for me. I talked the sheriff into giving me six months to find the real outlaw. I'm running out of time, though. More important, Bud is running out of time."

"You've gone to an awful lot of trouble based on your instinct."

"That's all I've got."

In that second, she understood his purpose. The pursuit of justice consumed him. She was right to focus his attention on the case once again. The sooner he found a lead, the sooner he'd be on his way. Discovering the truth drove him forward. The same way having a permanent home drove her to stay on the homestead, despite the obvious danger.

A chill breeze swept through the room, ruffling her papers. Elizabeth mustn't let regrets fill her heart. The past could not be changed. Jack had not appeared in the bakery all those months ago, sweeping her off her feet. Will had. Any longings that might sneak into her heart, any wistful dreams of a handsome Texas Ranger whisking her away, were foolish and dangerous. Everything she had rested on this desolate slice of prairie. This endeavor wasn't about watching Jack putter around the room, Rachel in his arms.

Her goal was to remind him of his duty, and motivate him to leave. "Why don't I read through these newspapers? See if there's anything interesting?"

Jack settled himself in the chair nearest the roaring fire he'd started in the grate. "It's your time. Do you have something I can read?"

Elizabeth stood and crossed to the bedroom. Jo had dozed off with the book slack in her hands. Elizabeth opened the top dresser drawer and dug beneath her clothes. She returned to the hearth room and handed Jack a book.

He propped the Bible open on one knee, his ankles crossed on a three-legged stool. Rachel sprawled over his chest. Elizabeth's gaze swung between Jack and the rear door. There really was no reason for him to be here. Why didn't she just demand that he return to the bunkhouse and save herself this torture? Save herself from the dream come to life? After all, the truce had been for dinner only.

Yet Rachel appeared so content in his arms. The baby struggled to lift her head, reaching out to grasp his silver star. The pin tugged at his shirt. Jack's mouth kicked up at one corner.

Elizabeth's soul crashed and soared at the same time, torn between the truth and what might have been. Despite the pain, she couldn't tear her gaze away.

Jack returned his attention to the Bible, studying the pages, his brow furrowed in concentration. Why disturb them to selfishly save her shattered heart?

Elizabeth spent the next forty minutes poring over the newspaper articles and making notes. She sketched out dates and times in one column, the bank locations in another. Below Jack's picture of the last bank robbery, she traced the route the outlaws had taken through the western territory. She lined up the wanted posters, but they offered little help. The outlaws had worn bandannas over their faces to protect their identities. Even the witnesses had given conflicting accounts of their heights and weights.

The crimes appeared to be random, like spokes on a wheel. There was no obvious trail, no distinct line from point A to point B. The times didn't match up, either. The outlaws struck at random intervals, giving no clue as to why they chose the particular banks to rob.

Stumped, she wrote down the events happening in the towns. There were church socials, local festivals and the occasional marriages and arrests. Her eyes drooping, she rested her head on the table. Something about the towns piqued her curiosity.

Jack woke with a start. Disoriented, he searched the still cabin. Rachel dozed in his arms, her tiny fists bunched beneath her chubby chin. Banked embers glowed red in the hearth. Alarmed by the unnatural quiet, he searched the room, then heaved a sigh of relief to find Elizabeth sleeping at the table with her head cradled in her arms. Escaped tendrils of blond hair curtained her face.

He rolled the baby into the crook of his elbow. Standing, he raised himself up on his toes to stretch his stiff leg muscles, then bustled around the cabin. He placed a dozing Rachel in her bed before clearing away the rest of the dishes. As quietly as he could manage, he gathered his newspapers and stacked them neatly atop Elizabeth's notes. Curious, he slipped her papers free. Her handwriting was neat and precise, her organization of the facts logical.

Jack rubbed the back of his neck with a sigh. The futile endeavor hadn't been a complete waste. He'd gotten his first decent meal in weeks, and his brief nap had left him more rested than he'd felt in a month of Sundays. The company of the pretty widow hadn't hurt, either.

He'd forgotten the soothing comfort of women. The tiny details that made a house a home. Elizabeth had set the table for company, just like he remembered from his youth. She'd even pressed the butter into decorated pats. A stamped cow adorned the yellow disks. A tablecloth embroidered with delicate pink roses draped the table. The frivolous touches stirred up memories he thought he'd buried long ago.

Rare longings for a home of his own surprised him with their intensity. He'd didn't want a family, a permanent place to live. He was content with his work, satisfied with his contribution to society. But the widow had him picturing a life where he returned home every night to enjoy a hearty meal before a roaring fire. A home where he watched his own children grow.

He stretched to release the painful knot throbbing in his neck. He'd chosen his given profession for a reason. He didn't want to be tied to the family ranch like his brothers, buried beneath the uncertainty of droughts and blight. Held prisoner by weather and fate. He controlled his own destiny. And, right now, he controlled the destiny of an innocent man. If he forgot that, he surrendered his honor.

Elizabeth and her daughter had unleashed his protective instincts, that's all. These unsettling emotions were a reaction to his failure to locate the real Bud Shaw. The delay presented an opportunity to feel useful, needed. Nothing more. He'd quiet these disturbing yearnings for home and hearth once he found proof that Elizabeth's husband had been involved with the outlaws. There was something here. He just knew it.

If he found his gaze lingering over Elizabeth's soft lips, his heart catching at her infectious laugh, his reactions were the natural result of a man isolated from the comfort of a woman's company for too long. He'd steeled himself from the crushing loneliness of life on the trail before, and he'd harden his feelings once again.

When he could avoid the task no longer, he touched Elizabeth's shoulder. She blinked at him, her eyes sleepy and unfocused.

His hands trembling, he brushed the hair from her forehead. "It's late. I'll see you tomorrow."

Her eyes flew open. She stumbled to her feet. He reached out a hand to steady her. Swaying, she leaned into him. Her gaze searched the room while she pressed a hand to her forehead. "Where is Rachel?"

"She's snug as a bug in a rug."

Elizabeth blinked sleepily, brushing the wrinkles from her skirt. His mouth suddenly felt as dry as the west Texas desert. With her eyes blurry from sleep, her shirtwaist rumpled and her hair tumbling loose, she was the prettiest thing he'd ever seen. Loose waves of hair framed her face in a halo of light. A becoming hint of pink tinged her cheeks. A thousand different words came to mind, but not a one of them lent her justice.

"Gracious, I must have fallen asleep." She ran a hand over her eyes. "Rachel is probably due to be fed and changed soon."

A lump of regret lodged in his throat. Not trusting himself to speak, he nodded. He vowed never again to torment his older brothers about their fierce devotion to their children. For years the thought of being tied down to kin had struck him as stifling and restrictive. He finally understood.

Standing here, staring into Elizabeth's questioning blue eyes, the thought of living in one place for the rest of his life didn't seem so threatening anymore.

She blinked at him expectantly, as if waiting for him to say something.

"I'll, uh. I'll just be going. Thank you for dinner."

"You're welcome."

She smiled then, wide enough to reveal those overlapping teeth. His heart hammered against his ribs. Sleep had washed away her usual reticence, leaving her open and vulnerable. A very male part of him wanted to sweep her into his arms, to wipe away the lines of worry that furrowed her brow each day, to care for her. He yearned to be the man she leaned on.

Jack fisted his hands. He wasn't a rancher or a farmer. He was a man whose whole life revolved around travel. Even if he trusted the widow's motives completely, he was still a Texas Ranger. Wandering and family life didn't mix well. Jack had no rights here.

He had to remind himself of his purpose. His instincts had never failed him before, and every nerve in his body screamed that the answers to his questions were hidden on this isolated homestead. If her husband had been involved, if he had financed their marriage with stolen money, then the truth threatened to shatter her world.

He didn't want to choose between Elizabeth and Bud Shaw, but the answer was obvious. This wasn't about love and land and a tiny baby girl. A man's life dangled in the balance.

He caught sight of a knitted blanket draped over the back of the kitchen chair, Rachel's basket sitting on the seat. There was one thing he needed to do before he left for good. Before the decisions he had to make destroyed any chance of peace for either of them.

CHAPTER ELEVEN

Elizabeth knew something was wrong the minute she reached the bottom step out the back door. An eerie hush had settled over the prairie. Not even the wind blew to rattle the hook dangling from the hayloft. She stumbled back up the step again, leaning one hand on the railing as she peered into the distance.

No shadows stood out on the horizon, no ominous clouds hung in the distance. A muffled thump sent the hairs on the back of her neck standing on end. She waited. When nothing out of the ordinary appeared, she took another cautious step.

A crack sounded overhead followed by a shower of snow. Elizabeth shrieked, slipping and stumbling until, in her haste to escape, she teetered backward, flailing her arms and sitting down hard on the first step. Heart pounding, she scrambled to her feet.

Her gaze snagged on a broken tree branch

dangling above her head. The heavy weight of snow had snapped the limb. She pressed a hand to her breast with a sigh, slumping against the handrail. "Gracious, I've become a simpering ninny."

Feeling foolish for her cowardice, she retrieved her pail and set off for the barn. She'd had a revelation the night before, and she was anxious to share her newfound discovery with Jack. Her footsteps quick and light, she almost missed the trail of red splotches crossing the freshly cleared path.

Paw prints accompanied the bloody trail, disappearing around the edge of the barn. *The chicken coop!*

Elizabeth lifted the hem of her skirts and set off at a run. The prints looked fresh. A stray dog most likely. She rounded the corner and stumbled to a halt.

Myrtle's brown feathers with their distinctive white tips littered the ground in a sodden mass. "Oh, you naughty thing," Elizabeth sniffled. "I told you escaping the coop would only get you into trouble."

She dug her nails into her palms. Myrtle might have been an annoying nuisance, but the poor thing didn't deserve to end her life as dinner for a stray dog. Elizabeth straightened and stomped around the chicken coop, her boots crunching through the icy drifts, determined to scare away the beast that had eaten her mischievous bird.

She lifted her pail. A dark form crouched in the snow. Her heart leaped into her throat, strangling her angry words.

An enormous gray wolf bared its fangs as a low growl reverberated in its throat. Elizabeth took an involuntary step backward. A mammoth dusky paw inched closer. Her frantic gaze skirted the clearing. She had nothing to defend herself with except the flimsy tin pail clutched in her mittened hand.

She'd encountered enough ruffians in New York to realize bullies sensed fear. Drawing herself up to her full height, she sucked in a shaky breath. "Go away," she hollered. "Bad wolf."

The beast snarled in reply.

"I said shoo!"

Another beefy paw moved toward her in the snow. The animal slunk forward, its belly scraping on the frozen ground.

So much for acting fearless.

She gauged the distance to the barn door. How desperate and hungry was the wolf to be searching for food this early?

Myrtle's crimson blood darkened the animal's snout, chilling Elizabeth. Where was the rest of the pack? Had this one become separated? Was it rabid?

Her mind raced with possibilities. If she dashed to the safety of the barn, she still had to lift the heavy T-bar and shove aside the bulky door. The mangy beast would have her in shreds before she accomplished the task.

A furtive movement caught the corner of her eye.

The barn cat hissed.

The wolf swung its scruffy head at the distraction.

Elizabeth whirled, floundering in the deep snow, hampered by her long skirts. Not risking a look behind her, she dashed away from the barn. When the wolf's fierce yelps didn't sound any louder, Elizabeth chanced a glance over her shoulder. The cat had clawed its way up the side of the henhouse to perch on the roof. Beneath the overhang, the wolf danced in the snow, bounding from side to side, jaws snapping.

Elizabeth skidded to a halt on the cleared path. Gasping, she pressed a hand to the stitch in her side. The house sat to her left, the bunkhouse and Jack farther to the right. Dare she lead the wolf to the house, even though the distance was shorter?

The unmistakable gallop of padded feet pounded behind her, coming up fast.

A plaintive howl spurred her into action.

At the sound of Elizabeth's scream, Jack dropped his level and leaped over the carved wood pieces littering the floor. He fastened his gun holster around his waist while bolting to the door. In one swift movement he grasped his rifle from its perch and burst onto the porch.

He slammed into Elizabeth with enough force to send them both sliding toward the shallow stairs. He caught her around the waist as they stumbled to the floor. Unable to cushion her fall, he jerked to lessen their blunt landing. Angling his body, he cracked his elbow against the wood, his sights focused on the animal bounding toward them. Ignoring Elizabeth's cry of pain, he aimed the rifle and fired.

The wolf yelped, its forward momentum halted as if it had smacked into a brick wall. Jack glanced around the uneven clearing formed by the three homestead buildings, searching for the rest of the pack. Where there was one animal, more were certain to follow.

With raw fear rushing through his veins like a river current, he jerked Elizabeth to her feet. Half leading, half carrying the stunned widow, he dragged her into the shelter of the bunkhouse.

Only when the door was safely closed and the latch firmly in place did he allow himself to search her trembling form for any signs of injury. Tears pooled in the corners of her eyes.

Jack ran his hands down her arms. "Are you hurt?"

"I'm fine, but —"

Relief shuddered through him. He folded her in his embrace, wanting to wrap her in his warmth. With a muffled sob, she buried her head in his shoulder. Rocking her gently, he murmured soothing words against the delicate curve of her ear.

"I must see to Rachel and Jo," she said, her voice muffled against his shirt. She wrenched free of his arms.

He managed to reach over her shoulder and slam the door before she exposed them both to certain danger. "You can't go outside. Where there's one wolf, there's bound to be more. We have to be sensible about this."

"That wolf killed Myrtle," she declared.

He pressed his forehead against hers. "I'm sorry about Myrtle."

"I'm just so mad."

She actually stomped her foot.

Sighing, Jack let her collapse against his

chest. "I bet the old thing stuck in that wolf's craw and choked him. Don't cry."

"I refuse to cry. I didn't ever used to cry." She tipped back her head, her pale blue eyes standing out against her ashen face. "Having a baby has ruined me. I haven't stopped crying in months. It's ridiculous."

"You're tired, that's all. Things will look better when you get some rest."

"No. I'm not going to think like that any longer. Things have to change, now, or not at all. From this moment on, I will no longer be a simpering watering pot."

She set her chin in a stubborn line.

"You're the bravest woman I've ever met." Once again he found himself wanting to rid the earth of every wolf and every danger that dared threaten her safety and peace of mind. "Wait here."

He circled through the bunkhouse, peering out each window to ascertain the level of danger. Three more wolves paced around the clearing. Fresh paw prints crisscrossed the snow, indicating additional animals.

Jack spun the gun chamber. He had six rounds in his pistol, and more than three animals circling the homestead. They could wait it out in the bunkhouse until the wolves resumed their search for food elsewhere. He cut a glance at Elizabeth fidgeting near the door. No chance of that. Keeping a mother separated from her baby was out of the question. They'd have to make a dash for it.

He considered his options. The safety of three females depended upon him. If the pack was bold enough to attack the chicken house in broad daylight, he had to assume the worst. With food scarce for the winter, the pack was growing bolder. Gray wolves rarely attacked during the day.

He reloaded the rifle with quick efficiency while Elizabeth paced the floor, chewing a thumbnail and peering out the windows every three paces.

"It's only been a few minutes?" Her tremulous voice rose at the end like a question. "They should be safe, right?"

She didn't have to say the names. "Rachel and Jo are fine." He slid back the hammer. "If it came down to a fight, I'd put my money on Jo against a wolf any day."

Her face blanched. Jack leaped to his feet and wrapped his arm around her shoulder. "Don't worry, they're fine as long as they stay inside. I haven't met a wolf yet who can unlatch a door."

"But what if Jo decides to check on us? What if she opens the door?"

"I've never known two females so intent

on creating trouble in their own heads."

"I'm not looking for trouble. I'm planning for the worst."

Jack gave her shoulder a quick squeeze. "We're going to run the distance between here and the house."

Pulling away from her, he stilled his racing thoughts, drawing into himself, into the place where emotions and feelings weren't allowed. A place where logic ruled.

Emotions clouded judgment, and poor judgment got people killed.

He carefully let the hammer down, squared his shoulders and settled his hat on his head. "How many wolves have you counted?"

"I can't tell for sure. They weave in and out of view." Her head snapped up. "Will the rest of the farm animals be safe? Do you think they'll get into the barn?"

"Everything is locked up tight."

Relief flitted across her face. "I think maybe five or six wolves. I can't tell for sure. They all look the same."

The twenty or so yards to the main house might as well have been a mile. Jack could manage the distance without much worry, but with Elizabeth, his options were restricted. "I'm going to step onto the porch and fire off a few rounds with my pistol to scare them off, then we're going to make a run for the house. Stay behind me and don't look at anything except where you're going."

He handed her his rifle. "You've already managed the shotgun. This isn't much different. It's a Winchester Repeater. After you fire off the first shot, you've got a toggle action to load the second bullet. Ratchet back the lever arm. Make sure you hear the next round snap into place before you . . ."

Her eyes had glazed over and her face was blank.

"Uh." She frowned at the gun. "A toggle action what?"

"New plan." He cocked the rifle, dropped the next ball into place and returned the gun. "You've got one shot. Make it count."

She nodded, her gaze fearful but determined.

He propped the rifle against the wall and tugged on her hands. "Take off your mittens or you won't be able to pull the trigger."

The minute their bare hands touched, his heart skipped over three whole beats. The barriers he had erected weakened. Taking a deep breath, he leaned his forehead on the door. A gentle hand touched his shoulder.

"What's the matter?"

"Nothing. We're going."

Determined to fight the distraction of her gentle touch, Jack handed her his gun. He grasped the doorknob, then paused. He caught Elizabeth around the waist and pressed a quick kiss to her lips. "Just follow me. You'll do fine."

She stared at him, bemused. He couldn't help himself. He kissed her again. The soft press of her lips, the way her body yielded, swaying into him, inflated his courage.

"For luck," he said.

Right then, he felt like he could conquer the world.

Elizabeth didn't know if her quickened pulse was from the thought of facing down a pack of predators, or Jack's astonishing gesture. The minute he'd released her, his face had gone blank.

"Are you ready?" he asked.

The stock rested against her shoulder as she carefully aimed the sights away from him. For the second time in so many weeks, she risked shooting a Texas Ranger.

"I'm ready."

Jack cleared his throat. "Dear Lord, keep us safe."

"Amen," she murmured, wishing she had more words of wisdom to offer.

He strode onto the porch first, firing off two shots in rapid succession. Elizabeth winced. He gestured to the left. "Keep an eye out that direction. I'll focus on the right. Go!"

Together they dashed across the clearing toward the cabin. Elizabeth struggled to keep her footing on the slick snow and still hang on to the rifle. As if attuned to her speed, Jack kept pace with her.

A wolf bounded around the corner. Before she blinked, the animal lay dead from Jack's bullet.

He reached the porch first, then shouldered his way through the door and shoved her inside ahead of him. A rasping howl sounded behind them. The barn cat raced across the clearing, a mammoth gray wolf close on its heels.

Jack bounded down the stairs, firing another shot. The wolf collapsed to the ground. The barn cat reached the bunkhouse, safely clawing its way up the porch support. To Elizabeth's horror, a dark form appeared behind Jack.

Gritting her teeth, she leveled the rifle and fired. The bullet caught the wolf in the hind quarters. The animal bellowed in pain, writhing in the pinkening snow. Jack pivoted on one heel and fired another shot, stilling the animal's struggles.

"What's going on out there?" Jo shouted. "Is everyone all right?"

"Don't worry," Elizabeth called. "I'll explain everything."

Disturbed by the noise, Rachel whimpered. Elizabeth swung her gaze between Jack and the open door to the back bedroom. He loped up the stairs, brushed her aside and secured the door.

She expelled her pent-up breath. After another quick glance at Jack to ensure he wasn't injured, she rushed to retrieve Rachel. Moments later, she returned to the kitchen, bouncing the infant on her shoulder.

Jack perched on a chair, casually inspecting his weapon. The daft man didn't even have the sense to realize he'd narrowly escaped a fatal mauling.

She paced before him. "Why on earth did you risk your life to save that silly cat! You might have been killed." Her voice caught on the last word.

He bent his head over the rifle. "I knew how upset you were over losing Myrtle. I didn't want you to lose the cat, too. You'd never keep the mice out of the feed bin."

Her anger evaporated as she realized he'd actually been thinking of her the whole time. "I suppose she did save my life."

"Myrtle?"

"No, the barn cat. Maybe it's time I actually name her."

Jack appeared confused at the rapid change of subject. "You're not still mad?"

Elizabeth pinched her lips together. "Of course I'm still angry. I'm furious. That was foolish and foolhardy. You might have been injured."

"I'm fine. See." He swept one hand down his chest. "Nothing happened. Tell me something. Why are women so bent on arguing about stuff that never happened?"

"And why are men so determined to make even the simplest task a feat of danger?"

She slammed into the bedroom with a huff. If she lived to be as old as Methuselah, she'd never understand men.

CHAPTER TWELVE

Jack perched on a three-legged milking stool, his hands clasped before him, his knees bent almost to his nose. The barn doors had been opened to the corral, letting the farm animals enjoy a rare slice of winter sunshine through fluffy white clouds dotting the brilliant blue sky. Ely McCoy paced before Jack's view of the sunny afternoon, his arms folded over his barrel chest, a scowl darkening his heavily bearded face.

"Strange business," Ely said.

"Yep," Jack replied.

The McCoys had appeared Sunday afternoon, distraught over the numerous gunshots fired and frantic to check on the women. Upon their arrival, the realization of Jack's continued presence at the homestead hadn't sat well with Ely McCoy.

" 'Spected you'd be gone by now," Ely repeated for the third time in so many minutes.

Jack sighed. "Couldn't leave the women alone."

"Yep." Ely bobbed his head. "I s'pose that'd be a problem."

The bearlike man resumed his agitated pacing. Jack was being called to task, and though he had a fairly good idea of the offense, Ely had yet to voice his exact displeasure. Jack's confusion stemmed from Ely's failure to form a coherent sentence. The neighboring farmer had paced and muttered for the better part of the last half hour. Every so often the burly man paused, opened and closed his mouth a few times as if preparing to speak, then muttered something unintelligible and set to pacing again.

Jack puffed a warm breath into his cupped palms and chafed his hands together. He cleared his throat to defend himself, only to be halted by Ely's stinging glare.

Partially visible behind their father, the McCoy children roughhoused around the corral. One of the smaller boys climbed up the sturdy corral rail, spread his arms and plunged face-first into a snowdrift.

Jack jerked to his feet. "Your son!"

Ely swung around, then shrugged. "That fence will hold."

Jack pressed one hand to his throbbing

temple. "It's not the fence I'm worried about."

The youngest McCoy child, Adam or Abraham, had already scrambled back into position. His legs splayed for balance, he leaped into the air and belly flopped onto the packed snow.

"Doesn't that hurt?"

Ely shot Jack a look encompassing both incredulous shock and weary resignation. "Iffin' it hurt too much, I guess they wouldn't do it anymore, would they?"

Settling the stool back into place, Jack resumed his submissive posture with a roll of his eyes. The man had a point.

Ely set to pacing again, his fists braced beneath his biceps, highlighting beefy arms encased in a heavy wool coat. Jack blew out a long breath. If the farmer was going to pummel him, Jack sure wished he'd get on with it. The waiting was turning out to be more torturous than the punishment.

"My wife!" Ely shouted.

Jack winced.

Noting the reaction, Ely lowered his voice to a less booming decibel. "My wife sent me over here. She's concerned with the, um, the arrangements, you see."

Jack decided it was time to change the subject. "You've got a curious lilt to your voice, Mr. McCoy. Where are you from?"

The brawny man visibly relaxed at the innocuous question. "County Cork, originally. My da came over during the blight." He scrubbed at his chin, staring into the distance, past the boisterous antics of his children.

Jack's attention remained riveted on the tableau playing out before him. The oldest boy planted his knee into his younger brother's back, then set to shoveling handfuls of snow down his collar.

"Get off me, Caleb!" the squirming boy shouted.

Aha, Jack finally had names for all three boys present. Thank heavens they'd left the toddler at home. Jack shuddered at the thought of an even younger boy in the mix.

"Make me, Abraham," Caleb shouted.

The middle child, David, ignored his brother's antics, climbed back up the railing, and plunged backward into the snow. Jack recoiled from the bone-shattering leap. The boy scrambled to his feet and scurried back up the railing, ice still crusted in his light brown hair and eyebrows.

Unable to watch the raucous horseplay any longer, Jack turned away. Even from the barn, a muffled thump sent his bones aching in sympathy. He faced the corral again.

Didn't those boys feel pain?

"Pa!" the middle child shouted from his supine position in the icy snow. "Can I ride the cow?"

"No, you may not, David. Now sit up. You've landed on your brother."

Jack craned his neck. Sure enough, David rolled over to reveal a red-faced Abraham. Jack blanched at the boy's woozy rise to his feet, but Abraham appeared otherwise unharmed from his ordeal and Ely certainly didn't seem concerned.

Evidently their father hadn't been as distracted as he appeared. Jack mentally noted that interesting character trait for future reference.

"Now where were we?" Ely continued.

Jack tore his gaze from the corral. "I believe we were discussing your wife."

"Ah, yes. Don't get me wrong. Mrs. McCoy is grateful for all you've done. But things have gone on a bit too long if you get my drift."

Jack wasn't sure he got anything. The conversation kept wavering between cordial discourse and thinly veiled threats.

"Yep. Strange business," Ely repeated.

"Strange business," Jack echoed, resigned. If you couldn't beat 'em, you might as well join 'em. "Strange business."

Ely planted his hands on his hips. "The missus thinks of Mrs. Cole like her own daughter. The poor thing came out here wet behind the ears, with no one to show her the way. That Will wasn't good for anything but holding up a fence post."

Jack raised an eyebrow.

"Not to speak unkindly of the dead," Ely quickly added. "But I don't cotton to a man who leaves his woman all alone that long. This here is dangerous country. Up until a few years ago, we had Indian uprisings. No siree." He shook his head forlornly. "This land is no place for a woman alone."

Finally, someone who understood what Jack was dealing with when it came to the widow. "Can't you talk some sense into her?"

"Me?" Ely jabbed a thumb at his own chest. "I hear it enough from the missus. We've had this conversation every day in the months since Will's death." Ely's voice took on a falsetto ring. " 'You go over there and get that poor girl, Ely. If something happens, it's all your fault, Ely.' " The beefy man pinned Jack with a fierce scowl. "What am I supposed to do? Throw her over my shoulder and drag her back like a sack of feed? I don't think so."

"Can't Mrs. McCoy —"

"She's tried. Believe me." Ely threw up his arms, as if petitioning the heavens. "Believe me, she's tried."

The three McCoy boys had ceased their roughhousing long enough to finish building a snowman. Caleb snatched Abraham's hat for the top, and David snatched it back. Abraham danced between the two brothers as they tossed the stocking cap over his head. The younger boy finally socked the snowman in frustration, sending its crooked coal smile exploding to the ground.

"So are you going to marry her, or what?"

Jack blinked. He'd lost the thread of conversation during the snowman's destruction. "Excuse me?"

"You heard me, Ranger. What's it going to be?"

"Well — uh — that is — I — uh," Jack stuttered.

"That's what I thought." Ely hung his head, swinging his bearded face from side to side. "Now you've gone and made things difficult for me."

Here comes the pummeling.

Jack scrambled off the stool, knocking it to the haystrewn floor. He knew how much Elizabeth treasured the McCoy friendship, so he couldn't very well hurt the older man. Calming this not-so-gentle giant was going to task his powers of mediation. "We're both reasonable men. I can assure you, everything has been perfectly proper. Just ask Jo."

"She's not exactly fit as a fiddle. How's she supposed to know what the two of you are doing in the barn and the bunkhouse?"

Heat crept up Jack's face. One kiss was hardly improper. It wasn't even a kiss really, more of a peck. A comforting gesture from one friend to another. There was nothing improper in that, was there?

Ely squinted one eye at Jack. "Is there something you want to tell me, Ranger?"

"No, no," Jack replied briskly. Once again, the situation had spiraled out of his control. "Listen, even if I wanted to marry Elizabeth, I'd be no better husband than Will. My job is mostly in Texas. I'm always gone. I can't remember the last time I stayed in one place more than a few days."

"I can," Ely interjected. "Feels like you've been here half the winter."

This time Jack knew a telling blush had reddened his cheeks. "As soon as I have a new lead, I'll be gone."

"And we all know that could take a while. You must be one incompetent lawman. After all, you practically shot a pregnant woman."

"I did not almost shoot Mrs. Cole. There

was an unfortunate misunder —"

"I guess there's always the doc." As if suddenly bored by the conversation, Ely rubbed his beard.

Jack glanced around, unsure what Doc Johnsen had to do with anything.

Ely slapped Jack on the back, nearly sending him to his knees. "You've just stumbled onto the perfect solution. If the two of us can talk Mrs. Cole into marrying the doc, it'll save us both."

Jack's stomach dipped. "Save us?"

He pictured Elizabeth and the fair, curly-haired man standing side by side. They made a striking pair, both of them blessed with blond hair and those Norwegian blue eyes. Their children would probably look like the cherubs he'd once seen decorating a church ceiling in St. Louis.

A sudden need to punch something tightened Jack's fists. Doctors made terrible husbands. Always leaving at odd hours to attend sickly patients, exposing themselves and their families to a plethora of deathly illnesses.

Ely grinned, revealing an enormous gap-toothed smile. "Well, sure. With Mrs. Cole married to the doc, the missus will stop telling me what I should and shouldn't be doing, and I don't have to bash your face in."

"Doc Johnsen seems like a nice man," Jack replied weakly. "But I think Elizabeth already turned him down."

Ely quirked one bushy eyebrow. "I see how it is."

"How what is?"

"Nothing, nothing at all, my good man. We're a team now. I'm grateful not to have to kill you."

"Me, too," Jack replied, unsure what else to say.

He felt as if he'd agreed to something, made a covenant, but he wasn't quite sure about what.

Off in the distance, the McCoy boys appeared to have formed a truce. Abraham rolled a new head onto the battered snowman. They laughed and playfully chucked handfuls of snow at each other. Once again Jack's thoughts drifted back to his own brothers. There wasn't much snow in Paris, Texas — but they'd managed plenty of mischief just the same. That curious longing for home surfaced again, rising like a tide of paralyzing emotion, threatening to drown him.

Suddenly Jack realized what he'd agreed to. He'd just agreed to find Elizabeth a husband.

■ ■ ■ ■

Ely McCoy paced before Elizabeth, his hands crossed over his chest, his forehead scrunched into a frown. She had the uneasy feeling she was being chastised for something, but she wasn't quite sure what.

"Mr. McCoy," she began. "Why don't you have a seat and tell me what's wrong."

The bearlike man slumped onto a ladder-back chair, splaying the support legs. He thoughtfully rubbed his beard, unaware of the strain he placed on his seat. She'd never seen him so talkative before, or so agitated.

"The missus and I are worried about you."

"There's really no —"

"I won't be hearing none of that. People look out for one another around these parts, and Mrs. McCoy thinks of you as one of her own."

"That's very kind —"

"It would do us both good if you moved to town. Why there's a mercantile, and a livery and a bank. Even a doctor." Ely's cheeks bloomed a brilliant shade of red.

Elizabeth tilted her head to one side. She had no idea why mention of the town doctor would cause him embarrassment.

Mr. McCoy cleared his throat. "A doctor

is good to have around when you've got young'uns."

"I'm sure you're right —"

The large man leaped to his feet. The chair sprang back into shape. "The missus is up nights pacing the floor and muttering. She's fretting about you and the baby out here all alone. And if she's fretting, I don't get any rest."

Elizabeth clasped her hands together. She'd assumed since she was self-sufficient, never asking for help or needing assistance, then she wasn't a bother to anyone. The muscles in her shoulders knotted with tension. It appeared she was wrong in her assumptions.

She'd never considered how her actions might affect her neighbors. "I didn't mean to be a burden."

Mr. McCoy waved his hands in denial. "You're not a burden, lass. But if something were to happen to you, the missus and I would never forgive ourselves."

His pleading words tugged at her conscience. She pursed her lips, avoiding his pleading gaze. No one needed to worry about her. She'd been doing just fine on her own. Even with the addition of Rachel's birth and Jo's unfortunate accident, they'd gotten along well.

Of course, their continued self-reliance had a lot to do with Jack's help. He managed the work of three men.

"Look, Mrs. Cole, if something happens to you, your young'un is all by herself. What if it was you that took that tumble off the back steps? And no one was here to help you? That baby needs a mother. A father. It's time to do the right thing."

Elizabeth sniffled, blinking back tears. She thought she was doing the right thing. She *was* taking care of her child, maintaining the farm and the animals. Didn't anyone appreciate the time and energy she'd invested in running her household? Didn't they understand how much she needed a home? This home? Certainly Jack didn't empathize. And now her staunchest supporter, her dearest friends, were asking — no *telling* — her to leave.

"Ah, no," Mr. McCoy moaned. "Now don't go and do that. You're a fine mother and we all love you. It's because we think so highly of you that Mrs. McCoy wants to see you settled. The doc has a two-story house with leaded windows and everything."

"I'm sure he has a very nice house."

Relief swept across the large man's bearded face. "See, it's all settled now. The Ranger and I both agree."

Her spine stiffened. "Agree about what?"

"That you should move to town, find yourself a nice fellow with a private cistern." Ely slumped back into the chair, clutching his drooping head with both hands.

"A what?" She wasn't so much angry any more as confused.

"A private cistern for rainwater." Mr. McCoy massaged his fists over his eyes in tight circles. "But that doesn't matter. He's a fine-looking fellow and I'm sure this land will benefit someone else. Why you've got a pump right in the kitchen. No fetching water from the well."

Dawning understanding finally cleared her muddled thinking. Elizabeth had a good idea where this conversation was headed, and she didn't want to pursue the subject any longer. "Thank you so much for your concern. I'm so grateful to you and Mrs. McCoy for all that you've done. I'll do everything in my power to ease your worry."

She stood, forcing Mr. McCoy to rise.

"Excellent," he said. "Then it's all settled." Lifting his arm, Ely tugged back his sleeve to reveal a patch of red, flaky skin. "Say, when you see the doc, could you ask him what he thinks this might be?"

"Perhaps you'd best ask him yourself." Brushing at her skirts, she glanced out the

back window. "Your boys appear to be starting a small fire. You might want to check on
that."

"Yes, yes. Of course." Mr. McCoy rolled
his sleeve back into place. "It'll be nice to
finally get a full night's sleep."

With a great yawn, he shuffled out the rear
door, avoiding her eyes. Elizabeth followed
his exit, then pressed her back against the
closed door. Mr. McCoy's words rang in
her ears.

So Jack Elder thought she should move to
town and marry a man with his own cistern?
The nerve of him.

Her blood simmered as she crossed to the
bedroom to check on Rachel. The infant
rested on the bed next to Jo. Will's trunk sat
in the corner. Elizabeth straightened her
back and stared.

She wasn't going to put off searching the
contents of that trunk any longer. She'd
break the lock if she had to.

She slanted a glance at Jo, relieved to note
the girl couldn't see over the edge of the
mattress. Elizabeth didn't know what she
was going to find, but she didn't want
anyone else looking.

"Jo, how do you and your family spend
Sunday?"

Elizabeth gently tested the truck lid. The

latch sprung free. Bemused, she sat back on her heels.

The bed support squeaked as Jo shifted. "We don't do anything much in the winter," the girl replied. "In the summer we go into town for church. Ma spit-shines the boys and browbeats them into submission. Afterward, we usually exchange pleasantries with the other families. Sometimes there's a potluck and Ma always brings her famous chocolate cake."

Elizabeth flipped up the trunk's sturdy black lid, disappointed to find a stack of neatly folded shirts. She'd expected to discover something much more flagrantly revealing. Perhaps that was why Will hadn't bothered to lock the trunk. He'd taken all the secrets with him. "Do you ever work around the farm?" she asked.

"No, sirree. The tradition around here is pretty strong. It's a day of rest."

Elizabeth bent her head with a sigh. She'd always worked on Sunday. Always. Growing up, the girls in the orphanage had never been allowed to take a day of rest. The work had never ended. "What if you didn't know about this tradition?"

"I suppose the Lord is more concerned with what you do once you've received His calling."

Elizabeth hadn't had a lot of choice in the matter growing up. In order to set a good example for Rachel, she'd conduct her life much differently. "You're very wise, Jo."

Gingerly lifting Will's shirt from the trunk, the stench of his overpowering cologne wafted out. Nausea rose in her throat. She thrust the shirt aside. A tissue-wrapped package fell to the floor. She carefully opened the bundle, astonished to find a familiar, bright gold tassel.

The decoration appeared to be the same one used to tie back the scarlet-velvet curtains on the Pullman car she and Will had taken across the country. Elizabeth thought back to that fateful trip. She'd been fascinated by her first train ride. The rail car had been sumptuous and opulent, a far cry from the stark plaster walls of the orphanage.

She'd oohed and aahed over every minuscule detail until a sharp rebuke from Will had spoiled her fun. He'd spent the rest of the trip cajoling her into a better mood, but his weak attempts had been filled with derision. He'd jovially mocked her, rubbing his cheek against the red-velvet curtains and playfully twirling the gold-threaded tassels like ropes. Yet despite his obvious contempt, he'd kept one of the decorations. Had even stored the memento in his trunk for sentimental reasons. Or had he planned on mocking her further? Confused by Will's purpose, she rewrapped the mysterious tassel.

"Jo, what sort of traditions does your family have for celebrating the Sabbath?"

"Ma usually makes a cold supper, and mostly we sit around and read the Bible. I know I shouldn't say this, but sometimes it's real boring. Still, it's nice not to have to work so hard one day of the week."

Elizabeth supposed young people looked at it differently, but a day filled with quiet contemplation sounded absolutely heavenly. She felt around the edges of the trunk, discovering a sheaf of papers stuffed into a side pocket.

She reluctantly tugged the stack loose and leafed through the pages. The documents had an official, aged look with browned edges and scrollwork writing. She separated one of the pages out for a closer look. Emblazed across the top was the word *Homestead.*

That was it? Paperwork showing the purchase of the land and outbuildings from the previous tenants?

"You still here?" Jo called from over the side of the bed.

"I was just going through some clothes."

Elizabeth tucked the documents into their snug pocket. All this time she'd been terrified of the trunk's contents, when there'd been nothing but clothes and paperwork inside. Jack was right again. She sure spent an awful lot of time worrying for nothing.

Jo shifted on the bed. "I sure hope my brothers don't accidentally burn the place down. That Abraham is a real firebug."

"Mmm-hmm," Elizabeth murmured, her thoughts distracted.

Will might have been a gambler, but he'd also worked. She had no reason to doubt the money used to purchase the outbuildings had come from anything but his railroad pay.

"My pa sure was interested in how much time you and that Ranger spend together. Alone. He musta grilled me for twenty minutes."

"That's nice."

If she sold the property and moved, the sheriff would find someone else to bother. She certainly wouldn't be marrying the doctor with his private cistern, but she'd have a modicum of security, nonetheless.

"Anyway, I told him not to worry. Told him the two of you mostly bickered and avoided each other."

Elizabeth dug deeper, pulling out a burlap sack with the initials W.F. stamped on the coarse, twill threads. She tugged the drawstring loose to reveal a wad of bills.

Her heart plummeted. She sat back on her heels with a sigh. Just what she needed — more money. She stuffed the bills back into the bag and shoved them into the bottom of the trunk. How could she use money gotten from dishonesty? Was she guilty by association?

"You're awful quiet," Jo called.

Elizabeth stood, brushing her hands together. Perhaps she'd donate the extra cash to the local church. "I think it's about time I started some traditions of my own. We have leftover turkey from yesterday. I'll make sandwiches and we can all eat together."

Jo scooted her legs to the edge of the bed, and gingerly set her feet on the floor. She clung to one of the bedposts until she gained her balance. "I think I'm going home with Pa tonight."

"Are you sure you can make the trip?"

Jo limped her way to the dresser. "You've been real nice and all, but I need to get home and help with chores."

The thought of caring for Rachel without Jo's gruff guidance left Elizabeth frozen with

273

doubt. "JoBeth, the world is not going to come to a standstill without you."

"You, either."

Elizabeth started at the note of censure in Jo's voice.

The younger girl caught Elizabeth's gaze, her spruce-green eyes full of determination. "I can't be worried about you and my own family all at the same time. You know how much I love working over here, but I can't keep splitting my time."

Elizabeth folded her arms over her chest. "You don't have to help out. I don't want to be a burden to anyone." She knew she was being childish, but finding the money had rattled her. What was the right thing to do?

"It's not that at all," Jo denied. "But I've done a lot of thinking since I've been laid up. If I'm at home, I feel like I should be here helping you out, and if I'm here, I feel like I should be at home."

Regret pierced Elizabeth's heart. She sympathized with Jo's confusion, and it pained her to acknowledge the part she'd played in Jo's turmoil. There was one way to ease everyone's fears.

"Don't you worry about a thing." Elizabeth smoothed the quilt and busied herself with fluffing the pillows. "You take care of your family. We'll be just fine."

"No, you won't." Jo limped over to lean on the bed. "Don't you see? We're already behind on all the chores, even with Jack's help."

Elizabeth visualized the papers in the trunk. The wad of bills in the burlap sack. "Well, there's good news for all of us. I'll be moving to town when the weather clears."

She'd be moving to town, but not to Cimarron Springs. The memories were too raw, and her late husband's reputation too vivid. She'd been a burden on the McCoys for too long. It was time to start over.

CHAPTER THIRTEEN

"If the three of you want to start a fire," Elizabeth patiently explained to the McCoy boys, "why don't you join Mr. Elder down by the creek bed? He's burning the wolves' bodies."

"Nah." David lifted one shoulder. "We already thought of that, but he said we had to stay ten paces away from the flames. What fun is that?"

Elizabeth blew out a long breath. Only one evening had passed with her unexpected company, yet she could no longer tolerate the raucous McCoy boys. After months of living in isolation, their rowdy behavior and incessant arguing had driven nails of pain into her skull.

She braced her hands on the scarred surface of the worktable. Removing the boys from the house was proving more difficult than she'd anticipated. "It's probably better that you stay in the house with the baby.

Burning those carcasses is bound to be grisly and disgusting. And the stench." She wrinkled her nose. "I bet the stench is nauseating."

Though his arms remained in a stubborn knot over his chest, Abraham's head swiveled in her direction.

Elizabeth brushed aside the flapping ends of a freshly laundered flour sack. The boys had been "helping" her with the laundry since first light, stringing sheets and nappies from a knotted rope stretched across the parlor. The constant commotion rattled her nerves. She'd felt nothing but relief when they'd disappeared halfway through the chore. Her solitude had been short-lived. They'd sheepishly returned with a basket full of Jack's shirts.

One of their pranks had gone amuck, and they'd drenched the Ranger's tidy laundry with coffee. After much begging and cajoling, Elizabeth had agreed to wash and iron the shirts as long as the boys promised to stay out of the bunkhouse — and muck out the barn stalls as punishment. All three had eagerly agreed to her terms. No one wanted to face the Ranger's wrath.

Unfortunately, they'd finished her punishment far too quickly. There wasn't enough muck to keep them busy all afternoon.

Elizabeth noted the spark of interest in Abraham's eyes at the thought of a potentially disgusting experience. "Watching the flames devour those carcasses is bound to be quite foul," she continued. "Best you boys avoid such a disturbing task."

David sat up straighter, his face bright with anticipation. "Do you think there's gonna be blood?"

"Buckets."

The ensuing stampede of young McCoys nearly bowled her over. She watched their mad dash across the clearing toward the creek bed with weary resignation before licking her finger to test the iron's heat with a sharp sizzle. A better person might have felt remorse for hoisting the boys off on the unsuspecting Ranger, but in the quiet solitude of the still cabin, Elizabeth decided she was *not* a better person. Idle hands gave the McCoy boys far too much opportunity to think up new trouble. Keeping their fertile imaginations occupied kept them out of trouble.

Rachel cooed and smiled, kicking her tiny sock-clad feet free of her blanket.

"I'll never understand boys," Elizabeth spoke to the smiling baby. "Why would they choose to spend the day at such a repulsive task when there's a darling little sweetie to be fussed over?"

Rachel caught her hands together, exclaiming in delight at her trick. Each day brought new wonders. Elizabeth marked each milestone with awe — Rachel's annoyed grimace when the bathwater was too cold, her wide-eyed delight when Jack lifted her in the air above his head while Elizabeth fretted. She'd become so attuned to her daughter, she often woke in the wee hours of the night, straining to hear the soft flutter of Rachel's breathing.

Even mundane chores took on a new significance as Elizabeth toiled to create a perfect home. She hadn't thought she was capable of experiencing such a deep, abiding love, such depth of pride and affection. Caring for the newborn had unleashed wells of soul-aching emotion. To her dismay, with the diamond-sharp feelings came an unexpected fear, the realization that love came with the uncertainty of loss.

Elizabeth pressed her cheek against Rachel's. "Do you know what I read in the Bible last night? 'For I know the thoughts that I think toward you, saith the Lord, thoughts of peace, and not of evil, to give you an expected end.' I think that means the Lord has plans for us to prosper. What do you think?"

Rachel gurgled in reply. Elizabeth shrugged and returned to her task. In truth, she didn't mind ironing. The chore was pleasant and warm in the winter's cold, and watching the wrinkles melt away from the crisp cotton gave her a rare sense of accomplishment. She hummed a merry tune, flashing cheerful smiles at Rachel in her basket. For reasons she couldn't explain, her mood had lightened, her smile was more at the ready.

Beneath her protective gaze, the baby's face screwed up and grew a brilliant shade of red. Moments later a distinct odor drifted from the basket.

Elizabeth set the iron aside with a resigned sigh, then reached for the smiling infant. "You seem awfully proud of yourself for such a dubious accomplishment."

With practiced care Elizabeth changed the nappy, and stepped out the rear door to rinse out the soiled cotton. She returned inside, startled to smell the faint scent of something burning.

She bolted to the stove, relieved to find nothing out of place. She glanced around and gasped in horror at the source of the pungent odor. The iron had slipped from its trivet and onto Jack's laundered shirt. Heart pounding, she darted across the room and grasped the rag-wrapped handle. To her horror, a black triangle darkened Jack's shirt.

Jo limped into the room, dressed in her usual drab, oversize boy's clothes. "You burning something in here?"

"Just the usual." Elizabeth instinctively stuffed the ruined shirt into the extra laundry basket at her feet.

"It's good to see you up and about," Elizabeth said to cover her furtive movements, her voice a touch shrill.

"I'm not up to racing speed."

Though Jo still walked with a distinct limp and a permanent grimace, her wounds were healing well. Mr. McCoy had decided to delay his trip home until today in order to give his daughter plenty of time to rest before the grueling ride through heavy snow atop the McCoy's sturdy draft horse.

Jo leaned heavily on the table. "I feel like I've been run over by a stampede of buffalo. It's good to be up, though. Thought I'd go check on the boys."

"I've sent them down to help Mr. Elder."

"Now that was downright cruel. What did that man ever do to you?"

Elizabeth quirked an eyebrow.

"I guess he had it coming." Jo took a hesitant step forward, resting her weight gingerly on her injured foot. "As long as he has his gun, I'm sure he'll be fine."

Elizabeth wiped the sweat-dampened hair from her forehead with the back of her hand. "They're not bad children. Just full of energy."

"You're too soft." Jo leaned over and adjusted the eyeletlace bonnet covering Rachel's head. "Looks like her peach fuzz is falling out. I bet she's going to be a blonde, just like you." Jo touched her own dark braid with a forlorn sigh. "Jenny at school says the boys prefer curly blond hair."

Elizabeth slanted a curious glance at the younger girl. "Any boy worth his salt is more interested in a girl's heart than the hair on her head."

"Don't matter none to me, anyway. I'm never gettin' married."

Elizabeth grinned. The heated denial was telling. "You might change your mind later."

"I doubt it." Jo straightened. "Would you ever get married again?"

Unbidden, an image of Jack flashed into Elizabeth's mind. She blinked the affectionate memory away. "We weren't talking about me. We were talking about you. Someday you just might meet someone who makes you change your mind."

"Well, I ain't met him yet, that's for sure."

Jo wrapped her serviceable coat around her slim shoulders. "Why did you marry Will?"

Elizabeth rested the iron on the trivet, giving it a shake to ensure it was secure, then adjusted Jo's collar. "Because he was the first man to notice me. I was in love with the idea of love. I just wanted to belong someplace, to someone."

"*We* love you. You always have a family with us. And you're never alone in God's love."

Elizabeth blinked. "I didn't know that then. I do now."

She worried over the dropping temperature until the younger girl practically shouted in frustration.

"I'm fine," Jo declared. "Now stop fussing."

"I'm sorry. It's just that I feel responsible. If you'd been home with your family instead of here with me, you wouldn't have been hurt."

"If I'd have been home with the boys, they probably would have pushed me down the steps. By accident, of course."

"They'd never harm you on purpose!" Elizabeth suspected the McCoy household was a good deal more hazardous than her own. "Just promise me you'll be careful. I've had enough of accidents and disasters to last a lifetime."

"Well, don't have any more children," Jo snorted ruefully. "And especially don't have any boys."

The two of them laughed as Jo stuffed her battered slouch hat over her ears and limped out the rear door. Elizabeth leaned over the sink to track her painful progress to the barn. Smoke from Jack's fire floated in the distance, curling above the treetops into the overcast sky. Recalling his quick kiss before they'd dashed across the clearing, she pressed her fingers to her lips.

She'd lain awake wondering what he meant by the gesture. Hours later, she'd finally decided the kiss meant nothing. She should have been relieved, but instead, she'd spent a restless night tossing and turning. Her thoughts had lingered on each of their encounters, from the first moment he'd stormed into her life, until the moment he'd risked his life to save her mangy barn cat from the wolf's sharp teeth.

Perhaps living in town wouldn't be so bad, after all.

Without Jo or the boys, and with Rachel sleeping soundly, the house felt eerily silent. Elizabeth finished up the last of the ironing and put away all the laundry. Everything except Jack's blackened shirt.

The baby woke from her nap, fed contently in the cradle of Elizabeth's arms, and promptly fell back asleep. After tidying the house, Elizabeth set about making another batch of kolaches. Jack had enjoyed the pastries earlier. She folded the blackened shirt and placed it atop the pile in the laundry basket at her feet.

Her experience with Will had taught her that men could be awfully particular about their belongings. She'd just about convinced herself that everything was going to be fine, when Jack stepped through the front door.

She whirled around, spilling a glass of milk.

"I'm hiding from the McCoy boys." He glanced furtively over one shoulder. "They had that little one tied to a chair this morning. Lord help me, but I don't know how those three are still alive and kicking."

Elizabeth sopped up the advancing spill. She'd been thinking the same thing earlier. "I believe they were playing outlaws and Texas Rangers when they tied David to the chair. Perhaps you should take that as a compliment."

"They were playing 'who can make the most noise.' "

A sudden thought had her glancing out

the back window into the clear afternoon sky. "You didn't leave them tending the fire alone, did you?"

His eyes widened. "Not hardly. I had them crack through the ice in the creek and carry buckets back to douse the flames. They won't be able to start a fire in that spot unless we get ourselves a hundred years' drought. And I should be dead and buried by then."

She laughed, but the sight of his folded shirts in the basket at her feet dimmed her joy. "I've made kolaches."

"I thought I smelled something tasty."

Her attention snagged on the laundry basket.

He followed her furtive gaze. "Say, are those my shirts? You didn't have to wash them."

"Actually, I did." Her knuckles white, she laid two plates on the dining table. "The McCoy boys were in the bunkhouse pretending to be soldiers when one of them decided to dare the other two to drink coffee. Turned out the brew wasn't as appetizing as they'd supposed. One of them spit a whole mouthful over your shirts."

Jack scowled. "Well, I hope they're the ones who cleaned up the mess."

"Yes and no. I sent them to the barn to

286

muck out all the stalls."

"I suppose that helps. But it still sticks in my craw that they made you wash up after them."

"I don't mind. Except. Well." She pulled her lower lip between her teeth. "Except there was an accident."

She lifted his ruined shirt with stiff, numb fingers.

He frowned in confusion. "What's wrong?"

"Well . . ." She gathered her courage and handed him the shirt.

Dawning awareness spread across his face as he unfurled the cotton to reveal the singed triangle. To her burgeoning relief, he appeared more confused than angry.

Then his face hardened, and his lips twisted into a thin, white line. "You have a scar. A triangle on your forearm. I saw it that day in the barn. Show me your arm."

Elizabeth felt the blood drain from her face. She backed away, bumping against the stove. "Wh-what?"

He advanced toward her with relentless determination. Fear warred with her disappointment. She'd thought he was different. He stepped closer. She flung up her arms to cover her face.

He grasped her arm and tugged her sleeve

until he revealed the arrowhead scar on her arm. "There's no way this was an accident. I can tell by the placement. Who did this to you?"

Elizabeth reached to cover the mark, but he brushed her hand aside.

She ran the tip of her tongue over her parched lips. "None of your business."

He angled his head, forcing her to meet his gaze. "You cower away from me like a whipped dog. I've never hurt you, not once. Someone did this on purpose."

She shook her head, tears of shame welling in her eyes.

"Why?"

The question felt more like an apology, and she couldn't bare the pity in his voice. "It wasn't his fault. Will was usually quite kind. He'd come home from his job tired and hurt. He'd been drinking. He wasn't the same."

"Did that happen often?"

"No, of course not."

"I'm not a fool, Elizabeth."

She twisted away. "None of this is your concern."

"Elizabeth." He rested his hand on her shoulder, the sensation heavy and comforting. "You can't hide out here forever. You're trapped by your own fears."

The warmth of his hand steadied her. "Don't be silly. Living out here all alone is more frightening than anything I've ever done before." She bit out a humorless laugh.

"You're afraid of yourself. Afraid of getting close to people."

"Now you're being foolish."

He brushed his thumb against the bare skin of her neck. Elizabeth shivered.

"It's not just the things that happen to us that keep us awake at night," Jack said. "It's the part we played in our own mistakes. I've rescued people over the years, and you know what haunts them? They can't let go of their own infallibility. They obsess over every detail, every perceived mistake. They can't let go of the past, asking themselves why they didn't trust their instincts, retracing their actions, questioning their decisions. You have to stop blaming yourself."

Her throat tightened. "I don't blame myself."

"You're lying."

Her eyes burned, but she ruthlessly blinked away the tears. She'd traveled to Kansas full of foolish dreams and false hopes. At some point during the journey, she'd stopped living in the present and pinned all her hopes on the future. *Everything will be different when . . .* How many times had she repeated those words? Even now, she was trapped in her dreams of the future. *Everything will be different in the spring. Everything will be different when the snow clears. Everything will be different when . . .*

She tipped her head to the side, pressing her cheek against Jack's knuckles.

"Look at me," he pleaded.

Though her heart ached, she lifted her head and shrugged off his hand. This growing dependency on Jack had to stop. He was leaving. Soon. The more she came to rely on his help, the more she came to crave his touch, the harder their parting would be. To Jack, she was simply an obstacle to his case. For her, he'd come to mean a great deal more.

Busying herself at the stove, she wiped down the castiron surface, carefully arranging her pots and utensils for supper. "I need to check on the baby. Jo sewed the most atrocious rag doll, but Rachel just adores the horrible thing. . . ."

She didn't resist when he pulled her into his arms. He was warm and strong, a balm to her aching heart.

"Tell me about him."

"I'd rather not," she spoke, her words muffled in the smooth leather of his black vest. "Living in the past is a dull and lonely business."

He set her back, his hands still clasping her shoulders. The distance separating them felt like an ever widening chasm.

His hand glided through her hair. " 'Let us therefore cast off the works of darkness, and let us put on the armour of light.' "

She inhaled the scent of wood fire on his shirt, pungent, familiar and comforting.

He sighed. "Sometimes the only way to bury the past is to pull it out into the open first."

The baby whimpered.

Relieved to focus her attention on something else, Elizabeth turned away to pick up Rachel and hug her close. "I don't know if that's such a good idea."

"Maybe it's the best idea."

She gently bounced the baby on her shoulder. "I'll think about it."

Will was the father of her child. Her husband. She'd cared for him once. Gossiping about him to a stranger felt like a betrayal of his memory — a betrayal of her daughter.

She pressed Rachel into the hollow of her neck. The baby cooed and rooted at her cheek. The infant's trust, the unabashed joy she showed at even the simplest activities lent Elizabeth courage. Perhaps she *had* been too hard on herself.

Living in the past might be a dull and lonely business, but wallowing in the present was no better. Maybe she should take up Jack on his offer and purge herself of all the bitter memories. Maybe then she could concentrate on the good times she'd shared with her late husband. He was her past, and it was time to concentrate on the future.

Jack regretted asking her to share this glimpse into her past, even while he hungered for knowledge about her life. To his surprise, she'd offered only a token resistance before she'd started talking. Though his heart ached, he forced himself to listen. After all, he'd asked for this — begged her to tell him about her past.

He didn't dare question his need to understand what her life had been like, how she had arrived on this Kansas homestead. Even the tiniest details haunted him. He woke up each morning with her image crowding his thoughts. The way her hair curled around the temples, the way she chewed on a thumbnail when she was nervous.

Watching her care for Rachel enchanted him. Mother and daughter shared a special bond, a secret communication that intrigued him. There was even a familiarity in the way they smiled.

He'd put off taking the steel box and its curious mix of watches and rings into town because he wanted to avoid the truth. He'd stayed one more day just to catch a glimpse of the widow smiling.

She wasn't smiling now, and he was the cause of her somber mood. She kept her back turned while she worked at the stove. "I told you before about how my father opened a bakery in New York. He had difficulty supporting us after the shop burned down. We moved several times, but the work was never steady. Then one day he didn't come home. We waited for days. He'd never done anything like that before. Some fisherman discovered his body in the river."

Jack yearned to comfort her, but she kept her back turned, scrubbing at the black cast-iron surface of the stove as if she might rub away the memories, as well.

"My mother wasn't well. She'd taken ill on the ship from England, and I don't think she ever fully recovered. The conditions on board were foul. People died every day. We considered ourselves lucky to have survived the trip at all. Anyway, after my father died, she grew worse." Elizabeth paused, he studied her profile, her bleak expression. "I

293

tried to hide her illness from the other tenants in the building, I tried to take care of her myself, but one day the nuns from the orphanage showed up and took me away."

Her revelations gave him insight into her character. She'd fought to care for her mother alone, just as she fought to remain on the homestead, alone. She considered self-sufficiency a virtue.

"Did you ever see your mother again?"

"Once." Elizabeth swiped at her nose with a sniffle. "She was very ill. She asked me to forgive her for letting them take me to that awful place."

Bitter resentment laced her words.

"You can't blame yourself for something that happened when you were a child."

Elizabeth shook her head. "I was so angry, I refused to forgive her. She died before I could tell her I was sorry." She pressed her hands to her cheeks. "I'm an awful person and God has punished me for it."

Jack leaped out of his chair and crossed the distance in two steps. He turned her to face him and clasped her shoulders. The anguish in her pale blue eyes humbled him. Without a second thought, he cradled her in his embrace.

Watching her suffer unleashed a fierce protective instinct within him. "God loves you. The Lord doesn't punish people, Elizabeth."

She sobbed into his vest. "You're wrong. He does. He took away my mother. He took away Will."

Her late husband didn't sound like much of a loss, but Jack held his tongue. "That's not the way it works."

She strained away, not quite meeting his eyes. "Will was handsome and charming. I'd never had anyone notice me before. I was overwhelmed by the attention. And he never seemed to want for money. I liked that he bought me things. It had been so long since I'd had anything nice. He made me feel special. Like I mattered to someone."

The walls closed in around Jack. His lungs hurt from the effort to breathe. "You're loving and kind. You're a hard worker. I can see why he wanted to marry you."

She snorted softly. "It was a whirlwind courtship. I worked for a baker and he didn't like Will hanging around the shop all the time. He gave me the sack. I didn't have any place else to go. Will took me to the courthouse that morning and we were married. A few hours later we were on a Pullman car headed West. Everything happened so fast, I didn't have time to consider what I was doing, or where I was going."

Jack forced himself to think like a Ranger instead of an infatuated fool. She was vulnerable, but she was also part of his case. The more she revealed about her late husband, the more convinced he became of the man's guilt. "Why did Will risk his life the night he died? The sheriff said the creek bed had almost washed out."

"He was leaving me." Her chin tilted up a notch. "I'd told him about the baby the day before. He was angry. He didn't want the responsibility of children."

Jack seethed with impotent rage. The source of his fury was beyond justice, beyond vengeance. "Yet he married you, brought you all the way to Kansas and bought this homestead. What did he think was going to happen?"

"I think he wanted to do a lot of things, he just didn't have the courage to see them through. I was like a toy to him." Her lips twisted into a sad smile. "Will bored easily with toys. He was bored with me almost from the beginning."

"You didn't do anything wrong. The sin lies with your husband. He took a vow to stay with you, and he broke his promise to God. What happened up on that creek bed was an accident."

"It's just that every time I pray, things

seem to turn out wrong. I prayed for a husband, and God sent me Will. I prayed for a child, and my husband deserted me rather than care for his growing family. I prayed for Will's return, and God sent me his body to bury." She ducked her head. "I'm afraid to pray any more. For anything."

Jack tucked his knuckles beneath Elizabeth's chin and gently forced her to look at him. Tears swam in her eyes, darkening the pale blue color. "The Lord knows what's in your heart."

"That's what I'm afraid of," she whispered. "I'm not pure of heart."

"No one is. We can't change the past, but we can make a better future. It's where you're going in your faith that counts, not where you've been."

Jack should know that better than anyone. He'd spent his entire life searching for justice, but evil still walked the earth.

She pressed closer. Voices sounded outside, indicating the return of the McCoy boys. Jack made a sound of frustration in his throat. He and the widow had unfinished business, and he was determined to settle things before he left. With the homestead overrun by McCoy boys, finding a quiet moment was going to be difficult.

At the sound of footsteps nearing the

house, she pulled away from him. "Thank you, for everything. I'm all right now."

She swiped at her eyes.

"We can finish this conversation later."

"There's no need. I'm perfectly fine."

Any fool could see she was lying.

Jack was no fool.

Jack hated being right sometimes. He kicked another stump into place. The McCoys, sensing his dark mood, were giving him a wide berth. They were helping their father build a new ladder for the loft.

He touched his cheek where Elizabeth had brushed her thumb against his skin. He'd been mule-kicked all right.

Ely McCoy was correct. Elizabeth needed to be protected. She needed to marry a nice man who wanted a family. Jack recalled all the bachelors in town who had offered for her hand. No wonder she'd been reluctant to accept a proposal after her husband's death. She probably feared a repeat of her first marriage.

Doc Johnsen was a good choice for a husband. He held a respected job. He was handsome and intelligent, everything Elizabeth could ask for in a man. Yet she'd refused his offer of marriage once before. No doubt she was gun-shy after her first experience. Perhaps if she moved to town and they courted properly, she'd change her mind.

Jack forced himself to imagine the two of them together, the widow and Doc Johnsen. Elizabeth deserved better than a rat like Will Cole. How much more was there? How much had she left out about her life?

At least the doc worked around Cimarron Springs. He wouldn't be traipsing all over the country, leaving her alone for weeks at time.

Jack swung the ax. The thought of Elizabeth married to another man tore at his insides. He swiped at his forehead with the back of his hand. What other choice did he have? He'd told Ely the truth. He wasn't husband material. If Jack wasn't going to care for her, Doc Johnsen was a good choice. She was too beautiful, too fragile beneath her bravado to be left all alone. And Rachel needed a father. Someone to dandle her on his knee and shoo the boys away when she grew older.

The next crack of the ax split the three-foot stump clean in half.

"You okay, Ranger?" Ely spoke from behind him.

"Swell."

Jack resumed his attack on the hapless stump.

"I can't wait to get home to the missus," Ely spoke loud enough to be heard over Jack's steady *thwack-thwack-thwack*. "I'm telling you. When I was younger, I never once thought about settling down. Then I saw Mrs. McCoy in the mercantile. She was picking out a pair of white cotton gloves."

Jack glanced over his shoulder. "Does this story have a point?"

"Sometimes I get stuck on a goal. And when I can't achieve that goal, I start to thinking that there's no way out." Ely tugged a fragile white cotton glove from his pocket. "I look at this, and I know nothing else matters."

Jack turned his back on Ely's somber gaze.

He was doing the right thing. He always did the right thing. "There's a pile of brush over by the creek bed. If we clear it out today, the widow will have enough kindling for the rest of the winter."

"Takes more than a fire to keep a body warm some days."

"I know what I'm doing."

"I hope you do." Ely sighed. "You can't punish a dead man, and you're not going to get another chance to make this right."

Jack thought of Bud Shaw. With Will Cole

dead, Elizabeth was his only chance at discovering the truth. "I ran out of chances a long time ago."

CHAPTER FOURTEEN

"Jo." Elizabeth glanced up from settling the last loaf of bread dough in a pan to rise. "Can I get your help in the bunkhouse before you leave?"

"I don't know if we're ever going to leave now," Jo replied. "Pa and Mr. Elder are down by the creek bed pulling up a stack of brush for firewood."

Elizabeth rolled her eyes. "Will started that project last spring. He piled a mountain of brush in one spot, and then lost interest. I don't ever recall seeing him work so hard."

"Musta been hard on those girly hands of his."

"JoBeth McCoy!"

The girl stuck out her tongue. "Don't you go scolding me. That man wasn't good for anything but telling tall tales and keeping the saloon in business. I'm glad he's gone."

Elizabeth pressed the heels of her hands

to her ears. "Don't say that. Don't ever say that."

She didn't want permission to think ill of Rachel's father. She'd made her own peace, hadn't she? The sound of his name barely stirred feelings of regret in her chest. Yet she worried the sins of the father might rest on Rachel's tiny shoulders. The baby was innocent of Will's wrongdoing, and speaking ill of the dead wasn't going to solve anything.

Jo's smile faded. "I didn't mean to upset you, Mrs. Cole. You said we were going to the bunkhouse?"

"I'm sorry. I've been emotional ever since the baby was born. I hope I never have to cry over something real, because I've used up all my tears." Elizabeth concentrated on draping towels over the rising dough. "Mr. Elder was searching for bank robbers when he arrived here. I've read all the newspaper accounts, and I keep feeling like there's something I'm missing. He's got his clippings tacked to the bunkhouse wall. Maybe if we put our heads together, we can figure out what's bothering me."

Jo passed Elizabeth a wet rag. "I'm not sure if I can help, but it's better than keeping the boys out of mischief all afternoon."

After wiping her hands clean, Elizabeth

tugged her apron strings loose. She plucked Rachel's rag doll from a shelf and handed it to the smiling baby. Chubby hands grasped the soft material and pulled it into her mouth.

Elizabeth grimaced at the odd toy. Two mismatched arms jutted from the overly round body. A pair of sausage legs strained at the seams. Offset eyes perched above a button nose and cross-stitch mouth. Elizabeth found the resulting combination of uneven stitching gruesome, but Jo had labored for days over the project, and the baby adored her new toy.

"Let's go, then," Elizabeth said, forcing determination into her voice.

She snuck a glance at the clock ticking on the mantel. They didn't have much time before the men finished their chores. An hour at most.

Together she and Jo crossed the clearing, their attention drawn to the blood-streaked snow. Elizabeth adjusted Rachel's laundry basket on her hip, careful not to disturb the warm blanket stretched over the top to keep out the cold. They paused in front of the bunkhouse door.

Jo lingered on the porch. "Feels wrong to go inside without Mr. Elder here."

Elizabeth took firm hold of the doorknob.

"This is my home, and Mr. Elder is an uninvited visitor. There's nothing wrong with the two of us entering *my* property."

As she breezed into the building, anxiety at odds with her brave words tightened in her chest. Elizabeth sucked in a lungful of air. There was no reason to feel like an interloper in her own home. "See, there's no reason to feel uncomfortable."

Jo followed with a resigned shrug. Elizabeth set the basket on the nearest bunk, almost tripping over a pile of neatly stacked wood on the floor.

Jo nudged the pile with her square-toed boot. "What do you suppose this is?"

"Firewood?"

"I don't think so." Jo knelt for a closer look. "He's cut and sanded all the pieces. Looks like he's going to build something."

Elizabeth plucked a length of wood from the stack. Someone, Jack she presumed, had painstakingly carved a pattern of ivy into the sanded piece. "Why on earth is he in here whittling? It's not like he can carry something so large when he leaves."

Angling another piece of wood to one side to catch the light, Jo leaned in. "I guess maybe he's bored."

Suddenly exhausted, Elizabeth slumped on the bed next to Rachel. She wasn't the sort to keep a man's attention riveted. The pile of wood might as well be stacked to the ceiling for all the excitement she provided.

Had she made a mistake in confiding in Jack? Even though they were destined to part, she wanted him to see her differently. She wanted him to enjoy her company.

She stuck out her lower lip and blew a breath, ruffling the hair resting on her forehead. He'd listened to her tale of life with her late husband, his expression somber and closed. She'd thought he was concerned, now she realized he was indifferent. Who wanted to spend time with a sniveling woman lamenting her life?

She didn't know what he thought about her checkered history, and she didn't want to find out. Revealing her past had been cathartic, but the truth of her own accountability had made her sick inside. No matter what happened, she was through making foolish, impulsive choices. From this moment on, she'd think before she acted. She wasn't the only one affected by her decisions.

Jo moved across the room to peer at the newspaper clippings. "These are all railroad towns." She glanced at Elizabeth while she jerked a thumb at the wall. "You think the outlaws bought tickets like regular folks?

How funny is that? Maybe they just rode into town like carpetbaggers, robbed the bank, then climbed right back on the train with the money."

"Don't be silly." Elizabeth flashed a grin at the mental image of bandanna-clad men lugging tattered satchels overflowing with money onto a fancy Pullman car. "Someone would recognize them."

"I don't know." Jo rubbed her chin, lost in thought. "The best place to hide is in plain sight. I can always fool the younger boys with that one. People see what they expect to see, not what's really there."

Once again, something struck Elizabeth as familiar about one of the outlaws. "Jo, do you recognize this fellow?"

The younger girl grimaced. "They all look the same to me."

Elizabeth's shoulders slumped. They *did* all look the same. The artist hadn't given the men much detail. She traced her finger along the towns Jack had underlined. The names were all familiar, but Will had been a railroad man. Of course he'd mentioned the names of the towns. She squinted, forcing a pattern to emerge in the dates or the routes the outlaws had taken.

Jo studied one of the reports, her nose inches from the paper. The type had nearly rubbed off with repeated handling. "As far as I can tell from this account, the people who lost out most were the saloon owners. I mean, they certainly complained the loudest. Says here they were counting on all those railroad boys getting their money and spending it on liquor." She planted her hands on her hips. "I bet one of them railroad boys stole that money. They'd have known the bank was going to have extra cash for payroll."

A railroad man. Elizabeth ran her gaze along the neatly displayed clippings, taking in the sketched picture of the bank. A sickening dread pooled in her stomach. She recalled the burlap sack in the bottom of Will's trunk. The initials W.F.

The last bank robbed had been a Wells Fargo. The bank where the outlaws murdered Jack's sister-in-law.

She backed away from the truth, physically and mentally, desperate to deny the evidence. Just because Will had worked for the railroad didn't make him an outlaw. His money had come from gambling. A lot of men supplemented their income by playing cards. Will was only violent with people weaker than him. She didn't see him storming into a bank. Towns sprouting up around the rail lines were teeming with unscrupulous people desperate for money.

There was no reason to believe Will had earned his extra income any other way. "Everybody in that town knew the railroad payday. For all we know, one of the saloon owners stole the money."

Considering the motives of transient workers eased Elizabeth's tension.

"Yes, but look at this." Jo motioned to one of the yellowed clippings.

Elizabeth reluctantly leaned forward.

"See." Jo pointed to an article farther down in the paper. "The railroad was building a mighty large bridge. Says here the area swelled by almost two hundred men. And here, look at this. They were digging a tunnel straight through the mountainside. That brought almost three hundred men to town. And where this last robbery took place, the railroad was laying new line through some rough terrain. That's gotta bring in almost a hundred men."

Jo pursed her lips, her expression thoughtful. "You know what I think?"

"No," Elizabeth replied weakly.

"First off, all these robberies took place when there was a big railroad project in the works."

The idea that had been nagging Elizabeth suddenly took shape. She grasped for an innocent explanation. "So you think transient workers robbed those banks?"

"Nah." Jo shook her head. "I think it was someone looking for a bank with lots of money. See here." She pointed to the rail schedule at the bottom of the page. "Payday isn't until the fifteenth, right? But the train doesn't run until the sixteenth. Only there was a rockslide, which set the schedule back another two days. That meant the money came in late, on the eighteenth. Look at the date the bank was robbed."

"The eighteenth," Elizabeth whispered over the blood pounding in her ears.

"Whoever planned those robberies knew plenty about the railroad. They knew the schedules, they knew what projects were being built, and they knew the payroll dates. This new line here was scheduled to start on the twentieth. There's a notice about the ribbon-cutting ceremony, but the robbery took place a week before the work started."

Hope flapped its delicate butterfly wings in Elizabeth's chest. "Then the pattern doesn't work. Someone who worked for the railroad would know there was no extra money in the safe."

Jo grinned from ear to ear. " 'Course the pattern still works. Says here there was a brawl the day before the robbery. According to this article, the men arrived a week before the ribbon-cutting. Whoever robbed that Wells Fargo knew the men were coming into town early. He also knew they'd be receiving a stipend for living expenses before their first paycheck."

The butterfly wings ceased flapping. "A stipend?"

"Yep. They paid my Uncle Pete a whole paycheck in advance when he moved to St. Louis. Called it stipend."

Elizabeth's stomach flipped.

"It's all right there in the type," Jo continued. "The fellow that planned these robberies was no construction worker. He was a fellow whose hands never got dirty. Sending a telegraph to the Santa Fe rail offices would give Jack a few names. It wouldn't take much to piece things together after that. Just figure out who was running those projects. Simple as pie."

Spots formed in the corners of Elizabeth's vision. She sank weakly onto the cot next to Rachel. "He's a smart man, Mr. Elder. I'm sure he's already thought of that."

Her late husband had never dirtied his hands with anything but dollar bills. He'd never been talkative about his job, but his fingers had always been covered in ink stains. He oversaw the movements of work-

311

ers, or something along those lines. Elizabeth rubbed her temples, desperate to refute the evidence. Yet everything made sense. Will's absences, his endless supply of money. The wads of bills he'd left behind.

Her husband had been a bank robber.

"I see your point." Jo tapped her forehead. "Even the Ranger's not that dumb. 'Course, they were probably looking for someone on site. A foreman or a laborer. What if it was a paper pusher? Didn't Will do something like that?"

"He scheduled trains and work crews."

"You all right, Mrs. Cole?" Jo asked. "You've gone real pale."

"I'm fine, Jo. It's nothing."

Perhaps Will's involvement had been periphery. He never even shot game, could he have shot an actual flesh-and-blood person? A sharp pain throbbed behind her eyes. Had the outlaws blackmailed Will into giving them information about the railroad schedule?

"Look here," Jo exclaimed. "A deputy even shot one of the outlaws in the leg. Sounds like those boys weren't very good at their job."

"When was that?"

"Looks like the end of May."

Elizabeth unconsciously touched the scar

on her arm. The shooting had occurred just prior to Will's return from Colorado. He'd been angry and out of sorts. And hurt.

He'd been limping because he'd injured his leg.

Her husband was the fourth outlaw.

What did it matter now? Will was dead. His justice was in heaven.

Jack was searching for Bud Shaw when he should have been looking for both Will Cole *and* Bud Shaw. Why reveal her discovery at this point? Her husband was beyond revealing his secrets. She certainly didn't know where to find Bud Shaw, and Will was gone.

How had she missed the signs of Will's activities? The truth had been obvious. *I've made excuses for him all along, that's why.* The first time he'd appeared outside the bakery to accompany her to the market, he'd walked a half pace ahead of her the entire distance. Even from the beginning he'd been leaving her behind. She'd made excuses for him from the start — instead of trusting her instincts.

Jack trusted his instincts.

She chanced a glance at Rachel chewing contentedly on her rag doll. The baby studied her surroundings with wise, solemn eyes. As Will's wife, what were the consequences for Elizabeth, for her child? If the sheriff could seize her land because of Will's cheating, what would he do if he discovered Will was an outlaw?

She stumbled out the bunkhouse door into the sunlight, blinking her eyes against the bright afternoon.

Jo followed her outside. "You don't look good."

"I just needed some air. Go back inside." She needed time to collect her thoughts, to make decisions for her and Rachel's future.

Instead, Jo brushed past her and loped down the shallow stairs. "Say, are you cooking something again? There's smoke coming from the house."

Plumes of smoke billowed from the window across the way. Elizabeth's heart leaped into her throat. An acrid smell teased her senses. She gripped the porch rail. "Stay with the baby!"

Desperate to retrieve her homestead documents, she lifted the hem of her skirts and ran. If the house burned to the ground, she still had the bunkhouse and the barn. But without those papers, she had no way of proving ownership. She bolted up the stairs and jerked open the door. A wall of hot air singed her cheeks. She threw her arm over her face against the advancing black cloud and dashed through the kitchen. Fire licked at the parlor walls. Flickering orange sparks danced behind thick heat waves.

Lungs burning, she felt her way to the bedroom, then slammed the door behind her, blocking the worst of the acrid smoke. She plunged forward and smacked her hip against the dresser. Rubbing at the painful sting, she knelt before Will's trunk and tugged on the handle.

A gray cloud curled beneath the door and snaked up the walls while she searched. Her eyes and nose watered. She frantically dug through Will's clothes until she located the sheaf of papers. Clutching the precious documents to her chest, she surged to her feet. With the room enveloped in a thick haze, she blindly groped her way back to the exit.

As she touched the brass knob, fiery pain enveloped her hand.

Glass shattered to her left.

Jack slapped the rump of the sturdy work horse hitched to the enormous stump he and Ely were struggling to pry from the ditch. "We're almost there."

The winds had picked up, whipping at the branches and driving dust into his eyes.

Ely McCoy tugged on the harness, his massive biceps bulging as sweat trickled down the side of his bearded face. The horse's forelegs stumbled to find purchase at the top of the rise. The animal tipped and bucked the next ten feet, dragging the stump over the crest before jerking to a halt.

Ely collapsed onto the ground, resting his elbows on his bent knees. "I'd like to dig up that fool Will Cole and give him a piece of my mind. Then I'd bury him back down again."

Jack slapped his hat against his thigh. A cloud of dust billowed from the brim. "I'm not sure how that's going to help us clear this brush."

"Why on earth does a man go to all the trouble of piling trees at the most impassable dip in the creek bed?"

"I dunno. Maybe he was letting the wood dry. This area is protected from flood. The waterline doesn't go up the embankment this far."

"It's still an idiotic place to gather brush. Why not just drag the branches up the shallow side?" Ely pressed a hand to his knee and surged to his feet. "That man didn't have the sense God gave a dandelion."

While Jack couldn't help but agree, he kept his own council. "Either way, we've cleared out most of the brush. One or two more trips and the pile will be cleared. The extra wood should keep the widow set through spring."

"If I live that long." Ely squinted into the distance. "Say, that's awful thick smoke coming from the house."

Jack glanced up from his stooped position down the embankment from where Ely stood. Dark gray tendrils lapped at the sky before blustery wind scattered the curling plumes. "Looks like chimney smoke to me. Nothing unusual about that."

Jack grasped a bundle of branches and tugged. The pile loosened, sending him stumbling back. He flailed his arms to catch his balance. After bracing his feet against the frozen earth, he straightened, then arched, pressing his fists against a tight muscle in his back. His gaze snagged on a dark hollow revealed by the brush he'd just hauled aside.

Crouching, Jack peered into the dark entrance of what appeared to be shallow cave.

"Mr. Elder," Ely called.

Jack glanced over his shoulder. "What is it?"

"I think those boys have gone and started a bonfire." Ely muttered something Jack couldn't quite make out. A moment later he hollered, "I'll be back in a few. I'm going to tan those boys' hides."

"Take your time," Jack called back, his attention drawn to the cave. He yanked free the dried grass and twigs covering the mouth, revealing a much larger opening than he'd first suspected. With a surreptitious glance over his shoulder to ensure Ely had left to check on the boys, he knelt down and felt his way through the entrance.

Sunlight illuminated the first five feet. Pitch darkness lay beyond. Jack reconsidered. He'd most likely find a hibernating animal in there, and animals weren't too keen on being awakened. He slanted his gaze up the hill at the neat pile of brush. Someone had deliberately arranged those tree limbs in front of the cave opening. Someone who didn't want the entrance seen by passersby. That someone certainly wasn't a bear or a raccoon.

Crawling through the entrance, he winced as dampness seeped through his pants, icy cold on his knees. Undeterred, he pushed through the darkness, bumping his hand against a sharp metal corner. Wind whistled past the entrance. Humid, stagnant air settled in his lungs. Jack reached into his pocket and pulled out a match.

With a scrape on his boot, the match sizzled to life. Flickering light exposed dangling tree roots. The shallow ceiling prevented him from standing or even sitting fully upright. The space stretched no wider than a horse stall. A pile of boxes appeared in the dancing shadows before him. As the flames touched his fingers, Jack blew out the match with a muffled curse. He lit another, and strained forward until he could make out the writing.

Wells Fargo.

He grasped the handle with his free hand as he shook out the second dying match. Unless he wanted to burn off his own fingertips, he had to drag the cases into the light.

Using his heels as leverage, he scooted backward to the mouth of the cave, towing the sturdy boxes behind him. The heavy boxes dug into the soft soil. His muscles strained at the awkward position. The pulled tendon in his back screamed in protest. An eternity later, he emerged into the sunlight, gasping. A fine layer of silt dusted his skin and clothing. Slumping onto his haunches, he took a moment to catch his breath. The scent of burning wood teased his nostrils.

A dark leaf fluttered onto his bent knee. He brushed it aside. The leaf crumbled into ash.

Jack leaped to his feat.

A haze of smoke billowed in the air above him.

His chest seized. *Elizabeth.* All thoughts of outlaws and loot fled his brain. Arms heaving, he sped up the hill. Flames licked the sky as he approached the house. Jo and the boys pumped water from the well into buckets.

Ely shattered the bedroom window with an ax. "She's in there!" The burly man threw his coat over the cut-glass edges.

Jack added a fresh burst of speed. Ely didn't need to say the name. Elizabeth was trapped in the house.

With a boost from Ely, Jack shimmied through the window. Smoke stung his eyes. His coat snagged on a shard of glass. Wrenching the material free, he jumped to the floor. Elizabeth appeared before him.

She gasped and coughed, burying her nose in the crook of her elbow. "I tried to leave through the kitchen, but it's too hot."

"Get away from the door."

He yanked the wedding-ring quilt from the bed and threw it over the sill, adding a cushioning layer to Ely's coat. "I'll lower you down. Ely is waiting."

Cold air rushed into the room, feeding the fire. Jack swept her into his arms. She scooted her feet over the ledge, her arms still wrapped around his shoulders. Her heavy petticoats crowded the narrow space. Jack shoved them through the opening. He slid his hands down her ribcage, then carefully lowered her into Ely's waiting arms.

The trunk in the corner snagged his attention. Smoke drifted toward the ceiling, revealing clothes strewn over the floor. Elizabeth had obviously been digging through the contents. Jack knelt and lifted one of the items. Even through the growing haze he made out a man's shirt.

She'd risked her life to rifle through her late-husband's clothing? Why?

Especially when all the loot was safely hidden outside.

CHAPTER FIFTEEN

The front room was completely destroyed along with most of the kitchen. Only the pantry and the bedroom had survived serious damage, but heavy smoke saturated every surface. Most of the food stores were ruined, and the structure itself was unlivable.

Elizabeth crouched in the wagon, Rachel snug beside her, the space was lit by three warming lanterns. Both sets of barn doors had been flung open during the chaos. The McCoy boys huddled together on the far side of the corral while the three horses and the milk cow stomped and snorted in the midst of the commotion. Jo sulked on the bunkhouse porch.

Though the fire had mostly burned itself out, fiery embers still drifted into the sky. From Elizabeth's vantage point at the back of the house, the structure appeared almost normal. If she circled around to the front, the true damage was revealed. The image of the porch roof caved into the parlor had burned into her brain.

The open barn doors framed the clearing formed by the three buildings. A scattered pile of her possessions littered the space. Ely and Jack had shattered the window in the bedroom and managed to save everything they could grab, including her, before suffocating smoke had overwhelmed them.

In a desperate attempt to save the outbuildings, Ely and Jack filled buckets from the well, splashing water onto the chunks of burning debris fluttering off the main house.

The sheltering branches of bare trees stood silhouetted against the setting sun, black and scorched. She tucked the blanket tighter around Rachel's basket, then scooted off the back of the wagon.

Jack caught sight of her, dropped his bucket and crossed the clearing. "How are you holding up?"

"I'm fine."

With a somber wave of remorse, she realized she spoke the truth. Nothing touched her anymore — not the blustery cold stinging her cheeks, not the blackened remains of her home, not even the blisters on her palm smarted any longer. She was more than fine, she was numb.

Jack lifted her hand. "How is your burn? Does it still hurt?"

Elizabeth shook her head. Feeling as if she were outside her own body, she studied the charred remains of her life and felt . . . nothing. "I used to wonder who planted all those trees. I think Hackberry Creek might be the only place in Kansas with grown trees. When I first saw the spread, I thought the house was real fine, but I fell in love with the trees first. I'll miss them most when we move to town."

"You can always rebuild."

"We both know that will never happen."

A beam cracked and popped, tumbling into what had once been her dining space with a shower of orange sparks.

Still nothing. Not even a twinge.

Jack cleared his throat.

"I'm not lying," she defended herself. "After Jo's accident, and then the incident with the wolves, well, I realized you were right. You and Mr. McCoy and Jo. I can't stay out here alone any longer. Once spring comes, the work will be too much to manage on my own. Jo has her own family to attend. She can't keep splitting her time between here and home and school. I wouldn't feel comfortable hiring a stranger to help."

Jack shrugged out of his coat and wrapped the heavy wool around her shoulders.

Shivering, she touched the collar. The pungent scent of wood smoke wafted from the saturated wool. "I thought Texas Rangers wore long slickers."

"I bought the coat off a retired sailor earning his way toward a train ride to the desert. He said he was tired of winter, and never planned on seeing snow again. Told me this was the warmest coat he ever owned."

The heavy wool sealed out the biting cold. Her fingers tingled as warm blood pumped through her veins. "He was right. I don't think I've felt this warm since September."

Ely shouldered his way into their conversation, his lips set in a hard line. "The boys claim they had nothing to do with this fire, but I don't know if I believe them."

Elizabeth nestled deeper into the safety of Jack's residual warmth. "I'm certain the boys wouldn't lie."

"I can't say for sure either way," Mr. McCoy growled. "Usually the little one will tattle on his older brothers, but he's keeping his mouth shut this time." Ely ran a thumb and forefinger down the length of his beard. "I don't know what to think."

He swiveled around to face his daughter. Jo lounged forlornly against the bunkhouse railing. "Did you see anything?"

She shook her head. "We were only gone about twenty minutes."

"In the barn?"

Jo flipped one heavy mahogany braid over her shoulder. "The bunkhouse," she replied with a sullen glare at Elizabeth.

If Jack noticed Elizabeth's sharp intake of breath, he didn't say anything.

Instead, he drew his dark brows together, his hazel eyes inscrutable. "Looks like the fire started in the parlor near the woodpile. Those boys are full of energy, but I don't see them doing anything this deliberately cruel. Must have been an accident."

"I just clipped the wicks this morning." Elizabeth brushed her cheek against the wool collar to brush aside a stray lock of hair. "None of the lamps were lit. I'm sure of it."

Jack's gaze skittered away. His hand crept over his pocket, as if he was unconsciously hiding something. Elizabeth's scalp tingled.

"Maybe the lamp fell over after the fire started," he replied. "There's no way to tell for sure."

"Why don't you talk to them?" Ely jerked his head to where the boys had disappeared behind the barn. "I've already got them shaking in their boots. We'll let that gun on

326

your hip do the rest."

Jack's gloved hand slid farther down his thigh, protectively covering the weapon. "Bring the boys around."

Elizabeth studied the Ranger. This was the first time she'd seen him don his weapon. There was a new determination in the set of his jaw.

Ely stomped across the clearing, his arms swinging resolutely. He returned moments later with the three boys trailing in his wake, their heads bent, their feet dragging in the soot-darkened snow.

"Boys," Jack spoke, his voice firm but kind. "Tell me what happened here today."

Caleb swallowed audibly. "I don't know. Honest. We went back down to the creek bed to see if we could find any wolf bones in the bonfire. David heard a wolf bone in your pocket brings good luck."

Ely guffawed and rolled his eyes. Jack shot him a quelling look.

"Maybe that other man did it," Abraham squeaked.

Jack's head snapped around to face the boy. "What man?"

The three adults and Jo closed the circle around the cowering boys.

Abraham's frightened gaze darted around the group. "There was a rider earlier."

"Why didn't you say something?" Ely demanded.

"He was just riding through. He headed toward the creek bed, so I figured you'd see him, too."

Ely swung his gaze around the clearing as if the man might still be lurking in the shadows. "We didn't see anyone."

"Did you girls see a rider?" Jack snapped.

Elizabeth and Jo exchanged a guilty look. "We were in the bunkhouse trying to piece together the bank robberies," Elizabeth began. She needed more time to gather her thoughts before she decided what to do with the information they'd discovered. "Is the bunkhouse safe? Rachel needs to be out of this cold."

Jack gave a distracted nod. "The women will stay there tonight. Ely and I will patch up the roof for the short term. The boys will sleep in the barn. We're burning daylight and it's only getting colder."

"There are more beds in the bunkhouse," Elizabeth pointed out. "It makes more sense for the boys to stay in there."

"The barn is too cold for Rachel, and Ely and I aren't exactly equipped to take care of a baby."

"Fine." Elizabeth scowled at his withering expression. "Rachel, Jo and I will stay in the *warm* bunkhouse tonight."

"Fine." Jack started toward the barn.

Elizabeth hesitated for a moment, then fell into step beside him. "Thank you for coming after me."

He swiveled on one heel, his expression thunderous. She sucked in a sharp breath.

"What's so important in that trunk that you risked your life?" he demanded.

"The homestead documents. The deed to the house."

His rigid shoulders deflated. He rubbed a weary hand across his eyes. "I didn't mean to yell at you. I just thought . . . nothing. Never mind."

He stomped away, leaving Elizabeth dumbfounded, and more alone than she'd ever felt in her whole life.

Jack ached to comfort Elizabeth, but with night rapidly descending, he worried they'd lose any chance of discovering more clues to the source of the fire. He didn't have time to ease the betrayal he'd seen in her eyes. The hurt caused by his harsh words. Realizing how close he'd come to losing her had unleashed a raging fury that hadn't yet dissipated.

Jack eyed the ragtag bunch of McCoys milling around the clearing. He faced Ely.

"Do you have room at your place for the animals?"

"Some."

"Enough for the milk cow and the chickens?"

"Should be."

"Excellent." Jack glanced at Elizabeth to see how she was taking the news. She held Rachel, gently rocking the sleeping infant. The wind whipped at her hair, tugging blond tendrils loose from the tight bun at the nape of her neck. Her detached gaze speared him like a lance.

He envisioned the woman in Texas after the Comanche raid, setting the table for her slaughtered family, wearing the same dulled expression. His throat tightened. A body could only take so much.

"Okay, then," he continued, yanking his muddled thoughts back to the present. "We're losing daylight. I'm taking Abraham to check for prints before this wind destroys any evidence of the boys' story. The rest of you can move Mrs. Cole's belongings into the barn."

He chanced another glance at Elizabeth, but she appeared oblivious. Numb. His heart went out to her. Jack stepped forward, drawn by a force more powerful than his own good sense. He knew what he wanted:

he wanted her to trust him.

Abraham jumped ahead of him, blocking his way.

"Over here," the boy pointed excitedly into the distance. "Come on."

Jack tore his gaze away from Elizabeth. He'd had his suspicions for days, but he'd done nothing. Her husband was the real outlaw, and he finally had the proof. Jack also had a suspicion someone else knew about the hidden money. If he'd faced the truth sooner, none of this would have happened.

And he still didn't know what Elizabeth was hiding. Was it her suspicions, or her involvement?

"C'mon," Abraham urged him forward.

He and the boy traced a path around the side of the house. Away from the distraction of Elizabeth and the fire, he realized his feet had turned to blocks of ice. He recalled the wistful look in her eyes as she'd nestled into his coat for comfort. He understood how she felt. He sometimes wondered if he'd ever be warm again.

After twenty minutes of fruitless searching, he and Abraham stumbled over the barest hint of animal prints in the drifting snow.

The boy shouted, jumping up and down at the proof of his innocence. The edges of the prints were ill-defined, but the tracks appeared to be from a large animal. A horse. They followed the spotty trail to the creek bed where the tracks veered left.

As if the rider had deliberately avoided Ely and Jack as they worked.

Jack circled the clearing in ever-widening arcs. The incessant wind howled through his brain, muddling his thoughts. His lips grew numb with cold. He kept picturing Elizabeth's haunted expression, the white cotton glove in Ely's pocket, the sun setting over the Texas sky. The widow had avoided the sheriff's involvement on more than one occasion. How much did she suspect? Why wasn't she willing to trust him?

He was about to declare the source of the tracks inconclusive when a divot in the snow snagged his attention. He crouched. The charred remains of a cigarette had melted into the ice. A check of the paper wrapping and a slight whiff indicated the Durham brand.

Digging into his pocket, Jack retrieved the curious item he'd discovered in the parlor. Side by side, the Durham cigarette he'd found in the house was an exact match for the one he'd just retrieved from the snow.

The animal tracks were definitely from a horse. And the man riding that animal had mostly likely started the fire. Jack searched the horizon. There weren't too many places to hide along the desolate prairie. A rider might escape detection by riding down the creek bed, away from him and Ely. Not exactly the easiest path.

"Abraham," Jack said. "Do you know if Mrs. Cole has a sled in the barn?"

"Yep. But one of the runners is broken."

Jack blew out a long breath. "You go back up to the house. I have something to take care of, then I'll be right there."

Abraham bobbed his head and bounded through the snow. Jack set off for the creek bed. He thought better of his action, and pivoted on his heel. Glancing up, he discovered Abraham staring at him from a few paces away.

"We didn't do it," the boy declared, his head canted at a forlorn angle. "We didn't set that fire."

"I know."

The boy's shoulders straightened with relief. "You'll tell that to my pa, then?"

"Of course I will."

Abraham jerked his head toward the main house. "Let's go, then."

Jack cast another look at the creek bed. He'd like to explore that cave once more. What else would he find in those boxes?

More money? More evidence?

Will Cole always rode a distinctive bay mustang.

That crotchety old sheriff had actually managed to stumble onto the truth.

The same questions swirled through Jack's head. How much did Elizabeth know? Did she know her husband had stashed stolen loot for a gang of bank robbers? Would his feelings for her change if she was involved?

Jack pinched the bridge of his nose. He didn't know what to think.

She'd been terrified from the moment he'd burst into her life. He'd always assumed her fear had been directed at him, but what if something more sinister had frightened her? What if she was being blackmailed?

If she'd known the money was in the cave, surely she'd have steered him and Ely away from clearing the brush. Yet when they'd mentioned the task this morning, she'd only smiled, her pale blue eyes clear and innocent. She couldn't have known about the money, or she'd have been terrified of discovery.

He glanced over the rise at the charred remains of her house. He had the uneasy feeling someone else knew of Will's involvement, and they were looking for that money.

His chest constricted. He'd found the loot and the real outlaw. Yet he had the uneasy sensation he'd just lost. And he'd lost big.

Elizabeth pulled down the galvanized tub and flipped it over onto the floor. She clambered atop the metal dome and stretched until her fingers closed around the rough wooden slats of the crate containing Will's saddlebags.

"Jack's gonna be real mad when he finds out we're in the main house," Jo called from the kitchen. "He gave mighty strict instructions about staying outside."

"I told you to wait outside," Elizabeth grumbled.

"If you don't have to listen to instructions, why should I?"

"At least be careful and stay out of the parlor. And the bedroom."

Elizabeth harrumphed as she set the box on the floor. She tore open the flap, then paused. What she didn't know, couldn't hurt her. "I want to see if we can salvage any of these canned goods."

For the next few minutes she puttered around the pantry, rubbing her towel over jars blackened with soot. All the while the saddlebags rested near her feet. When she'd discovered the Bible, something had bothered her. Will never did anything without a purpose. And he certainly wasn't a religious man. A Bible was innocuous, innocent. No one would search through the pages if the book was discovered. She certainly hadn't. If Will had left behind any clues to Bud Shaw's identity, she owed it to Jack to look.

Mustering her resolve, Elizabeth wiped her hands and knelt. She tugged on the leather flap and pulled out the Bible. A neat row of hand-written names adorned the inside cover. The Cole family tree. She ran her finger along the cascading history. One name in particular caught her attention — Bradford Shaw.

A sudden memory shocked her upright, Jack's voice, *Is he in there? Where's Bud Shaw.*

Bradford and Bud. A coincidence?

"We need to get going," Jo urged.

Elizabeth shoved the Bible into the saddlebag. "We're having a fresh chicken for dinner tonight. We might as well have one last celebration before we close up the house for good."

She stepped into the kitchen and grasped a soot-darkened pan from its neat perch on the wall.

"Thank you," Elizabeth said. "For everything. For taking such good care of Rachel and me. For lining up the pots by size."

"That was Mr. Elder. He's awfully fussy for a man."

Jo accepted the pot from Elizabeth's limp hand. "I'm going to miss having you close like this. But it'll be fine. We'll see each other every Sunday at church when the weather is nice. And maybe after school. Next year is my last."

"Of course we'll see each other." Elizabeth folded Jo into a quick embrace. "I never thanked you properly for helping me out the night Rachel was born. I don't know anyone as brave as you."

The girl's cheeks bloomed crimson. "I didn't do anything special."

"Of course you did. Do you remember when you ordered that Ranger around?"

Jo worried the braid draped over her right shoulder. A smile kicked up the corner of her mouth. "You should have seen his face."

The two of them giggled.

Elizabeth smiled. "I imagine Mr. Elder wishes I *had* been a bank robber."

Jo's giggles erupted into outright laughter. "He probably would have preferred being shot."

"Those big strong men could never survive having babies."

"We're worth more than rubies."

"Amen," the girls spoke in unison.

Unable to find a moment alone to speak with Jack, Elizabeth spent the next day salvaging what they had retrieved from the house. She separated the items she planned on giving to the McCoys from the items she planned to auction. Kneeling on the hay-strewn floor, she emptied the remainder of Will's belongings from his trunk and replaced his clothing with Rachel's.

In order to air out the worst of the acrid smoke, they stretched her clothing on lines outside to flap in the gentle breeze. Elizabeth retrieved her wedding dress and re-wrapped the satin gown in sheets of tissue paper. She'd have little use for such a fine outfit in the future, and the memories associated with the beautiful dress were best left to the prairie winds.

She tucked a note to Jo inside the lace-edged bodice and stacked the box against the stall wall. Someday, Jo would need a courting dress. Elizabeth hoped the younger girl would heed her advice and trust her own heart when choosing a husband. Turning, Elizabeth surveyed the items she'd be taking with her to town. She'd whittled her possessions down to a trunk and satchel. Her entire life in a tiny heap — just enough to start over fresh, someplace far away.

She crossed the length of the barn just as Jack draped a blanket over something in the wagon they'd moved inside for loading. He straightened at the sound of her footsteps. If she didn't know better, she'd think he looked almost guilty.

"What are you covering?" She peered over the edge.

His gaze didn't quite meet hers. "Just a couple of hay bales. You can throw a handful under the wheels if the wagon gets stuck in the snow. Hope you don't mind me packing them. With the animals over at Ely's, I don't suppose they'll be much use here."

"Remind me to tell Mr. McCoy that he can gather the rest of the bales if he needs them."

Jack leaped down from the wagon bed.

"Sure." He rested one hand on her trunk. "Is that all you're bringing to town?"

Elizabeth shrugged. In the chaos after the fire, she kept putting off telling Jack what she'd discovered about her late husband. This was her opportunity to blurt out the truth, to admit that nothing here truly belonged to her since she didn't know what had been purchased with stolen money.

The words stuck in her throat.

They'd been getting along so well, she

didn't want to lose even one minute of their limited camaraderie. She'd confess once they arrived in town. "I'll be staying at the boarding house until Rachel and I can find a new home. I can send for the rest later."

"Seems like a baby needs more stuff. Strange how the littler they are, the more they seem to need." He paused for a moment. "I have something else you can bring."

He motioned for her to follow him to the work area. As they approached the space, the pungent odor of varnish stung her nostrils.

Jack skirted aside, revealing a gleaming wooden crib resting on a drop cloth. "I found a tin of varnish in the cupboard there. I cut up one of the trunks in the bunkhouse. I figured you'd need this more." He rubbed the back of his neck. "I don't know much about carpentry, but the joints are real solid. Should hold a baby just fine."

Tears pricked behind her eyes. The pieces she and Jo had seen in the barn had all been assembled. Carved ivory decorated the head of the crib in an arched leafy trail. Jack hadn't been bored. He'd been making Rachel a gift.

"I just thought the baby should have something besides a drawer and a laundry basket." He scuffed at the floor with his boot.

Elizabeth knelt and studied the piece.

Jack stuck out a warning hand. "You'd best not touch it. I don't think the varnish has dried yet."

Resisting the temptation to run her fingers over the wood, she rested her hand on her chest. The painstaking detail he'd carved into the piece enchanted her. "So that's what you've been doing all morning. I wondered where you disappeared to."

That same shadow of guilt crossed over his face. "Yep."

Elizabeth folded her hands together. Her whole life was slipping away. She was leaving everything behind — everything that was familiar, all the little things that had brought her so much joy over the past few months. Even the memories of Will seemed to fade into the past. They were hazy and distant, out of focus, while the good times stood out in sharper relief.

"Do you like it?" Jack asked, a heartbreaking note of doubt in his voice.

Contentment swelled in her chest. "The crib is beautiful. Thank you."

"You're welcome." He sighed, his shoulders relaxing.

"You've been such a blessing to me."

"Anyone would have done the same."

"You and Jo are too stubborn for your own good."

"I'll agree with you about Jo, but I like to think of myself as decisive, a man of action."

Elizabeth smiled at his posturing. "Not to mention modest and unassuming."

"I never was one to hide my light under a bushel."

I have fallen in love with him.

The truth struck her like a lightning bolt. The process had happened so gently, she hadn't noticed the signs. The way her heart flipped when he entered the room, the way her thoughts strayed to fond memories of his kisses, the way she had begun to think of the three of them as a family. The source of her melancholy finally made sense. She had given her heart to a dream.

Elizabeth blinked. Falling in love slowly was much more binding and endearing than instant infatuation. "Do you think you'll ever marry?"

She regretted the question before she even finished speaking.

Head bent, he considered her question. "I'm not good husband material. My job is my life, and my job requires me to travel. I'm never in one place for too long."

"Of course."

"I suppose I could always settle down and become the sheriff of some sleepy hamlet. I could arrest the town drunk every Friday."

"And let him out of jail every Sunday for church?"

"Well, of course! As town sheriff I'd consider it my duty to rehabilitate the disorderly."

He was joking with her, to put her at ease, and she appreciated the effort. "It's getting late. If I want to make it to town before sunset, I'd best finish packing up the rest of the things we salvaged from the fire." She thought about the fire. "Say, did you find out anything about the man Abraham saw? Mr. McCoy said you discovered tracks by the creek bed, but he didn't appear concerned."

A look she couldn't quite read flitted across his face. "I didn't." He hesitated. "But I don't think you should stay here any longer than necessary. I don't like the idea of a stranger lurking around."

Elizabeth suppressed a shudder. "Me, either."

Jack moved to stand before the stall. "Do you think this horse can pull the wagon all the way into town?"

"She's stronger than she looks."

Jack patted the mare's muzzle. "Seems like

all the gals on this farm are stronger than they appear."

"I believe you've just compared me to a horse. I don't know whether to be complimented or insulted."

Jack laughed good-naturedly at his own gaff. "Point taken." His expression grew somber. "Do you have the resources to move to town?"

He hadn't said the words outright, but she knew he meant money. "Will left us set pretty well."

Her answer didn't seem to comfort him. "I'll drive with you into town."

"Of course."

"You know you can always trust me," he spoke quietly.

My husband was a bank robber.

She longed to confess what she'd discovered in the Bible. About seeing the name, Bradford Shaw. They'd all teased and tormented Jack for barging into her home all those weeks ago, but he'd been right all along. Her husband was involved. He was also dead.

A distinctive bay mustang.

Will had won the horse from Mr. Peters, the owner of the mercantile, in a card game. Once again her late husband's activities had come back to haunt him — and her. He'd covered his tracks well. In the end, his vanity had done him in. A less flashy horse might have garnered less attention.

With the weather and the heavy load, the long wagon trip to town was bound to take two hours at least. She didn't think she could stand sitting next to the Ranger with the weight of Will's betrayal hanging between them.

Jack couldn't do anything until he reached town, anyway. She'd wait until they arrived, and give him the Bible when they separated. She didn't know if Bud Shaw was guilty or innocent, but she owed it to him to let Jack find out. She had to do everything she could to ensure an innocent man didn't hang.

Suddenly chilled, she pressed the back of her hand to her forehead. Jack could wire the Santa Fe railroad line and get a copy of Will's work schedule.

She wasn't sure how deeply Will had been involved in the scheme, or how his actions would affect her. Maybe one of his relatives had been involved, and he'd been too loyal to turn in his partner. Either way, Jack needed to track Will's job schedule. Once the truth was revealed, she'd face the consequences. She was an outlaw's widow, and Jack wasn't the marrying kind.

As for her love, she had the rest of her life to mourn that loss.

CHAPTER SIXTEEN

Twenty minutes later, a somber group gathered in the center of the clearing. Jack chafed at the delay, anxious for the journey. He didn't want any distractions while he questioned Elizabeth. Instinct told him he was close to a breakthrough with her.

Mr. McCoy held the milk cow by a knotted-rope tether. "I'll miss you, lass. But we'll be up to town before you know it." He shifted in the snow. "The boys and I will come back tomorrow for the rest of the animals."

"Don't forget the barn cat." Elizabeth wrapped her arms around her body and rubbed her shoulders. "She saved me from the wolves. I'd hate to think of her out here all alone."

"I've got some salted fish. We'll lure her back to our place, all right. It'll give the boys something to do other than wrestle one another."

"Are you certain you have enough room? Won't this be too much of a burden?"

"We can always use another milk cow around the place."

"Of course."

"Of course."

Jo stepped forward and pumped Elizabeth's hand. "I'll see you in church."

Elizabeth nodded, but her gaze shied away. Jack's instincts flared.

Ely embraced the widow in a bone-crushing bear hug, tears shimmering in his eyes. "You take care of the little one, lass. And take care of yourself. Don't you worry about a thing. We'll keep an eye on the place while you're gone. Looks like this weather is about to break. It'll be spring before you know it. Don't forget to ask the doc about my rash."

"I will." She grinned indulgently. "Thank you, for everything."

"Get on with you. It's going to be dark soon."

Jack assisted her onto the plank-wood carriage seat. Rachel's basket rested on the floor with the baby tucked snugly inside. Tethered to the back of the wagon, Midnight snorted and balked, as if offended by the subservient position. Jack clambered up beside Elizabeth and slapped the reins to wake up her tired old mare. The horse jolted forward.

They lumbered to the end of the drive. Elizabeth touched his sleeve.

"Wait," she said. "I want to take one last look. I want to remember this."

The worst of the damage centered on the front of the house, lending the scene a neglected, forlorn appearance. The wind whipped the hair loose from beneath her bonnet. The strands snapped at her eyes.

Jack cleared his throat. "I'm sure someone will rebuild."

"Someone has been rebuilding this place for more than thirty years. Maybe it's cursed."

"There's no such thing as a curse. This is a harsh land. Everyone who lived in this house left the prairie a better place."

"Except for me."

"You did your best. That fire wasn't your fault."

"Then whose fault was it?"

Jack shrugged.

He had an idea who had caused the damage, but he wasn't ready to confide in Elizabeth just yet. Will had probably bragged about his escapades, and someone was looking for the money. The boys had seen the man, and Jack had seen evidence of a rider.

He'd started to tell her about the cave a hundred times, but the words stuck in his throat. He wanted her to trust him.

Using the evidence he'd discovered as proof of Bud Shaw's innocence, he'd telegraph the jail in Texas once they arrived in town. He still wasn't sure why Will had chosen to steal Bud Shaw's identity, but it really didn't matter anymore. He'd have the sheriff keep an eye on the homestead in case the man who started the fire returned.

The grueling miles to town passed in tense silence. Jack attempted to start up a conversation a few times, but Elizabeth mostly ignored his overtures. She stared into the distance, somber and distracted. When the town's smokestacks appeared on the horizon, Jack reined the horse to a halt. "I'll ride Midnight the rest of the way."

He swung out of the driver's seat. "You okay to handle the reins?"

He spoke to her bonnet as she bent to retrieve something from beneath the seat. Straightening, her expression pinched, she held out a book.

"I should have told you sooner." She cleared her throat. "But I didn't know how."

Realizing she held a Bible, he frowned. "Told me what?"

"This belonged to Will. I think maybe he

350

was related to Bud Shaw. There's a family tree. A man named Bradford Shaw is Will's first cousin. It can't be a coincidence."

His heart sank. "How long have you known this?"

"Not long. The Bible was tucked away in Will's saddlebags. I never went through his things until after the fire."

"Your husband has been dead for eight months."

"I don't expect you to understand." She rubbed her temples beneath the rim of her bonnet with mittened hands. "You've got his whole family laid out in the front of that book. I'm sure you'll be able to prove Bud was involved because he and Will knew each other. They were cousins. . . ." She paused. "There's more."

His head throbbed. *Emotions clouded judgment, and poor judgment got people killed.* "How much more?"

She scooted toward the driver's seat. "Check the Santa Fe work records for Will Cole. You'll find proof my husband was involved with his cousin. Will scheduled work crews for railroad projects near the banks robbed." She lifted the reins to spur the horse forward. "That's all I know."

Jack slammed the brake into place, preventing her from fleeing. "Why didn't you

351

say something sooner?"

She'd known for days, maybe even weeks, and she hadn't trusted him with the truth. She didn't trust him. Despite everything he'd done for her, she'd never trusted him.

Her face averted, Elizabeth sighed. "Jo put it all together earlier this week. I know I should have told you sooner, but the fire —"

Despite her lack of faith in him, he forced himself to think like a Ranger. Since the moment he'd discovered proof of Will's involvement, he'd been wondering why the man's name hadn't surfaced during the investigation. "We checked all the railroad crew managers. Will's name never came up."

"He wasn't a foreman. He only put together the schedules. Will had access to information on payroll and large projects. He knew exactly when the banks had the most money. He knew when the trains were delayed, when the projects started, everything." She met his gaze, her clear blue eyes stricken. "And he always had money. Too much money for a working man. I lied to myself all along. I made excuses for him. Especially after I found out how much he gambled. Some of the people in town thought he cheated."

Comprehension slammed over Jack. "How

could I have been so stupid? We checked foremen and managers. We never once considered a pencil pusher."

He circled to the back of the wagon and grabbed Midnight's reins.

Elizabeth twisted in her seat. "Tell the sheriff he can auction off whatever is left on the property." Her bonnet shielded her face. "He knew Will was a cheat. He's been wanting the property since Will died."

Jack winced at the stark pain in her voice. "We'll settle up with the sheriff later."

"Aren't you listening to me? You don't have to worry about hanging an innocent man anymore. Will was related to Bradford Shaw. They were first cousins. They must have been working together."

Jack knew exactly what had happened. Why Will Cole had assumed Bud Shaw's identity. All the puzzle pieces fit. Every loose end came together. The two men looked alike because they were related. The resemblance had confused the witnesses.

Jack looped the reins over the saddle horn. "There were only three outlaws — Slim Joe, Pencil Pete and your husband."

Angry with his own stupidity, he fisted his hands. He'd been sitting on the proof for months. *A distinctive bay mustang.* He'd followed the trail of a man riding a distinctive bay mustang all the way through Texas to Colorado to Kansas. The horse had been on at least four different trains, several witnesses had attested to that, but no manifest had ever indicated the presence of the animal.

Jack had assumed the rider bribed the workers, but a railroad employee could get away without signing the manifest.

Elizabeth's husband was guilty as sin, only she refused to believe it. "You're right about one thing, Mrs. Cole. There's a man sitting in jail, set to hang in less than three weeks. But he's definitely innocent." Jack lifted his head. "Your husband was impersonating Bud Shaw."

Elizabeth frowned, her face as pale as the snow sweeping across the prairie. "Will wouldn't betray his own kin."

"It was the coward's way out. Your husband *was* Bud Shaw. He framed his own cousin."

Her breath puffed clouds into the chill afternoon. "That's absurd. They must have been partners."

"Did your husband take his horse with him when he traveled?"

"Always. Will said he didn't like the mounts the livery provided. He liked to stand out."

"I'll prove it to you. Show me something with your husband's handwriting."

"My papers are in the trunk."

Elizabeth brushed aside his proffered hand, leaped off the wagon seat and circled around the bed. Jack tugged the trunk until it rested on the edge and flipped open the lid. He stood aside, allowing Elizabeth access. While she searched, he snatched his own documents from Midnight's saddlebags.

After rummaging for a few moments, she pulled out a sheaf of papers. "There."

Jack flipped through the pages. He brushed the snow from the wagon bed and laid her documents beside the sheet he'd torn from the hotel register. "Bud Shaw signed his name on the register at the hotel in Texas. Look at that handwriting. It's the same man."

"How can you be sure?"

"The slant of the letters is the same. Look at the *W*. Will puts a flourish on the end. Even you have to see that."

"The signatures are similar," she replied. "I'm still not certain they're the same man. Why didn't Pencil Pete declare Bud's innocence? Certainly he'd know the man wasn't involved."

Jack stepped onto the back of the wagon.

"This is why Pencil Pete kept quiet."

He whipped off the tarp and revealed the stash of Wells Fargo boxes. "I found these on your property."

"No!"

"I discovered them in a cave by the creek. This is why Pencil Pete was so all-fired-up arrogant. He thought your husband was coming back to bust him out. Except Will never made it back, did he? Come to think of it, I don't believe Will ever planned on busting his partner out of jail.

"See, that's what's been bothering me this whole time. Why did Will make a trip down the creek bed in a storm? I think your husband was going to take the loot and run. After Pencil Pete and his cousin were hanged, he'd have all the money. No one was looking for Will Cole."

The betrayal in her eyes stabbed him like a lance.

"Everything you say makes sense," she spoke, her expression stricken. "I can't believe he was willing to let his own cousin hang for his crimes. But it must be true, right?"

"I'm sorry, Elizabeth. I know how much this must hurt. But all the evidence points to Will."

"Does this mean you can free Bud Shaw?"

He raked his hands through his hair. "Should be. Everything against Bud is circumstantial."

"What if I come to Texas?" she asked eagerly. "What if I testify that my husband was the third outlaw? That Will assumed Bud's identity?"

"It'd just be your word. They'd want some kind of proof."

"I suppose you're right." She climbed back onto the wagon seat, her movements stiff and weary.

For a moment she sat, hunched over the seat. Jack rubbed Midnight's haunches, unsure how to comfort her.

Then she jerked upright, snapping her fingers. "Bud Shaw was shot in the leg during a robbery in Colorado last spring. Will came home with a wound on his leg around that same time. Once you show the Rangers the stolen money and tell them where you found it, and Bud proves he doesn't have a scar on his leg, that should be enough."

"We better put you on the payroll. It's perfect. You won't even have to be involved."

There'd be no reason for her to accompany him to Texas.

His heartbeat stalled.

No reason for him to see her. Ever.

She adjusted the reins and sat forward.

"We'd best get his money to town."

"You can still come to Texas," he blurted.

"There's nothing for me there," she replied, her expression bleak.

I'm there.

The carriage surged forward. Jack whipped off his hat and slapped his thigh. What did he have to offer her?

Everything.

Love, marriage, a home and a family.

He'd never thought of himself as the kind of man to marry and settle down. Until now.

He mounted Midnight. Kicking the horse into a trot, he searched the horizon. They were safe. For now. But someone else was searching for that money, and money had a way of forcing men into desperate acts. It wasn't going to take long before they discovered the loot wasn't at the homestead. None of them were safe for long.

"Are you following me, Mr. Elder?" Elizabeth demanded in a harsh whisper. She glanced around the quiet mercantile, relieved no one had noticed their heated exchange.

"Where is Rachel?" he asked.

"I left her with Mrs. Wilmont from the boarding house."

"It's not safe."

"Of course it's safe. All the stolen money is at the bank."

"You and I know that." Jack circled her upper arm and tugged her behind a display of penny candies. "But the man searching for those Wells Fargo boxes may still think you have them."

After their discussion the previous day, she hadn't thought their next meeting would be a whispered conversation in the general store.

Glancing around, he slapped his hat against his thigh. "I didn't want to alarm you until I knew for certain. Pencil Pete escaped, and he's looking for the stash. I had some suspicions after the fire. When we arrived yesterday, I telegraphed Texas. Pete broke out of jail three weeks ago. That's plenty of time to make his way to Kansas."

"Why didn't someone tell you sooner?"

Jack snorted. "They sent the notice to the sheriff in town. Only he was too drunk to care. I don't know why Pete set the fire. I think it may have been an accident. I think one of the McCoy boys spooked him and he knocked over the lantern."

Panic sucked the breath from her lungs. "It's not going to take him long to figure the money isn't there."

"He's been watching the place for at least

a day. He's seen me. He'll assume I have the money."

"I'd better —"

"Mr. Elder!" a feminine voice called. "Mr. Elder, is that you?"

A pretty dark-haired woman with coffee-colored eyes rounded the corner, a bundled infant in her arms. "I can't believe it's actually you."

Jack frowned before dawning recognition spread across his face. "Helen Miller, as I live and breathe."

"I'm Helen Smith now." She and the Ranger shared an awkward embrace with the baby pressed between them.

"Mr. Elder," the woman exclaimed again as she backed away. "What are you doing in Kansas?"

"Working," Jack replied shortly.

The woman's violet calico gown enhanced her striking brown eyes, a crisp bonnet framed her creamy complexion. Helen Smith glanced curiously at Elizabeth. "Won't you introduce us?"

"I'm Elizabeth Cole." She stuck out her hand. "It's a pleasure to meet you, Mrs. Smith."

"Call me Helen. Any friend of Jack's is a friend of mine."

"And how do you two know each other?"

"That's not —" Jack began.

"It's all right." Helen interrupted with a wave of her hand. "Jack negotiated my release from the Apache when I was just a girl. They raided our settlement." The woman's expression clouded at the memory. "Without Jack's intercession, I don't know what would have happened."

Her whole body trembled. Sensing her mother's distress, the baby whimpered.

"It's my job." Jack scuffed his boot against the floor. "Everything turned out for the best. Looks like you've been busy."

The woman adjusted the baby to the opposite shoulder. Two spots of color appeared on her high cheek bones. "I'm a married lady, all right. My husband and I were visiting his sister in Wichita. We're on our way home now. Our train doesn't leave until tomorrow. Will you still be here?"

"I'm here for a few more days."

Mrs. Smith's face lit with pleasure. "Isn't that wonderful? We can catch up."

Elizabeth narrowed her eyes. Having a beautiful woman from Jack's past "catching up" with him didn't feel wonderful at all.

It wouldn't hurt to remind Jack that Mrs. Smith was a *married* lady. "How old is your baby?" she asked pointedly.

The woman's attention immediately

turned to her child. "This is Mary. She's almost four months old. I can't believe how quickly she's growing."

Helen turned down the blanket and revealed a plump-cheeked, adorable infant with enormous dark eyes. Elizabeth's heart melted at her obvious affection. Of course, Mrs. Smith wasn't interested in Jack romantically. How silly of her to be jealous.

"Mrs. Cole has a baby girl, too," Jack offered. "Maybe we can all have dinner."

"How wonderful!" Helen exclaimed. "We can compare notes. I feel so ill equipped to raise an infant sometimes. My mother died in the Apache raid. I miss her more than ever."

"I know how you feel." Elizabeth responded to the warmth in her gaze. She didn't have a rival, she had a friend.

They shared a knowing look. Once again Elizabeth was ashamed of her uncharacteristic bout of jealousy. She had no right to be jealous about anything. When you loved someone, you wanted what was best for them. Even if what was best hurt like a thousand bee stings.

Helen glanced at Jack, but she directed her question to Elizabeth, "I'll be looking forward to meeting your husband."

"Mr. Cole passed away."

Helen's expression immediately sobered. "I'm so sorry, Mrs. Cole. My family is planning on staying at the boarding house. If you need anything tonight, you just give me a holler. We women have to stick together."

Elizabeth's throat tightened. "That's very kind of you."

"Don't be silly. Jack and his family were there for me when I was alone. I don't know what I would have done without them."

The women exchanged a quick hug before Helen motioned to the door. "I'd best be going. My husband worries if I'm out of his sight for too long. You know how men are." She winked at Elizabeth, then turned to Jack. "Your brothers are going to be happy to see you home again. The way they sing your praises, you'd think you hung the moon and stars. Not that I'd ever disagree."

Jack squirmed beneath the praise. After Helen disappeared around the corner, out of earshot, Elizabeth turned to Jack. "I didn't know you were a negotiator."

"That's my specialty. I negotiate the release of Indian hostages. Not a real exciting job, eh?"

Elizabeth's heart filled with pride. "I can't imagine a braver or more noble job."

Jack set his hat onto his head. "I need to talk to you. Privately. I'll call on you at four.

Between now and then, stay close to the boarding house. I've spread word through town to look out for Pencil Pete. I've got men watching the train depot and the livery. But you've got to be careful."

"You be careful, too."

He blinked at the suggestion. The reaction shamed her. She'd never thought of the danger Jack faced every day, or what a solitary, and lonely, life he led. He spent his career looking out for others, putting his own needs last. That's what she'd done — she'd put Jack's needs last, as well. A man that special deserved someone just as special to love him in return. Someone without a past.

"Elizabeth, you do know I'll always protect you," he spoke earnestly.

"I know."

Everything that brought them together was destined to tear them apart. If she'd never married Will, she'd never have come West. If Will hadn't been an outlaw, Jack would never have appeared in her life. No matter what brought them together, one truth remained. An outlaw's widow made a poor prospect for a lawman's bride. Her husband had been a party to his sister-in-law's murder. How could his family ever forgive her, even if Jack somehow could?

Jack caught her gaze, his expression uncharacteristically grave. "A man gets to thinking sometimes, and he realizes his priorities have changed. Texas isn't such a bad place to settle down and raise a family. You know?"

"I know."

Her heart thumped madly in her chest. She loved him with a wild, desperate abandon. He wanted to take care of her. Just like he'd taken care of Helen, and Jo, and even little Rachel. Eventually though, he'd regret his decision.

She'd always be a reminder of Doreen's murderer. "You don't have to worry about me."

"I'm not worried." He lifted his hat and raked his free hand through his hair. "Of course I'm worried. But that's not the reason I hung around all this time." He paced the narrow aisle. "I'm sorry your late husband dragged you into this mess, but I never would have met you otherwise. And I can't be sorry about that. Once Pencil Pete is caught and Bud is cleared, none of this will matter."

Of course it mattered.

Everyone in his hometown knew about the outlaws. Even if they tried to hide her identity, there'd be no hiding her involvement from Jack's fellow Texas Rangers. People would wonder how much she knew. They'd speculate on her involvement. And Jack's family. She shuddered to think of their reaction to Will Cole's widow. She could live with scorn, but Rachel deserved better. Jack deserved better.

He stared at her expectantly. The tinkling bell over the door saved her from a reply. Half a dozen men streamed into the store, their hobnail boots drowning out any chance for further conversation.

With one hand on his front brim, the other hand on the back, Jack straightened his hat. "We'll finish this conversation later. Promise me you'll go right back to the boarding house."

Elizabeth flashed a watery smile. "I will."

"Because I'll be watching."

"I know."

She followed his exit. He wouldn't stray far. He had shadowed her every move for the past twenty-four hours. He was too honorable for his good. When she met him tonight, he'd ask her to marry him, of that she was certain. Elizabeth glanced at her hands. Was she selfish enough to accept his offer?

Maybe Jack was right. Maybe people would forget about her past. He felt something for her, maybe not love, but certainly affection. He cared for Rachel. He wasn't a man to enter into a bargain lightly. If he thought they could forge a future together, perhaps it was possible. In time, he might even grow to love her.

She stepped forward and placed her purchases on the counter. The mercantile owner, Mr. Peters, leered at her from his perch on a three-legged stool. He wore a crisp, white apron knotted around his waist. His black hair was slicked back, the comb marks still visible. He'd refused to serve her after Will had won his horse in a poker game, but that was months ago.

One of the cowboys approached the counter, his boots click-clacking across the wood floor.

Mr. Peters pointedly turned his back on Elizabeth. "You need any help, *sir?*"

The cowboy jerked his thumb in Elizabeth's direction. "She was here first."

"I ain't gonna take her blood money, *anyway,*" Mr. Peters sneered.

Elizabeth winced from his withering stare.

"The sheriff says your husband was a murderer and a cheat. Not that any of us around here are surprised. The sheriff says you're going back to Texas to hang."

Heart thumping, Elizabeth backed away

from the venom in his steady gaze. People rarely forgave, and they certainly never forgot. She was fooling herself to think she and Jack might share a future.

The cowboy blocked her exit. "You wanna have some fun before you hang, little lady?"

Mr. Peters spit on the floor at her feet. "Since they can't get at your husband, they gonna take you."

The cowboy licked his fleshy lips. "I can get you outta town without that Ranger knowing. Just say the word."

" 'Course, you'll have to leave the brat behind," Mr. Peters cackled.

Elizabeth elbowed past them, their jeers cut off by the slamming door. She didn't believe their lies, but she'd just received her answer.

Jack was better off without her.

Jack paced outside the parlor door, his hat in his hands. He'd rehearsed the speech a hundred times over the past few hours. Maybe even a thousand. His solution was perfect. Inspired.

He'd been in love with her from the moment he'd caught her crying because she hadn't named Rachel yet. Even when all the evidence told him she was protecting a man who didn't deserve her, his heart had known her innocence. He loved them both. She and Rachel were the puzzle pieces missing in his life.

He rapped on the door, tipping forward when the heavy weight swung open beneath his fingers.

Elizabeth perched on the edge of a spindly chair. Sunlight shafted through the windows, highlighting the golden amber in her hair. She turned slightly, just enough for the light to silhouette her profile. She wore a familiar white shirtwaist, its crisp cotton tucked into the wide band of a calico skirt. She kept her hands clenched in her lap.

Jack cleared his throat. "I've wired the boys in Texas. The judge is willing to review the evidence."

She appeared more fragile, the circles beneath her eyes darker than when he'd seen her this afternoon. She smoothed her skirts over her knees. "I wanted to apologize for not revealing my suspicions about Will sooner. I keep looking back, and everything is so obvious. I don't know why I didn't see it before. I guess I was fooling myself. If I didn't face the truth, I didn't have to face the consequences. Except Bud Shaw might have hanged because I didn't want people to know I was an outlaw's widow. I'm not proud of myself. I should have done the right thing straight away."

He worked the brim of his hat. "You were busy holding your family together."

"I suppose."

A sense of foreboding hung over him. He'd never seen her like this, quiet, almost cowed. "No one blames you for what Will did. It was his sin, not yours."

"I've been praying, you know." She pleated the blue calico draping her knee. "Praying for answers, praying for Rachel, praying for myself. I think that's all I've done for the past few days, pray."

"Did you pray for us to be together?"

"No."

The floor dropped out from beneath him. "You didn't?"

She faced him then, so breathtakingly beautiful he had difficulty concentrating.

"I finally understand. When you love someone, you want what's best for them. Even if what's best isn't you." She met his gaze, her expression distant. "You knew that all along though, didn't you?"

"No. I don't understand. I know you feel something for me."

"It took a lot of praying, but I know what I need to do. I always told myself that I was doing the right thing, that I was following God's path, but I wasn't. Not really. I was doing what felt right for me. I put Rachel and you, and even the McCoys, in danger because I was selfish. This time I'm going to do the right thing for everyone, not just me."

Her refusal to acknowledge his words pounded in his brain, a deafening pain that drowned out everything but his own shock and hurt.

I love you.

The words clogged in his throat. If he said them out loud, she still might reject him, and he couldn't bear her scorn.

She faced him then. "Remember that first night? The night Rachel was born? You made me a promise. Even then I knew there was something special about you. Something strong and honorable."

Jack swallowed around the emotion tightening his throat. He wasn't brave. He was a coward who couldn't admit his own feelings. "I'll take care of you, Elizabeth. I'll take care of you *and* Rachel. I'll raise her as my own."

"I know you would."

She stood then, moving away from him. Moving away from the future he'd only just begun to plan. Moving away from a life he'd only just begun to yearn. She didn't love him. His instincts had failed him. She'd rather be alone than be with him.

He pictured his future without her. He'd go back to his job, back to the endless travel, back to never putting down roots. How could it hurt so much to lose something he'd never had?

The desolate image jolted his courage. "I don't care if you don't love me. I have enough love for both of us. Marry me? We'll build a future together. You and me and Rachel."

She didn't even blink, didn't react at all to his declaration or his question. If anything, she appeared to grow colder, more distance. "No. I can't. Don't you see? Will is always going to be between us."

"Don't you feel anything for me?"

Silence answered his question.

Jack didn't know how a body could feel so much pain and still be standing. All the sorrow in his heart burned into his brain. He smashed his hat upon his head. "You lied to me. Maybe not in your words, but in your actions. You made me think you felt something for me."

Elizabeth rested one hand on the mantel, her gaze averted. "I'm sorry."

He was mad, no furious, with her for tying him up in knots. For making him love her, then turning away. He didn't want to talk to her anymore. He didn't even want to look at her.

He stomped toward the door then paused, his gaze riveted on the brass knob. "You *are* selfish, Elizabeth Cole. Selfish with your affection, selfish with your prayers and selfish with your love."

CHAPTER SEVENTEEN

"All aboard!" the conductor called.

The train chugged forward with an ever-increasing *click-clack, click-clack, click-clack* over the rails. Elizabeth perched on a velvet-covered bench, Rachel snug in her lap. Helen and her husband, along with their own baby, sat across from her. Elizabeth stared out the window. The prairie stretched white all the way to the horizon.

She hadn't seen Jack since last evening. She hadn't even told him she was leaving. Not that he'd even care anymore. Her refusal had driven him away for good, leaving a gaping emptiness in her chest that would never be filled.

The train was headed for Texas, and that was as good a place as anywhere to start over. The state was big enough that she'd never fear running into Jack, yet she knew she'd feel closer to him there.

She'd left the deeds for the homestead

with the town agent. Together she and Rachel would start a new life.

"Look at the brass fittings over the windows!" Helen exclaimed. "And the velvet benches. This is so much better than my first trip across the plains. In a wagon." She grimaced.

Her husband, a balding man with a round stomach and kind gray eyes, smiled indulgently. "And faster, too."

"I wish Jack hadn't cancelled our dinner last evening. I so wanted to catch up."

Her husband patted her hand. "He has his reasons."

Helen leaned forward and snagged Elizabeth's attention. "The whole town of Paris, Texas, is crawling with Elders. Their cattle ranch must take up half the county. It's a good thing they have so many sons running around to help care for the place. Those Elder boys are all so driven. *And handsome.*" Her husband rolled his eyes. "Why the Elder family built the church, the hotel and even the courthouse."

In a weak comparison, Elizabeth had forty dollars in her reticule. The same forty dollars she'd brought with her from New York. Her life savings.

She wore the original dress she'd donned to cross the plains nearly two years ago.

She'd stuffed the money Will had left, the ominous wad of bills, into Rachel's crib and placed the whole thing in a sturdy wooden crate in the baggage cart. Jack had refused to take the money, saying all the stolen loot had been accounted for. His refusal hadn't left her a lot of options on such short notice. She definitely didn't want to face the sheriff, especially after he'd been gossiping all over town. Carrying the money around in her satchel wasn't an option, either. The bills felt heavy and tainted. When she and Rachel found a new home, she'd find a suitable charity and donate the cash.

The train lurched. Gasping, Elizabeth flung out her arm to save Rachel's basket from sliding off the seat. The passengers grumbled. Heads popped up over seat backs. The train shuddered to a halt. A middle-aged woman in a dark burgundy gown lowered the window and peered outside. Her hat feathers fluttered in the cold breeze.

"Say," one of the passengers called, "what's going on?"

A uniformed conductor entered through the rear pocket door. "There's been a slight delay," the man called.

He held up his hands to still the cacophony of protests erupting from the passengers. "There's a dead animal on the tracks. We haven't built up enough speed to push it aside with the cattle guard. If I can get eight or ten sturdy, strong men, we'll drag it off and be on our way in no time."

Helen Smith's husband rose to his feet. He dropped a kiss on his wife's forehead before sidling down the aisle, his body angled to traverse the narrow path. Elizabeth smiled at the obvious affection between the Smiths. Helen's husband obviously didn't hold his wife's past, her capture by the Apaches, against her.

Prodded by jabs in the ribs from their wives, grumbling husbands shuffled into the cold. The railcar soon drained of able- and not-so-able-bodied men, leaving only women and children. Elizabeth glanced at Rachel.

With nervous chatter filling the car, the delay gave her unwelcome time to think. She *was* selfish. Just not the way Jack thought. She wanted more than anything to accept his proposal, but she could never face his family. Jack's sister-in-law was dead because of Will. Every time the Elders looked at her they'd be reminded of how Doreen died.

She'd convinced herself that leaving was the right thing to do. Why, then, did her decision feel so wrong? She pressed her check against Rachel's. Elizabeth's tear slid down her daughter's cheek.

She could go back and face Jack, confess her love and her fears. Her heart wrenched. Loving Jack wasn't the easy choice, but was it the right choice? Is this how her own mother had felt when she'd been forced to send Elizabeth to an orphanage? This soul-deep pain? All these years Elizabeth had wallowed in her own misery, never considering her mother's anguish.

Jack was smart enough to know his own mind. He wasn't a man who made rash, impulsive decisions. If only Elizabeth could say the same. She'd followed a man because of an infatuation. Not even two years later she was running away from love. She was forcing her child into a life of secrets and lies and running rather than face the consequences of her late husband's actions.

What was she teaching her daughter? That it was okay to run when life became difficult?

Elizabeth shot upright. She didn't know what she was going to do once she saw Jack, but she was going back. They were only a short distance from the rail station. How long did she have before the tracks were cleared? No matter what happened, she wasn't leaving without Jack's gift. He'd carved the wood with loving hands, and she wasn't going to leave behind his treasured present.

Elizabeth grasped the seat back. She scooted into the aisle and stood beside Mrs. Smith's seat.

"I need to get my crate from the baggage cart," Elizabeth said. "Will you watch Rachel for a moment?"

Mrs. Smith bounced Mary in her arms, her expression one of earnest concern. "Of course. What a delightful child. I know you're newly widowed, but there's no finer man than Jack Elder. If you don't mind my saying so."

"He's the finest man I've ever met."

Her resolute decision faltered. He deserved someone better than Elizabeth. He deserved to find love with someone who wouldn't jeopardize the career he treasured. Someone without a past. Someone he could proudly introduce to his family.

The train lurched. Elizabeth clutched the seat back for balance.

As if sensing the tension in Elizabeth, Helen covered her hand. "I don't know what happened between the two of you. It's none of my business. But I think you should know something about Jack. He never stopped searching for me. Even when everyone said it was hopeless. For three months he searched. When he found me, it took another three months to negotiate my release. But Jack never stopped trying, even when everyone told him to stop. Even when my uncle told him a child captured by Indians wasn't worth saving, Jack never gave up. There aren't many men who hold honor above their own needs."

That was the whole problem. "He deserves someone just as honorable as he is."

"He deserves someone to love him. That's all any of us wants or needs."

"That's what I'm counting on," Elizabeth's voice sounded unconvincing, even to her own ears.

"Jack told me something once." Helen squeezed her hand. "He told me, it's not the things that happen to us that define who we are, it's what you do about it."

Elizabeth realized one thing for certain. Even if they didn't have a future together, Jack deserved to know how much she loved him.

"Thank you," Elizabeth choked out. "I'll be right back. I have to make things right."

Her vision blurred by tears, she stumbled down the aisle and slid open the pocket door.

Glancing up, she blinked at the sky.

"I forgive you, Mother," she whispered. "You did what you thought was best, even though it must have torn you apart. Just like I feel now. I'm sorry I was so bitter. I needed to be a mother to understand the sacrifices we make for our children."

Clutching the chilly rail for balance, she placed her right foot on the second metal stair.

Jack was a good man.

Her left foot sank into the snow piled near the rails.

Knowing everything about her past, he'd still declared his love. He knew her secrets, the whole unvarnished truth, and he had offered to love and protect her. He'd offered to care for her child as his own. No, he'd begged her to let him care for Rachel.

He loved the infant and he wasn't ashamed to show his affection. The gruff Texas Ranger and her tiny daughter shared a bond forged the moment she was born. He loved Elizabeth. He'd said so, and Jack never lied.

Her right foot sank to her ankle in snow.

She had been scared of loving someone again, scared of picking the wrong man again. Frightened of ending up alone again. Terrified of losing her only love.

Wind whipped at her skirts.

Elizabeth pivoted to face the train. A fresh coat of brilliant red paint glimmered in the sun. Jack was right. She had been selfish with her love. Selfish because she was scared. And she wasn't going to be scared anymore.

Her decision made, she set off for the baggage cart.

An enormous hand clamped over her mouth. Rancid breath puffed against her cheek.

"I've finally found Will's little fancy piece," a gravelly voice spoke in her ear. "You'll show me where the money is, now won't you, love?"

Jack watched as men filed off the stalled train. Like a great metal snake, the cars stretched into the distance with the depot still visible. He knelt before the enormous steer splayed across the tracks. Lifting the animal's ear, he noted a bullet hole. The hairs on the back of his neck stood on end. Something was wrong. Surging to his feet, he strode back through the crowd, jostling his way toward the passenger car, only to find himself blocked by the steady parade of bodies. He shoved them aside.

"Easy there, fellow," one of the men

grumbled.

Jack slammed into the railcar, searching frantically for Elizabeth.

She was gone.

He bolted down the aisle.

"Jack," Helen called.

He whirled. "I have to find Rachel and Mrs. Cole."

"Don't worry. Rachel is right here."

Relief weakened his knees. For a moment he'd thought he lost her again. Elizabeth wouldn't leave her daughter behind. "Where is Mrs. Cole?"

Helen adjusted Rachel's eyelet-lace bonnet and grimaced at the baby's rag doll. "She was getting her trunk. I think she changed her mind about leaving."

His heart hammered in his chest. *She was coming back to me.* Once he'd discovered her gone, he'd raced to the station. He'd thought he was too late, until he saw the train chugging to a halt.

"Are you Jack Elder?"

Startled, he spun toward a lanky uniformed rail worker.

"I'm the train detective," the man said. "One of the coal boys thinks he saw that fellow you were looking for. Pencil Pete. Says he saw someone hanging out on the platform earlier this morning."

His worst fears realized, Jack drew his gun. "This train doesn't move until I say so. Not one inch. Understand?"

"Y-yes, sir."

Jack raced down the narrow aisle beneath the curious stares of the remaining passengers. Ripping open the door, he planted his feet on the metal stairs. Two pair of footprints marred the otherwise-pristine snow near the tracks.

He leaped to the ground just right of the footprints, careful to avoid marring the trail. The evidence indicated a small woman, and a much larger man.

Elizabeth had plunged right into Pencil Pete's hands.

Hushed voices sounded ahead of him. Jack flattened his back against the railcar.

"I don't have the m-m-money anymore."

Elizabeth's frightened voice tugged at Jack's heart. He tightened his grip around the gun stock. Charging into the situation with his guns drawn guaranteed certain disaster. No matter the personal cost, he had to remain detached. Sensible.

"The Ranger already found it," she continued. "He moved it all into town."

"I don't think so, missy," Pencil Pete grumbled. "I been following you, and I been following that Ranger. I seen him put the boxes in the wagon. You two were planning on double-crossing old Willy boy all along, weren't you? Did you kill him yourself, or did the Ranger shoot him so he could have Willy's bride . . . and the money?"

"It's not like that."

Her voice trembled so violently Jack had difficulty discerning the words. He clenched his jaw.

Pencil Pete guffawed. "I mighta believed you 'cept I also saw the sheriff in town. He was drinking over at the saloon. Drinking so much, he even talked about a pretty little widow living over by Hackberry Creek. That old sheriff jawed for hours, but he didn't say nothin' about a Ranger finding a stash of loot. So I asks myself, why didn't the Ranger turn over the money to the sheriff? Then I remembered the way that Ranger looks at you."

Jack pinched the bridge of his nose. He'd avoided telling the sheriff about his findings to prevent gossip. Looked like his plan had backfired.

He crouched. Under the railcar, he watched the scuffle of feet.

Pencil Pete shoved Elizabeth ahead of him. "Go on. I know the money is in the baggage car. I saw you loading something into a big crate."

Pencil Pete dragged Elizabeth toward the back of the train. Jack slid between the cars. He pointed his gun at the sky, his thumb positioned over the hammer. All the money was sitting in the bank vault in town. That outlaw was going to be mighty angry when he discovered a crib.

His mind racing, Jack stalked them to the baggage car. He leaned in, straining to hear their conversation.

"It's in here," Elizabeth said.

Pencil Pete tossed her into the baggage car. "Your husband always wanted the money. He sure did like his fancy things. Once Slim Joe shot that woman, though, Willy didn't want any part of the gang. Got yellow on us, he did."

Jack peered through the door. His back turned, Pencil Pete knelt before the crate containing the crib Jack had built for Rachel.

"I know you wouldn't lie to me, now would you?" The outlaw snickered. "Let's open this up and check."

Unable to wait any longer, Jack surged into the crowded space, his pistol arm outstretched. "Not another move."

"I wouldn't dream of it," Pencil Pete drawled, his left arm rising into the air. "If I moved, my hand might slip. I wouldn't want to blow this little lady's head off, now would I?"

Jack stilled. The outlaw's right hand remained out of view. Elizabeth gave a subtle nod of her head.

Pencil Pete held a gun on her. He cautiously rose to his feet. "We've got ourselves a real live stand-off here. First thing we gotta do is make sure this box is the right one. You wouldn't double-cross me now, would you pretty lady?"

Elizabeth shook her head. "Of c-course not. I'll sh-show you. Hand me the pry bar and I'll open it up."

Pencil Pete tipped to the side and grabbed the metal bar, keeping it just out of Elizabeth's reach. "You wouldn't be thinking about hitting me with this would you? Because if you get any funny ideas, I'll blow your head off. Then I'll take care of your man."

Elizabeth blanched. "N-no."

She accepted the crowbar with shaking hands. Jack appealed to her with his eyes to defy Pencil Pete's orders, but she ignored his silent urging and knelt before the crate. Time slowed as she pried open the cover and stuck her hand through the narrow opening. Sweat beaded on Jack's forehead.

A moment later she removed a large stack of bills.

"See," she said. "It's all in here."

Jack's eyes widened. If he wasn't mistaken, she'd revealed the wad of cash he'd refused to take from her earlier.

Elizabeth leveled her gaze at him. Jack winked at her clever ruse.

"Put it back." Pencil Pete licked his lips. "Now, then —"

A commotion sounded behind Jack.

"I'm the train detective," a man called. "What's going on here —"

His words choked off as Pencil Pete aimed his gun at Elizabeth's head.

"Well, looky here." The outlaw faced them, grinning as if the whole situation was some sort of lark. "We got ourselves a party. Lay your guns on the floor, boys, and kick them toward me."

Jack bit off a muffled curse. The train detective flashed him an apologetic grimace. Together the two men scooted their guns across the narrow space between piles of mail bags.

The outlaw crouched and stuffed the weapons into his pocket. "You're just what I need, detective man. You and that Ranger are going to drag this box off the train. Then you're going to board and be on your way.

I'll keep the lady with me. Just in case you get any ideas."

Jack ground his teeth together. "I'll kill you before I let you hurt her."

"Ain't that romantic? Don't you worry. I'll leave her safe and sound in Cimarron." Pencil Pete leered at Elizabeth. "If he's willing to take you without the money, he might even come back for ya."

Jack didn't believe the outlaw for a second. Once he and the detective reboarded the train, Elizabeth was dead.

The outlaw swiped at his nose with his filthy sleeve. "Get moving, boys."

Jack eyed the ashen face of the train detective. "Listen to the man. Let's get this over with."

The outlaw kicked the crowbar to one side. "Wouldn't want the two of you to get any ideas."

Since the stolen money would weigh more than a crib, Jack made a show straining as he lifted the crate. The train detective frowned before reluctantly following suit.

"You're gonna let Bud Shaw hang." Jack feigned a weighty groan. "Even though he had nothing to do with the robberies."

"I sure am." Pencil Pete cackled gleefully. "That Will Cole was smart. He had a cousin with a record of cattle rustling. Willy used his name and hid some money on the fellow's property. We counted on Bud getting caught all along. If any of us got captured, Will was free to break us out of jail. Then we'd all split the money hidden on his spread and let Bud hang. Not like he could identify any of us, since he wasn't even part of the gang."

Pencil Pete shook his head forlornly. "Except Willy didn't come back like he was supposed to. I had to break out myself. Now I'm the only one left, and all the money belongs to me."

Jack and the detective strained to the door. Pencil Pete pushed Elizabeth ahead of him. She tumbled to her knees. Impotent rage surged through Jack's blood. As the outlaw jerked her upright, she threw him a weak, encouraging smile that did nothing to alleviate his fears.

Jack jumped to the ground, then waited for the detective to join him. Together they yanked the crate over the edge into a snow drift. As he backed away, Jack sized up the situation. The outlaw kept the gun aimed at Elizabeth's head, his arm wrapped around her body. Something glinted at her side. She pointedly glanced down. Jack followed her gaze. She held the crowbar hidden in the folds of her skirts.

Pencil Pete shoved her from the baggage car. She floundered in the snow, struggling to rise to her feet and still keep the weapon hidden. The outlaw lumbered after her, his gun arm never wavering.

Jack kept his gaze locked on Elizabeth. She winked at him.

The outlaw snatched the back of her collar, hauling her upright. Jack lunged forward. Elizabeth twisted around, the crowbar arcing through the air. The blow glanced off Pencil Pete's arm. The outlaw howled. A wild shot split the air.

"Run," Jack yelled.

Elizabeth struggled to her feet.

Pencil Pete spun, aiming his gun at Jack's advancing form. Elizabeth clutched the outlaw's arm, hindering his aim. Pencil Pete backhanded her. Her limp body crumpled onto the snow.

Jack heaved toward the outlaw. Another shot exploded. Jack slammed the man into the ground. They scuffled, rolling in the snow. Pencil Pete was strong, but he didn't have the added power of Jack's rage. He threw the man onto his back and slammed his knee into the outlaw's chest, winding him. Circling the outlaw's wrist in a fierce grip, Jack pounded Pencil Pete's hand against the crate until the weapon sprang loose.

From the corner of his eye, he watched the detective scurry for the gun. Jack rolled away to give the guard a clear shot. Still dazed from the scuffle with Pencil Pete, he crawled toward Elizabeth's sickeningly still form.

Behind him, the outlaw flailed.

"I ain't going to jail again," Pencil Pete growled.

Another gunshot exploded. A grunt of pain preceded an ominous silence. Jack didn't need to turn around to know the outlaw had just met his maker.

He cradled Elizabeth's still form in his arms and tugged her bonnet strings loose. "Wake up, Elizabeth. Please, God, be all right."

Her eyes fluttered open. "Don't you yell at me. I just saved your life."

"I know you did." Tears of relief filled his eyes. He laughed and cried and hugged her in arms. "You risked your life to save me, fool woman."

"You saved me first. I guess we're both fools."

Jack gathered snow in his handkerchief and pressed the ball against the blood streaming from Elizabeth's forehead. "You lied to me, Elizabeth Cole. You know I don't abide liars."

She touched his cheek with her bandaged hand. "I love you, Jack Elder. That's the truth. If you're willing to marry an outlaw's widow, I'm willing to be a lawman's bride."

"Then I guess we're getting hitched."

"What about Bud Shaw?"

"We'll go back to Texas together."

"But what about your family?" Her expression dimmed. "I'll always remind them of what happened."

"You were a victim, just like Doreen. You have to give my family the credit for knowing that."

Tears streamed down her face. "If your brothers are anything like you, I won't worry."

"You gotta stop crying, or your face will freeze in this cold."

Elizabeth giggled.

Jack brushed the matted hair from her forehead, relieved to find the bleeding had slowed. "Why'd you put the money in the crib?"

"It's a long story."

"You've got the rest of your life to tell me."

Elizabeth's mouth tipped up at the corner. "You'd marry me still? Even though I hurt you so much?"

His heart pounded in his chest. "I'm awfully pigheaded not to have understood what you were saying. You thought by leaving, you were being noble and doing what was best for me. That's why you didn't pray for us to be together." Warmth flowed through his veins. "I love you. Don't you know you're the best thing for me?"

Blushing color livened her face. "I love you, too."

"I'm not like that fellow in the book, Mr. Darcy. I'm not one for fancy words or flowery speeches. But I can do some of the things he did, I can make things right for you. I can take care of you."

"You already have. I think I loved you from that first night. When you said —" she lowered her voice to a gruff impersonation of him "— Lady, you got a heap o' trouble, but I ain't part of it."

Jack grinned. "I kept wishing you were a big ugly outlaw with a pair of six shooters."

"And I kept wishing you were a tiny little midwife."

His heart thumping in his chest, Jack held her close. "I'm glad we didn't get what we wished for. Now will you marry me?"

"God gave me exactly what I prayed for. Not the way I planned, or the way I thought I wanted, but he gave me what I needed just the same. He gave me Rachel. And you. He gave me a family."

Drawn by the commotion, passengers streamed from the rail cars. The guard tossed his coat over Pencil Pete's body, shielding the gruesome sight from gawkers. Jack lifted Elizabeth into his arms.

Helen's husband rushed to meet them. "Is she all right? What happened? We heard shots. Is everything okay?"

Jack pressed a kiss to Elizabeth's lips. "Couldn't be better."

"Yep," Elizabeth replied, love shimmering in her pale blue eyes. "Couldn't be better."

"You look so beautiful." Jo stepped back and sighed.

Elizabeth stood in the kaleidoscope of light shining through the stained-glass church windows. "I can't believe I missed Christmas."

Jo had even worn a dress for the ceremony, albeit reluctantly. "You missed Christmas by a long shot."

Elizabeth smiled. "I've been busy this winter."

She and Jo had braided her hair and woven the thick ropes into a knot at the nape of her neck. An artfully arranged lace veil with a sprig of evergreen covered the bruise on her forehead.

Elizabeth patted her temple. "It was so nice of Mr. Peters to open up the mercantile."

"He's an a —"

"Jo," Elizabeth shook her finger in a warning. "I know he hasn't always been kind to me. But he made a special trip to the boarding house to let me know he had a dress fit for a wedding. He even found a new sack coat for Jack."

Elizabeth smoothed the satin fabric at her waist. The dress had only needed a few minor alterations. The two-piece ensemble had been ordered a year before, but never claimed. Packed away in the storeroom, the white fabric had aged to a delicate ivory. A fitted jacket nipped in at her waist, and three-quarter-length sleeves ended in a fall of lace. Additional lace edged the beaded, scoop-neck collar. Kid-leather boots peeked out from beneath the sweep of her ivory skirts. A modest bustle adorned the back, trailing the barest hint of a waterfall train.

Jo held out something in her hand. "There's no hothouse in Cimarron Springs, so I made you this."

A length of blush-pink ribbon had been wrapped around the base of a posy of pink fabric roses. The fluted ends dangled a foot below the tiny bouquet.

Elizabeth accepted the lovely present. "They're absolutely beautiful."

"Go on with you," Jo ordered. "I'm sure that Ranger is getting impatient."

Ely stepped forward and offered his elbow

to escort her down the aisle. He wore his best Sunday suit, a dark wool coat over neatly pressed trousers. Even his beard and mustache had been trimmed for the occasion.

He enveloped her in a rib-crushing bear hug. "We all love you, lass. Are you sure you want to move all the way to Texas?"

Elizabeth glanced up the aisle to where Jack waited before the altar, resplendent in his new charcoal-gray suit. "My family is there. According to Jack, there's going to be a new sheriff in town."

Ely wiped a tear from his eye with a loud sniffle. "You keep in touch, you hear?"

"I will."

They made their way down the aisle past a smattering of well-wishers. The Smiths had offered to hold Rachel during the ceremony. The infant wore her best pink dress and crocheted booties. A white eyelet-lace bonnet framed her cherubic face. Elizabeth paused long enough to run the back of her fingers along the baby's downy cheek.

Jo had scurried back to her seat, taking her place beside her mother. The four McCoy boys sat stiff in their seats, tallest to shortest. The youngest swung his feet and sucked on his thumb.

When they reached the altar, Ely nodded

and Elizabeth placed her hand in the crook of Jack's arm. Tall and handsome, his hazel eyes twinkled with joy. His new jacket stretched across his broad shoulders and his dark hair waved back from his forehead. He was the most handsome man she'd ever seen.

Her heart swelled so large, she feared it would burst from her chest in a shower of light. "I love you, Jack Elder."

"I love you more."

She grinned. "You better."

With a roll of his eyes, the minister cleared his throat. "Shall we begin?"

The couple stifled smiles and nodded.

"We are gathered here together —"

Rachel wailed her way into the ceremony. The small gathering turned at the commotion. Sighing resolutely, Elizabeth tugged her arm free.

Jack held up his hand. "I'll handle this."

He strode down the aisle and retrieved the red-faced baby from a fretting Mrs. Smith. Cradled in the safety of Jack's arm, the wailing ceased.

The minister released his pent-up breath.

Jack returned and tucked Elizabeth against his other side. "I've got my daughter. We're ready to begin."

"Oh, Jack." Elizabeth rested her head

against his shoulder. She had everything she'd ever prayed for. Beneath the sure knowledge of God's love, her family had come together.

Their daughter slept through the whole ceremony.

Dear Reader,

I hope you enjoyed Jack and Elizabeth's journey of faith and love as much as I enjoyed writing their story. I began this book with my own journey. I prayed that I was worthy of writing a Love Inspired book. Together with Elizabeth, I traversed a frigid, snowy winter and discovered my place in God's love.

This book will always hold a very special place in my heart. I never had a chance to meet my mother-in-law, Rita, but we both dreamed of writing for Harlequin. When I decided to write a romance, my in-laws gifted me with treasured boxes of her manuscripts. Rita inspires me to live each day to the fullest.

I love to hear from readers. Contact me at sherrishackelford@gmail.com, or visit my website and blog at sherrishackelford.com.

Sherri Shackelford

QUESTIONS FOR DISCUSSION

1. Elizabeth's first husband was jovial and kind when they first met, but soon revealed a darker side. Looking back, Elizabeth realizes there were signs of his true character all along. Have you ever known a person who turned out to be a wolf in sheep's clothing? When you look back on the relationship, can you see the early signs that may have been disguised by their engaging manner?

2. Elizabeth has had little spiritual guidance during her life. She worries her prayers are causing more harm than good. Can you think of ways your prayers have changed throughout your life as you grow and mature in your relationship with Jesus?

3. Even though Jo did a fine job of delivering the baby, she experiences strong emo-

tions in the aftermath. Can you think of a situation where you accomplished a difficult task, only to be emotionally overwhelmed hours or even days later?

4. Jack is furious when he discovers that Elizabeth has risked her life to find help in a blizzard. Can you recall a time when you were so worried, the emotion of fear manifested in anger?

5. Jo and Jack often bicker, though it's clear they have a mutual respect for each other. Why do you think they enjoy antagonizing each other so much?

6. Elizabeth wants a closer relationship with Jesus, but she's uncertain how to proceed. What advice would you give Elizabeth to help her on her spiritual journey?

7. Jack is fearful of developing a bond with Elizabeth and Rachel because of the horrors he's seen in his job. Do you think Jack was right to protect himself from pain?

8. Elizabeth initially hides the truth about her late husband from Jack. Is there ever a time when a lie of omission is justified?

9. Jack showed his love for Elizabeth in his actions before he admitted his feelings. Name some of the ways Jack showed his affection.

10. Elizabeth is able to forgive her mother when she is faced with her own difficult choice. Can you think of a time when your opinion changed because a similar experience gave you greater insight?

ABOUT THE AUTHOR

A wife and mother of three, **Sherri Shackelford** says her hobbies include collecting mismatched socks, discovering new ways to avoid cleaning, and standing in the middle of the room while thinking, "Why did I just come in here?" A reformed pessimist and recent hopeful romantic, Sherri has a passion for writing. Her books are fun and fast paced, with plenty of heart and soul. She enjoys hearing from readers at sherrim shackelford@yahoo.com, or visit her website at sherrishackelford.com.

The employees of Thorndike Press hope you have enjoyed this Large Print book. All our Thorndike, Wheeler, and Kennebec Large Print titles are designed for easy reading, and all our books are made to last. Other Thorndike Press Large Print books are available at your library, through selected bookstores, or directly from us.

For information about titles, please call:
  (800) 223-1244

or visit our Web site at:
  http://gale.cengage.com/thorndike

To share your comments, please write:
  Publisher
  Thorndike Press
  10 Water St., Suite 310
  Waterville, ME 04901